FIC   Martin, David
MAR   Lozell.

        Cul-de-sac.

                                13BT01635
$22.50

DATE			

CUL-DE-SAC

CUL-DE-SAC

DAVID MARTIN

 VILLARD   NEW YORK

Arabel, all the way

Cul-de-sac: Bottom of the bag

CUL-DE-SAC

1

THEY WERE ON THE COUCH NOW, IT HAD BEEN AN EVENTFUL HOUR AND Judith Rainey was finally quiet, her head resting on Donald Growler's lap while Judith's husband Lawrence perched on a nearby chair.

Growler asked why he did it but Lawrence didn't answer.

Night after night for seven years Growler plotted what he would do to the friends who had lied about him, sent him to prison . . . Growler imagining elaborate operas of vengeance, stages slick with blood, arias sung to pain. But not knowing *why* these former friends had stabbed him in the back had become worse than the betrayal itself, was like having a tiny voracious beetle lodged in his ear, eating its way to his brain, driving him mad.

"Larry, *why?*"

Unlike his wife who'd become hysterical under Growler's questioning, Lawrence Rainey managed to park himself in some sort of mental quiet zone. He was seventy-two, his wife Judith was sixty-seven, they'd been married fifty years. Whenever this was mentioned, announced in church last Sunday for example, the Raineys received warm applause.

"Was it the elephant?"

Lawrence continued staring into the middle distance.

"You found the elephant, figured with me out of the way you could keep it for yourself?" Growler asked, his voice quietly solicitous . . . this had been gnawing at him for all these years and he genuinely wanted answers. "Oh Larr-y." When Growler placed a hand on Judith's head and stroked her wispy hair, Lawrence began leaking tears. "You and Judy testified I was with Hope the day she was killed," Growler continued. "Why would you perjure yourselves like that?"

Lawrence stood. He wore flannel pajamas with prints of fish on them, bass and trout.

"*Sit,*" Growler commanded as you would a dog . . . and after a moment's hesitation Lawrence sat down again.

Growler said nothing more for the longest time, he was tired but in no hurry . . . the Raineys' living room silent except you could hear clocks ticking. Lawrence and Judith had been awakened past midnight by this man they'd known since he was a boy.

"I show you these?" Growler finally asked, drawing back his lips.

Astonishment caused Lawrence's jaw to drop, Growler laughing softly and telling him to shut his mouth.

Lawrence complied.

"Do you know where I can find Kenny Norton or Elizabeth Rockwell?" No response. *"Larry."*

The old man looked at Growler as if just then realizing someone had been talking to him. "I saw the photographs."

Growler's dark eyes widened, he sat up straight.

"I was . . . cleaning your uncle's room after he died." Lawrence's voice gravelly with age and emotion.

"And you found Hope's pictures?"

"In an envelope."

"Where are they *now?*"

"You were going to get off on a technicality unless we testified like they said."

"Like who said?"

Lawrence's wet eyes blinked rapidly.

Growler spoke excitedly, "Larry listen this is important, who told you to lie about me . . . who was in those pictures with Hope?"

He shook his head. "I didn't look, they were filthy and I didn't . . ." His voice lost to weeping.

With thumb and finger gently on Judith's chin, Growler turned her head to face Lawrence . . . whose weeping birthed a single wet sob as he demanded, "Why are you doing this!"

"Why am *I* . . ." Growler tried with some desperation to hold on to his composure. "Where are the photographs?" But his control was slipping away, his anger fueling itself. "What happened to the elephant, why all these goddamn lies about me!"

"I don't know anything," the old man pleaded.

When rage finally propelled Growler to his feet, Judith's head rolled from his lap onto the floor, turning a full revolution before stopping face-up at the slippered feet of her husband . . . raising both hands to his mouth like a child who's just spilled milk.

ANNIE SHOULD'VE KNOWN BETTER. SHE HAD IN MIND A MOVIE SCENE . . .
Paul opens the door, his eyes round with delight as he asks what in
the world are you doing here and she says I wanted to surprise you,
they embrace, music up, lights down, fade to morning.

Reality saw it differently. Paul for example hadn't even answered
the door and Annie was worried she might be stuck out here in the
country all by herself, after dark, no other buildings in sight. She'd
already sent away the Corwoods who gave her a ride up from
North Carolina, Annie now standing at the front entrance of a big
lonely building she'd cosigned to buy even though this was the
first time she'd seen it. She knocked again, called her husband's
name, then picked up suitcases and purse and went around to the
side of Cul-De-Sac.

That was the building's name. They'd bought it to renovate and
resell but the place was so big, so deteriorated, Annie wondered
how in God's name Paul ever intended to do all the work by himself.

She went to his old truck and looked in. Seeing it parked here
had given her the confidence to send the Corwoods on their way
. . . yeah Paul's here, she had said, there's his truck. Also Annie
didn't want them around to spoil the reunion scene she had in

mind. Paul didn't like the Corwoods, a florid couple in their fifties
. . . they drank and smoke and spoke frequently in sexual imagery.
Annie thought they were hilarious but the Corwoods offended
Paul's sense of propriety.

Like the entrance doors, the two doors at the side of the building were locked . . . no lights showing here either. The last time
Annie talked with Paul he said he was staying up every night until
three or four A.M. working on Cul-De-Sac's renovations . . . maybe
he chose this particular night to go to bed early. Annie raised a
wrist to take advantage of starlight, eight P.M. Fishing a little flashlight from her purse she soldiered to the rear.

Four doors back here not counting one at the bottom of
cracked concrete steps leading to a basement, Annie didn't intend
to try that door. The others were all locked but she found an open
window and shined her light in on a storage room full of cardboard boxes, broken wooden chairs, dented metal filing cabinets.

Without really making a decision about what she was doing
Annie pushed both suitcases through the open window, tossed in
her purse, then lifted a leg to the sill . . . no way to do this ladylike,
Annie's bare ass showing as the blue dress hiked to her hips. Paul
mentioned once that the dress made her look as fresh as morning
and it's funny how an offhand comment like that will stick with
you, Annie having now categorized this dress as Paul's Favorite.
She had on low-heeled black shoes and over the dress she wore a
denim jacket because mid-April was a lot colder up here in North-
ern Virginia than it was back down South.

Annie got caught half-in, half-out straddling the paint-flaking
windowsill in a way that felt rough and unsafe between her legs.
She laughed a little thinking how she might have to ask Paul to get
a splinter out, he'd want to know where, she'd have to say . . . just
then she dropped the flashlight. *"Damn."* Annie struggled the rest
of the way in. The flashlight was on the floor still shining. She retrieved it, her purse, the suitcases, then went through the storage
room, relieved to find its interior door unlocked. Curious though.
All the outside doors locked but a window left open to a room left
unlocked . . . almost as if an intruder had entered this way.

No, Annie told herself, don't start imagining things again . . . such as what she'd been imagining when she was pounding on the front door and calling Paul's name: that he had a lover with him, they were warm in bed while Annie was standing out in the cold, and this lover—bimbo, slut, bitch—was the reason Paul didn't want Annie to come up from North Carolina, not even for one visit during the entire month he'd been here.

Except Paul would never cheat, it wasn't in his makeup . . . Annie was almost sure of it.

In the corridor outside the storage room she felt sweaty hot but left the denim jacket on so she wouldn't have to carry it along with everything else. She checked walls for light switches, found one, it didn't work.

If an intruder had come in that open window, maybe he cut the electricity and crept up on Paul in the dark, murdered him . . . the killer still here in the building.

She shook her head, *stop it.*

Feeling scared but mainly feeling stupid for putting herself in this predicament, for thinking it would be a nice surprise to show up here totally unexpected, Annie made her way though mazelike corridors and hallways, all of them overheated, finally coming around to Cul-De-Sac's most dramatic feature: a central atrium reaching up three stories, all the way to the roof, with rooms and balcony-hallways on all four sides.

She didn't want to go up the steps to the second floor but what were the alternatives . . . start walking country roads looking for a telephone, spend the night in Paul's truck, sit on a suitcase and cry until morning?

Ready to take that first step Annie heard something, she shined her flashlight up the stairway and saw a man standing very still, looking down at her.

With a startled sound escaping the back of her throat she dropped everything and this time the flashlight went out when it hit the floor.

In the dark she heard his footsteps . . . not coming down the steps toward her as she'd expected but running away, hurrying along the second-floor hallway that also served as a balcony overlooking the atrium.

Annie shook the flashlight until it agreed to come on. He was gone, nothing but quiet at the top of the steps, as if Annie had only imagined seeing her husband. Hopeful, she picked up her things and resumed climbing that stairway to the second floor.

THE SHOWER WENT COLD, GROWLER CURSING AND STEPPING BACK OUT of the water stream. He'd hoped that a long hot shower in the Raineys' basement would refresh him but it wasn't having that effect, just as ending their lives hadn't particularly satisfied him. He'd been obsessing on vengeance for seven years but tonight's installment was turning out to be like the cocaine and pills and booze he'd been indulging since getting out of prison a week ago: momentary relief followed by an even larger hunger.

When the water turned warm again, Growler stepped back into the stream. The maddening irritant of not knowing why he'd been betrayed was even worse than before . . . who told Lawrence and Judy to perjure themselves at the trial, what happened to Hope's pictures? The police said no photographs were ever found, had Uncle Penny hidden them to ensure Growler's conviction?

The hot water ran out a second time, Growler stepping back again, cursing again, taking it personally that the shower was doing this to him. Nothing ever worked out, the whole world conspired against him, son-of-a-bitch anyway, that little beetle gnawing its way into his brain asking why, why?

The hot water returned, Growler dipping his head into the comforting stream as if to receive a blessing. Getting out of prison and discovering the elephant was gone had been the final betrayal that put Growler where he was tonight, that made him the murderer he was accused of being seven years ago.

"Decapitations are this man's signature," the prosecutor had told the jury.

"Decapitating animals," Growler murmured as he brought his hands up in a prayerful pose under his chin and folded his shoulders inward to take fuller advantage of the hot water washing away his sins. He used to cut the heads off dead animals he found, he never killed them himself, certainly didn't murder Hope . . . he loved her.

He was tired. He needed sleep or needed more pharmaceuticals to continue postponing sleep . . . so incredibly tired.

This time when the water went cold it took Growler's breath away and he leapt from the stall looking around for something to use on the shower head, to bust it apart, to punish it for mocking him. Then he heard the washing machine running and realized it had been robbing the shower of hot water . . . he'd put his clothes in to clean them of all the blood. Growler stepped back to the stall and sheepishly turned off the shower.

When the washing machine stopped spinning he transferred his clothes to the dryer. It was cold and damp down here in the basement, Growler hopping up on the dryer and hugging himself for warmth. He tried halfheartedly to jack off but nothing came of it, too frigging tired, then went back to scratching at that unreachable itch.

Uncle Penny must've convinced the Raineys to lie at the trial, Judith and Lawrence worked twenty years for Growler's uncle and would've done anything for him. But if they'd taken the elephant they wouldn't still be living in this little house, this crappy bungalow with shit-colored shingle siding. No, Kenny Norton, Growler's former best friend, was the most likely suspect in the theft of the elephant because Norton was the only other person who knew about the scam, he must've gone looking for the elephant after

Growler was sent to prison. And now Growler was looking for him
. . . but Kenny had moved a lot in the past seven years and had left
a cold trail.

When he closed his eyes they stung, Growler had been over
these possibilities a thousand times, ten thousand times. And although his innocence in the death of Hope Penner no longer mattered, because as of tonight he *was* a murderer, what still mattered
hugely was the goddamn elephant. His share of three million dollars would finance a way out of the country. *Who took it?*

Paul?

The dryer clicked off. Growler hopped down and took out his
clothes, they felt comfortingly warm as he slipped them on. Having stashed the Raineys' bodies in a closet upstairs he'd brought
their heads with him down here to the basement . . . not sure why
though. They were on the concrete floor, Growler lifting both lids
to put Judith Rainey's head in the dryer, Lawrence's in the washer.
He set the machines to their longest cycles but before closing the
lids Growler stepped back to the shower stall and retrieved a container of shampoo, the contents of which he squeezed into the
washer. The name of the shampoo amused him, Head & Shoulders. Or in this case just Head. It wasn't that difficult being a homi-
cidal maniac.

Growler closed the lids and turned the machines on, the washer
sounding okay but the dryer making a terrible racket. He rubbed
his weary face and felt along his teeth with an index finger which
he then sniffed . . . time to go home to Cul-De-Sac.

4

ANNIE SAW A LIGHT IN ONE CORNER OF THE HALLWAY-BALCONY THAT RAN around the second level of the atrium. Up on that second floor now, still carrying suitcases, purse, and flashlight, she kept a wary eye on the closed doors to her left and stayed well back from the railing on her right. The light in the corner was coming from under a door, which was fitted with a heavy metal hasp and padlock though of course the padlock wasn't closed because Paul was inside. She knocked tentatively. "Paul?" *Why had he run from her?*

He didn't know it was me. Of course! Annie had shined the flashlight on him but Paul didn't see who *she* was . . . he hadn't been expecting his wife.

She knocked harder. "Paul! I'm sorry for scaring you, it's me, *Annie.*" She tried the handle, it wouldn't turn.

A soft voice from the other side. "What're you doing here?"

Not the response she expected. "I came to surprise you. Stupid, I know. I'm sorry." *Why isn't he opening the door?* "Paul?"

"How'd you get here?"

"The Corwoods were coming up to D.C. and—"

"Are *they* here?"

"No, they dropped me off."

"You have to go back."

"Paul, open this door."

"You can't stay here."

"Open the goddamn door!" Annie could picture her husband's pinched expression, he disapproved of her cursing.

A lock clicked, the door opening slowly. Annie intended to throw her arms around him and give Paul a big kiss but, shocked by his appearance, she just stood there in the doorway and stared.

"You shouldn't have come."

"What's happened to you?"

He raised a hand to his face.

"You look like you've been beat up." When she reached for him Paul leaned away. "What happened?"

"Nothing."

The usual impression of Paul Milton might be that of a handsome young college professor on whom students, male and female alike, had crushes . . . five-ten but appearing taller because he was slender and long-legged, flat-stomached and smooth-skinned, blond hair and blue eyes, wire-rimmed glasses, a face that promised to remain forever boyish.

But that promise had been broken in the month since Annie last saw her husband, his face now haggard and hollow-eyed, his expression nervous and frightened. Bruises discolored his left cheek and temple, his left eye was blackened, his normally thin lips were swollen fat.

Usually fastidious about his appearance Paul was filthy, his hair so greasy it stuck together in clumps and didn't look blond, his jeans actually stiff having been worn so long without a wash. Paul's once-white shirt had big underarm stains, the outer rings dark brown, the inner ones urine-yellow. When Annie finally stepped close to hug him she could smell his rank body odor, his bad breath.

Paul endured the hug as if it were a medical procedure he'd been warned would hurt a little.

She asked again what had happened to him, he didn't answer and wouldn't look her in the eye.

"Have you seen yourself in a mirror?"

He mumbled something about putting in a lot of hours, not getting any sleep.

No, Annie thought, it's worse than that. She looked over his shoulder . . . the room, Paul's workshop, was large and tall-ceilinged, had obviously once been a library with hardwood paneled walls and floor-to-ceiling bookshelves that were now filled with power tools, some of them brand-new still in their boxes. This was an interior room, no windows. Most of the far wall was taken up by a massive fireplace of red brick, in the middle of the room was a big camel-backed couch covered in black leather cracked and split, horsehair stuffing sticking out in several places. Paul had apparently been using the couch as his bed, a blanket draped on one end, food wrappers and milk cartons on the floor.

He cleared his throat.

Annie waited but Paul said nothing. The old-fashioned cast-iron radiators around the walls must've been operating at full tilt because the room was stifling hot.

Bringing her things in she avoided looking at Paul, his condition made them both self-conscious. "Why is it so warm in here?" She took off the denim jacket hoping that Paul's Favorite Dress would earn a comment.

It didn't. He mumbled something about being cold all the time, Annie didn't catch every word. As if to illustrate the point, he tucked both hands deep into his filthy armpits and hugged himself.

"You bought new tools?" she asked, trying to keep her voice light and unaccusing.

"You can't stay here."

Annie went over and stood right in front of him. "Why not?"

"It's . . . not safe."

"You mean the building, the structure, isn't safe?"

Paul didn't answer.

"I'm not leaving until I find out what's wrong."

"Wrong," he said, repeating the word in a monotone.

"You look . . . like you've been through something terrible." He looked like a mental patient who'd been turned out on the streets without medication or hope.

"Cul-De-Sac," he whispered as if the name was a secret or terrible profanity.

"It's too much isn't it . . . too big to renovate by yourself."

"You have to leave."

She tried hugging him again but he went stiff in her arms. Annie drew back and smiled. "You're going to be okay, I'm here now and you're going to be okay. You said on the phone that you'd fixed up a bedroom and bathroom, why don't you show me where they are . . . I've been in that car—"

"Annie . . ."

"I'm here, I'm not leaving you." When she put an arm softly around him Paul began crying, Annie staying close, comforting him as you would a child. "Show me that bedroom and bathroom, I'd like to take a shower."

"Down the hall."

"Good." Annie picked up one suitcase, leaving the other for Paul, but when she got to the door he wasn't behind her . . . he'd gone to the other end of the room, to the fireplace.

Paul had his hand on the brick chimney. "Remember this chimney," he said . . . a request, not a question.

"Remember it?"

"Yes."

"I don't understand."

"Remember this chimney."

"Paul, I don't—"

"Just remember it."

"All right." When she turned to the door again Paul spoke her name. He was still touching the brickwork.

"Remember this chimney."

"Okay I'll remember it."

"Good." He seemed satisfied, coming over to Annie, picking up the suitcase on his way, even stretching his swollen lips in what might've passed for a smile. Annie smiled back but as soon as he went in front of her she lost that smile.

After they were out in the hallway Paul shut the workshop door, closed the hasp, and squeezed the padlock into place. Annie asked him why he was locking it but Paul didn't answer. He went to an electrical panel box and flipped switches, bringing on some lights, then led Annie halfway down one side of the hallway-balcony. Paul stopped and brought out a key ring, unlocking a door.

Although not as large as the workshop-library this room also had twelve-foot ceilings, one wall dominated by four huge floor-to-ceiling windows. The only furnishings were a chair, a table with a lamp, and on the floor a mattress that was covered with a sheet.

Annie walked to the windows thinking how dramatic they could be if they weren't covered with old shades and rotting curtains. "Which way do these windows face?"

"East. The bathroom's through there," Paul said, indicating a connecting door. He went back and locked the door to the hallway.

"Honey why are you keeping everything locked?"

He started to reply but changed his mind.

"Have you had break-ins?"

He shook his head and asked her if she wanted to take a shower or a bath.

"Shower I guess."

"I'll turn it on, takes a while for the hot water to get up here."

"Thanks."

Annie told herself everything was going to be fine, they'd each take a shower and then make love, afterwards Paul would explain what'd happened to him. She was in the middle of her cycle, the right time to get pregnant . . . which was part of Annie's motivation for plotting this surprise visit.

While Paul was in the bathroom Annie tried to make one of the window shades roll up but it was rusted tight. When she yanked really hard, the dirty shade broke out of its brackets and clattered to the floor putting up dust and half a dozen fat black flies that buzzed so persistently around Annie's face she was forced to wave them off with both hands.

Paul came running out of the bathroom looking first at his wife then at the uncovered window. *"What have you done!"*

"I thought it would be nice to get the morning sun but—"

"Oh Sweet Jesus," he muttered grabbing the old linen shade and holding it to the window as if it might stick there of its own accord.

When Annie put a hand on his shoulder he jumped like she'd struck him. "Paul, it's all right . . . leave the shade off."

But he kept struggling to rehang it, the linen tearing in his hands, several of the flies having landed in his greasy hair.

"Paul stop it."

He looked at her and finally conceded the futility of what he was attempting.

Standing at the window Annie couldn't see anything out there in the dark except a distant glow from a shopping center. "It'll be nice in the morning, to be awakened by the sun."

After moving her away from the window he went over and turned out the overhead light . . . the room now illuminated only by the light from the bathroom.

"What's wrong?" She chastised herself for asking it again, he obviously wasn't ready to talk yet. "I'll go take a shower." Annie stepped into the light from the bathroom doorway and turned, made sure Paul was watching, then slowly raised her dress. Once in a rare moment of sexual candor he had told her that the image of a woman slowly raising a hem and eventually revealing she was wearing no underpants . . . he found it powerfully arousing. Annie had used this information to great success on several occasions.

But now Paul watched her blankly. When he finally understood what she was doing he looked away in embarrassment. Annie felt ashamed of herself. She went into the bathroom and closed the door, realizing only later that she'd left Paul in the dark.

After showering quickly Annie wrapped herself in a towel and came into the bedroom to find that Paul had turned on the little lamp by the mattress . . . he'd also torn off a six-foot length of shade and had taped it to the window as far up as he could reach.

Before she could speak he pointed to the exposed upper portion of window and said, "See, you can still have the morning sun."

She smiled but also wondered what was out there he didn't want looking in. Cul-De-Sac had no neighbors within sight.

A section of water-stained window shade was still on the floor, Annie holding Paul by the arm and telling him the shade was an ancient map scroll, brown and rusty-red stains forming islands and isthmus-connected continents on a yellowing fabric sea.

Usually enchanted by Annie's fanciful stories he listened now with dull expression.

She kept talking, hoping to lighten his mood. Encouraging him to his knees she took her husband by finger on circumnavigations that led to encounters with parrot-feathered natives, escapes from nose-boned cannibals, to islands where the women were beautiful and bare-breasted and the men wore only the briefest of loin cloths.

He began softly crying.

She wrapped him in her arms. "Is it the money?"

He didn't answer.

Early in their marriage she withdrew everything she'd saved over the years to invest in Paul's dream of buying old buildings, renovating them, then reselling at a profit . . . the dream failing on that crucial third point. Creditors had shut them down in North Carolina and Annie still wasn't sure where Paul came up with the down payment for Cul-De-Sac, this decaying former hotel-hospital-asylum, this sixty-room monstrosity in the Virginia exurbs of Washington, D.C. . . . but when he left North Carolina a month ago to start the renovations he promised that this time he'd make them rich.

"If we have to," Annie said, "we'll declare bankruptcy, I'll go back to work, we'll start over again."

Paul had stopped crying but wasn't replying to anything she said.

"Nothing matters as long as we stay together." After Annie's father died, her mother married and divorced three times, each marriage more hateful, each divorce more acrimonious . . . Annie pledging herself not to repeat the pattern. She was with Paul for life.

He apologized.

She went over and opened a suitcase, bringing out a bottle of white white. "It's not champagne . . ." Annie produced two plastic glasses that had an unnerving tendency to lose their stems. "And these aren't crystal but—"

"Our anniversary," Paul said, closing his eyes and looking as if he might start crying again.

"Three years tomorrow . . . and another reason I pulled this silly stunt of coming here to surprise you."

"It wasn't silly." He sat next to her on the mattress.

"I even brought a corkscrew," she said, bending to search through the suitcase.

Paul touched her dark red hair and quoted from the Bible, "You are my refuge and my fortress . . . you cover me with your feathers and under your wings I find trust."

He had been a theology student, they'd met at graduate school and Paul sometimes joked that he gave up God for Annie. He was still a religious man and had remained active in what he called lay ministries, working with drug addicts and prison inmates.

As Annie looked into his soft and battered face she thought it telling that Paul had cast her as his refuge, his fortress, his winged comforter . . . instead of the other way around. She was the emotionally stronger of the two and also older, thirty-five to Paul's thirty. Strange that she should have married a younger man considering that since the age of ten Annie had been in love with someone fifteen years her senior.

When she came up with the corkscrew Paul said, "I'll go take a shower then we'll have the wine . . . I mean the champagne." He stood and took a few steps toward the bathroom before turning back to Annie. "I haven't . . . kept myself very clean."

She nodded.

"I feel . . . *vulnerable* when I'm in the shower."

"This is a big spooky place, being here alone at night I can see how you might—"

"I'm not alone."

"You're not?"

He came over and knelt next to her. Annie saw that one of those fat black flies had lodged in his hair, buzzing there, and while she tried to brush it loose Paul whispered to her, "Satan lives in Cul-De-Sac."

She didn't know what to say.

"Sometimes I open a door and he's *just standing there.*"

"Oh Paul . . ."

"I first saw Satan floating in a bathtub."

"Paul don't . . ."

"Last time I fell asleep, when I woke up his face was *right there next to me* . . . do you know what's hanging out of his mouth—"

"Please stop, you're scaring me."

He nodded. "Exactly."

"Paul . . . how long have you been like this?"

His eyes were large with a kind of terrified wonder, his whispering becoming even softer. "Sometimes he plays a piano, I can hear Satan playing the piano . . . but then I go looking and I can never find the piano. And he's always scratching at the walls, scratch, scratch, scratch . . . can you hear it, he's scratching now, you probably think it's mice but it's not, it's—"

She put a hand over his swollen lips.

∎   ∎   ∎

LYING NAKED ON the mattress, listening to the shower running in the next room, Annie got her mind in a twist wondering if Paul's mental breakdown was so severe he might kill himself . . . or even try to hurt *her.* He could come back in here, see Annie on the mattress, think she was Satan and try to kill her. It's terrible to be afraid of someone you love. Jesus.

Annie would've bet a million dollars she'd never fall asleep, too worried and frightened, but obviously she *had* slept because suddenly she was awakening to a dark room, the lamp by the bed out, no illumination from the windows, just a slit of light showing under the door to the bathroom . . . and a figure standing, looming, at the foot of the mattress.

"Paul?"

The figure made a sound, like a pig's grunt.

It was then she realized the shower was still running, Paul still in the bathroom . . . Annie shouting for him.

The intruder came down onto the mattress with her, Annie scrambling away but getting caught by the foot, being dragged close . . . he was incredibly strong and kept grunting, other animal sounds too, Annie thinking of what Paul had said about Satan, she wanted to call again for her husband but was too occupied trying to get away from—

He started laughing. "Who in the hell are you anyway?"

Annie kicked until he let go then she brought up the sheet to cover her nakedness before finding the lamp and turning it on.

He grimaced as if the light hurt. He had a long narrow face and large dark eyes, his black hair combed straight back. Wearing black slacks with a dark red shirt and heavy work boots, he was roughly Annie's age, average height and weight . . . could've been considered handsome, nose very straight and jawline strong.

"What are you doing here!" she demanded.

He stretched out, elbow on the mattress, head resting casually on one hand. "I asked first."

"I'm Paul's wife."

"St. Paul *married*?" He seemed amused but then his face darkened. "You see this is exactly what I was worried about, a man who keeps secrets from his partner."

"What do you mean . . . partner?"

"Where's the elephant?"

"*What?*" She wasn't sure she'd heard him correctly.

"The elephant, Mrs. St. Paul, the goddamn elephant."

"How do you know Paul?"

He abruptly yanked on the sheet pulling it from Annie's hands and exposing her breasts.

"Small tits but nice buttons."

She tried to get the sheet back, then crossed her arms over her breasts.

"How'd you like having them chewed on?" he asked, drawing back his lips to reveal teeth that were clean and straight but grotesquely large . . . like something out of a bad monster movie. He slipped a hand under the sheet. "You ever take it up the ass?"

"Paul!"

"I have."

"Paul!"

"St. Paul!" he shouted, mocking her. Then he stood on the mattress and started unbuckling his belt. "I'll show you something you ain't never seen."

"Please."

"Everybody begging for Old Scratch."

They both heard the shower shut off. He took his time looking over at the bathroom door and down at Annie before stepping from the mattress. "You tell St. Paul if he's double-crossed me on the elephant I will *personally* deliver his soul to hell." He went up on his toes and left the room like something on hooves.

■　　■　　■

ANNIE REACHED THE bathroom door just as Paul opened it, one towel around his waist, drying his hair with a second towel. "Boy that really felt good." He looked almost normal again.

"There was a man here!"

Paul's haunted expression returned.

"We have to get out of here!" Annie had already put her dress back on, wishing she had time to go through a suitcase for something more substantial to wear, for underpants and jeans and a heavy shirt.

"What'd he say?"

"He called you St. Paul, said something about an elephant—"

"Did he hurt you?"

"No but—"

"Did he show you what's in Satan's mouth?"

"What? Come on, we have to get out of here!" She was holding her purse, waiting impatiently for Paul to slip on his filthy pants and stained shirt. Annie kept an eye on the door to the hall . . . the intruder obviously had a key. How long had he been in the room before Annie awoke? What'd he mean about being Paul's partner? . . . She couldn't worry about any of that now, all she wanted was to be out of this awful place.

Paul took Annie's hand and led her from the bedroom, along the second-floor hallway-balcony. Although he flipped on light circuits at another panel box it was like trying to illuminate a pyramid's tomb with candles, the bulbs creating more shadows than light as the vast interior of Cul-De-Sac hungrily absorbed that light, wanting more. Annie was trembling, palms wet and mouth dry as she and Paul raced down the stairs, through the central hallway, to the front doors which Paul unlocked, then finally outside.

The relief jellied her knees, Annie breathing so deeply through her mouth that certain teeth were forced to acknowledge the cold night air.

As they hurried around toward the side of the building Annie turned and looked at the three levels of moonlit front porches supported by wooden columns and running the full length of Cul-De-Sac. When first driving up here with the Corwoods she'd thought the porches were charming but they looked sinister now . . . places for goons and vampires to heckle from the railings.

Reaching the old pickup truck Paul slid a key off the ring and gave it to Annie. She got in and started the engine. He closed the driver's door but then just stood there. "Go around and get in!" she told him.

"You find a motel, I'll—"

"Paul, get in this truck *right now.*"

"You go on, I'll be fine," he said with a calmness that, considering the situation, struck Annie as totally demented.

"Please get in, we'll drive right to the police—"

A panicked expression broke his serenity. "Don't go to the police, don't call them . . . promise me you will *not* contact the police

. . . if you love me, if you've ever trusted me, you have to promise you won't—"

"There he is!" Over Paul's shoulder Annie watched horrified as the intruder walked around the corner of the building.

Paul didn't even turn to look. "You go to a motel, call me in the morning—"

She dropped the transmission into gear and urged Paul to jump up on the running board . . . maddeningly he just stood there. "Look! Will you turn around and look, he's coming!"

Paul finally did turn . . . and when he faced Annie again his expression mixed pain and sadness, as if he regretted having to tell her, "No one's there."

ANNIE SPENT WHAT MIGHT HAVE BEEN THE WORST NIGHT OF HER LIFE IN a cheesy little motel room several miles from Cul-De-Sac. She debated for hours about calling the police but Paul had been so panic-stricken at the prospect of involving the law that Annie knew he had to be doing something illegal . . . probably in partnership with that awful man.

She called Cul-De-Sac off and on through the night, Paul not answering the phone until eight in the morning. Annie begged for an explanation but he remained frustratingly evasive, asking her to be patient for a few days and then all their troubles would be over, warning her not to return to Cul-De-Sac, reminding her again not to go to the police.

Annie washed the blue dress in the motel's bathtub and hung it over a heating vent to dry. She'd taken her purse when she fled Cul-De-Sac but left both suitcases and had to buy toothpaste and a toothbrush at the motel office.

Waiting for the dress to dry Annie got out her address book and looked up a telephone number, a contact in an old network she had established long ago to keep track of the man she'd been in love with for the past twenty-five years. Paul didn't know about this of course, Annie considered it a harmless indulgence because she never intended to see or speak to the man again . . . she just liked to hear about him occasionally, it comforted her to know he was still alive.

Annie punched in the number, a woman in Maryland. Waiting for an answer she realized she was feeling jittery, the prospect of talking about him again, saying his name.

"Hello."

"Barbara?"

"Yes."

"It's Annie Milton."

"Who?"

"Annie Locken," she said, using her maiden name.

"Annie!"

They spent several minutes catching up on news, Annie finally slipping in the question she'd called to ask, "Where's Teddy these days?"

"Cripes, you're not still tracking him are you?"

"I'd heard he was back in the D.C. area."

"Is that where you are now?"

"My husband and I bought some property here."

"And you're going to look up Teddy, introduce him to your husband . . . that should be cute."

"Do you have an address?"

"Annie, you know what kind of man he was when he dumped you, what kind of man do you figure he is now?"

The kind of man who can fix the trouble Paul's in, Annie thought.

"A tiger doesn't change his stripes," her friend said. "I'll give you the address but I hope you don't have any illusions . . . he'll be the same man he's always been."

A SERIOUS MAN WHO CARRIED HIMSELF CAREFULLY, THE LEGACY OF OLD injuries, Teddy Camel was fifty but looked more used than that. His face was weathered and road-mapped, lit by eyes that seemed to have blue lamps shining behind them. He ran cool, seldom raised his voice, didn't rattle . . . like he operated on the assumption he was the only man in the room armed.

Each day at noon Camel came into The Ground Floor where he was well known by the owner, Eddie Neffering. They had an arrangement. If Camel ever failed to show, Eddie would go up to the fourteenth floor and check to see was Camel dead or alive.

If he died the way he lived, alone, Camel didn't want his body to lie undiscovered until it gassed a stench along the hallways of the high-rise where he had his office and apartment.

Camel had been a cop twenty-seven years if you count his army tour as an MP. He'd been sent out on bad-smell calls, usually a dog or rat but sometimes a man. Camel didn't want to be found that way, strangers standing around covering their noses and mouths, cursing his stink . . . though you might wonder why . . . if he didn't care what people thought of him when he was alive why this concern of offending them in death.

As soon as Camel reached the bar Eddie brought over a bottle of beer and a glass. When Camel went to drink from the bottle, Eddie said he should pour it in the glass first. "Aroma enhances taste."

Camel smiled like it hurt to smile then drank from the bottle "Beer's warm."

"Cold kills taste."

"Where you all of sudden getting this gourmet beer information?"

Eddie shook his head. "Try to educate you . . . Hey you do your taxes yet?"

"When're they due?"

Eddie started to reply then caught on Camel was ribbing him. "You going to be one of those bozos standing in line at the post office come midnight?"

Camel grimaced another smile.

He and Eddie Neffering worked homicide years ago, they stayed friends . . . Eddie's the one who got Camel into this building. The vacancy rate was high and Eddie was tight with the building manager, negotiated a sweetheart deal on Camel's two-office suite.

"This guy does my taxes, he's a genius. I could—"

"It's all right, I'll file late."

Neffering shook his head the way your old man might if you're doing something stupid but now you're too old for him to slip off his belt and teach you a lesson, all he can do is shake his head.

Eddie was sixty to Camel's fifty, it frustrated the older man's sense of success that a talented guy like Teddy should've racked up so many failures . . . being cashiered out of the department a few years ago at what should've been the shank of his career, to name one. Camel was also bad with money, he'd sold his car last week to make expenses. And now he's not going to file his taxes on time?

Eddie was different, did things right. He owned the bar-restaurant on the ground floor of the high-rise, called it The Ground Floor and had his slogan printed on matchbooks and napkins: "Get in on The Ground Floor." It was a big place, like a ballroom. Eddie tried to make it more intimate by installing shoulder-high partitions and tall-backed upholstered booths. He wanted to keep the lighting dim but customers complained they couldn't read their reports and memos so Eddie put lamps in the booths.

The building was in an office complex that in turn was part of a shopping center, sixty acres of concrete marched by armies of shoppers and office workers and store clerks . . . they stopped in The Ground Floor for their morning coffee and bagels, came back for tuna salad sandwiches and iced tea at lunch, then in the evening after work, that's when the lights in the booths got turned off.

Unless he told Eddie otherwise, Camel was there every day at noon. This particular noon was Monday, April 15.

"You gotta get organized."

Camel agreed.

"You know what I'd tell you, you were my kid?"

"How you managed to father me when you were ten years old?"

"I'd tell you, you gotta plan your work, work your plan."

Eddie's kids apparently took to heart their old man's clichés, one son was an M.D., the daughter was a professional golfer number twenty-two last year on the tour, the other son was a real estate broker who if he didn't have more money than God it was close.

"When I think of the paperwork I used to do for you," Eddie said, meaning back when they were detectives.

"You carried me," Camel agreed.

"Not that you weren't a stand-up guy."

"We just operated differently."

"That's the gospel."

Eddie for example was smart about money. Retired after he got thirty in, he invested in this bar-restaurant while the building was still under construction. Eddie also kept close to his kids, he had grandchildren who adored him. Camel always said he could've learned a lot of what you call those life skills from Eddie Neffering.

Back when they worked together as detectives, if some citizen cursed Eddie he never took it personally, a supervisor reamed him out and Eddie didn't let it fester . . . unlike Camel who filed for future reference every slight against him.

He used to wake up mad at the world. He hated lies and liars with a depth of emotion usually reached only by religion and Camel still accepted as an article of faith that people are liars on the most fundamental levels . . . they lie for profit and self-protection, they lie recreationally and out of habit, people lie because they're bored with the truth. Camel had a talent, or a burden depending on how you looked at it . . . he could not be lied to. Once known in police circles as the Human Lie Detector he became semifamous because he could spot a lie the way you recognize your mother's face. The problem with Camel's talent, he couldn't turn it off. Most of us, there are times we prefer certain lies over the alternatives: *Stop worrying about it, nobody noticed . . . I came straight home, honest . . . I never loved anybody like I love you, baby.* And in these cases, even when we do suspect we're being lied to, we can offer a benediction: the benefit of the doubt. *All right darlin' I'm giving you the benefit of the doubt.* That blessing wasn't available to Camel. To him all lies, petty or grand, little white ones and big black-hearted ones . . . they were obvious, hateful, undeniable. After his marriage and career were undermined Camel tried to go numb to lies but that effort turned out to be like a dog trying to abandon the sense of smell. Tell Teddy Camel a lie and he knew it inevitably, instinctively . . . he could smell it on you.

Eddie got called down to the end of the bar where a group of young men, red ties and suspenders, were arguing about sports and needed a verdict.

It surprised Camel a guy like Eddie, old school, could get along so well with the modern young men and women who came into The Ground Floor. His customers listened carefully to his opinions, you could tell they had a lot of respect for the guy.

Maybe it was his size, couple inches over six feet, couple twenties over two hundred. Camel knew him back when he had hair. In compensation for what he'd lost on top, Eddie had grown a huge walrus-type, red-going-gray mustache that made him look like a jolly pirate. Most of his customers tended toward wispy, in their twenties and thirties, power wanna-be's, success-oriented . . .

maybe they thought of Eddie as an older brother or a big uncle, an ex-cop who could protect them if it came to that.

During the past few weeks several of the women who worked in the building had complained to Eddie that a guy was bothering them in the parking garage, making lurid remarks and miming masturbation. Eddie was taking down all the information and establishing a pattern, when the guy hit and what level of the garage he frequented and the type of woman he picked on . . . Eddie figuring he and Camel could set up stakeouts and catch this pervert.

When Neffering returned, Camel asked if there was any news on the weenie wagger.

But instead of answering him Eddie raised his chin and signaled with his eyebrows that someone standing behind Camel wanted his attention.

When Camel swiveled around on the barstool and saw who it was Eddie heard him give up a little grunt like the kind you hear at ringside when a body punch lands solid.

7

SHE SAID, "IF I HAVE TO TELL YOU MY NAME THIS TIME, I WILL BY GOD knock you on your ass."

From behind the bar Eddie laughed.

Camel said, "Annie Locken."

"Well you're half right."

He said nothing more, he just kept looking at her. She'd changed of course. When Camel last saw her she was a twenty-one-year-old college student, now she was a woman of thirty-five, but she still had freckles, blue green eyes, dark red hair, and, most important of all, the animations of her face were exactly the same. It had always seemed to him that Annie's face generated light.

"The lug ain't going to introduce us, I'm Ed Neffering."

She reached across the bar to shake his hand. "Annie Milton, nice to meet you." Her face was flush as if she'd run all the way in from the parking garage.

Eddie said, "How come since he got your name wrong you ain't going to knock him on his ass like you said?"

"Aw he didn't know I got married."

Camel wondered if she was going to tell Neffering how old she was when they first met. Not much embarrassed him anymore but that would.

When Eddie offered to buy Annie a beer she popped up on the barstool . . . they both looked at Camel but he was accustomed to people waiting in vain for him to say something.

Eddie brought a bottle and a glass, Annie telling him, "Great mustache."

"Tickles the girls."

"I bet it does."

Unlike some women she didn't cover her mouth when she laughed, Annie had teeth to be proud of . . . they were white and straight and when she laughed you could see those perfect teeth against clean gums and you could see her pink tongue too. Most people, you don't want to look too closely into their mouths but Annie could make you think maybe dentistry wasn't all that bad to take up as a profession.

Camel kept rejecting stupid things to say . . . you're a sight for sore eyes, what brings you to my neck of the woods . . .

A ream of office workers at the other end of the bar clamored for Eddie's attention, before he left he suggested that Camel take Annie over to a booth where they could have some privacy. Camel picked up the two bottles, Eddie telling him, "Take her glass, schmuck."

As soon as they got to the booth Annie found the lamp switch and turned it off. When Camel started to pour the beer she said she'd drink it out of the bottle.

"Eddie says you pour it in a glass first you get the aroma and that enhances the taste."

She laughed and kept drinking from the bottle.

In the low light her hair could've passed for black, the dimness taking none of the shine from her eyes as she asked him if he was surprised to see her.

"Fourteen years," Camel said.

"Fourteen years and you never returned a call, never answered a letter." She tipped up the bottle for a deep drink, Camel watching her long freckled throat. After putting the bottle back on the table she looked at him and said, "Not that I expected you would."

He didn't say anything.

"I was a sweet little piece of ass, wasn't I?"

Camel kept quiet.

"That's what you told me."

He remembered.

"When I wanted to marry you, that's what you told me . . . instead of saying yes, okay, Annie, I'll marry you, you said I was a sweet little piece of ass."

"What kind of trouble you in?"

She looked surprised then focused her attention on tearing the label from the beer bottle. "Do you remember something else you told me . . . you said if I was in hell and you could find your way there, you'd come get me."

He remembered.

"It's my husband."

"He hurt you?"

"*No.* But he's . . . I think Paul's having a mental breakdown and I think the reason is, he's involved in something illegal."

Camel waited for her to tell him about it.

She did . . . the building they bought in this area, her surprise visit up from North Carolina, Paul's wrecked condition, the intruder, Paul pleading with her not to contact the police. Then she started crying but so softly if you were watching her from across the room you wouldn't know it.

He brought out a clean white handkerchief.

"Sorry," she said, accepting the handkerchief which was ironed and neatly folded. "No sleep last night."

He nodded. "You want me to go out and talk with your husband, try to find this other guy, the one with the big teeth?"

"I don't know what I want you to do. I didn't have anyone else to go to, don't know anyone in the area . . ." After using the handkerchief on her eyes she refolded it. "This was in your left back-pocket wasn't it. A sharp pocketknife in your left front pocket . . . carbon blade, lockback. A few hundred dollars cash in your right front pocket. Am I right?"

He said she was close enough.

"I knew how you'd be dressed too. Old jacket, something tweedy and formerly expensive, faded blue oxford shirt, tan slacks, white socks, heavy black shoes. Same haircut from when you were what, thirty years old? I bet if I came over there I'd smell bay rum wouldn't I?"

He thought of telling her come on over and find out but instead said, "All I've done for the past fourteen years was get older."

"Still armed?"

"Always."

"I remember everything about you like it was yesterday."

He felt the same way about her. Everything . . . but most especially the ocean. For him Annie would always be the ocean.

She leaned forward. "Teddy—"

"This building you and your husband bought . . ."

"Cul-De-Sac." She drew back in her seat. "I had no idea until last night it was so big, so dilapidated. A massive square building, three stories of rooms arranged around an open center. Paul told me that originally there was a huge skylight illuminating the building's entire interior but it's been covered over and now the interior's so dark you can turn on all the lights and it still seems like you're in shadows.

"All I know about renovation is what I've learned being married to Paul for three years but just walking through Cul-De-Sac you can tell it would take a fortune to restore . . . some of the doorways have been bricked up, walls torn down, corridors full of junk, there's been vandalism, fixtures torn out, the plumbing would have to be replaced, new wiring. No way could we ever get our money back and it's too big of a job for one man anyway."

"You have any idea what your husband and this other guy might be involved in?"

"No. He kept mentioning *elephant,* is that some kind of drug term . . . like, *gimme an elephant of heroin?*"

Camel smiled in that peculiar way of his, as if squinting from the sun. "Not that I know of . . . your husband ever been involved in drugs?"

"No, Paul's a super-straight arrow. I was with him once when he was stopped for failing to signal a turn, the cop was very nice about it, issued a written warning . . . but Paul was a nervous wreck, like he was being arrested for murder."

Camel went back to wondering what it was exactly that Annie wanted him to do.

She emptied her beer bottle. "You think I could get something stronger to drink?"

"Sure."

"Large vodka?"

"How you want it?"

"In a glass."

Up at the bar, Camel asked Eddie for a double vodka rocks.

"I assume it's for your friend."

"Yeah."

When Eddie brought the drink he said, "You're happy."

"What?"

"Suddenly you're a happy man."

"I don't know what you're talking about."

"I ain't saying you got a big shit-eating grin on your face but you're definitely a happy man."

On the way back to the booth Camel realized Eddie was right.

STATE POLICE SUPERINTENDENT PARKER GRAY SUFFERED A TERRIFIC JONES
otherwise he wouldn't be doing this, not here in the office where
he could get caught. He'd tucked his tie into his shirt, now he was
rolling the chair away from the desk and leaning forward so he
wouldn't get any of the white powder on his clothes . . . it was already smudging three fingertips and a thumb, had already dusted
the blue cover of a statistical report Gray was using as a placemat
. . . virtually impossible to eat these powdered-sugar doughnuts
without getting the white dust everywhere. Gray had acquired his
addiction back when he drove patrol and every once in a while just
had to have one.

If the powdered sugar fell on your clothes and you tried to wipe
it off, that just made the mess worse, created a greasy white smear.
The key was to stay leaning over until you could . . . *shit,* the telephone. Keeping his head forward and using his unpowdered left
hand Gray picked up the receiver but didn't speak just yet because
his mouth was full.

"Superintendent Gray?"

"Mm-uh."

"I hope you remember me . . . Kenneth Norton?"

Gray almost choked, quickly licking the fingers and thumb of his right hand before reaching for his coffee cup.

"Hello?"

After he got a gulp of coffee down, Gray said, "I remember you sure, what's up huh?"

"Is Donald Growler out of prison?"

Gray felt his heart go funny. "Of course not . . . why?"

"For the past week someone's been asking around for me . . . called a place where I used to work, showed up at one of my old apartments. People who've told me this, they've described the guy and it sounds a little like Donald . . . except he's not giving anyone his name."

Gray stood and moved away from the powdered sugar mess waiting like a booby trap on his desk.

Norton asked, "Are you still there?"

"Yeah."

"If Donald's out of prison—"

"He's not."

"You promised me . . . if I did what you said, you promised me Donald would never—"

"This guy you say's looking for you, you don't know it's Growler huh?"

"No but—"

"I wouldn't worry about it."

"I *am* worried, I lied for you!" When Parker didn't comment, Norton pressed the issue. "You and your partner said Donald was guilty but he'd get off on a technicality unless I—"

"You're mistaken."

Shocked into a moment's silence Norton finally pleaded with the superintendent, "Don't do this to me, you owe me protection—"

"Mr. Norton, I don't owe you anything."

"If Donald's escaped from prison—"

"He didn't escape, I would've been notified." *Maybe,* Parker thought.

"Would you be notified if he was released?"

"He wasn't."

"But you don't know that for sure do you . . . *do you*? If Donald finds me, I'm dead—"

"He's in prison."

"I hope you're right!" Norton becoming screechy. "I hope to God you're right!"

After hanging up Gray moved quickly behind his desk to get to the computer terminal, unluckily catching the edge of the blue vinyl report cover he'd been using as a placemat, flipping it enough to puff up a mini-snow-cloud of sugar dust that powdered his pants just over the left pocket. "Fuck me," he muttered . . . a sentiment that after five minutes with the computer he found himself repeating.

ON CAMEL'S THIRD TRIP TO THE BAR FOR ANNIE, EDDIE ASKED HIM WAS she drinking them or spilling them . . . by the time she finished that third vodka her eyes were shining wet and her smile had slipped a few degrees off horizontal.

"I don't want to go back to a motel."

"You can stay with me."

Implications kept them both quiet for a moment, then Annie said okay. Camel suggested they leave now, get Annie something to eat and maybe she wanted to take a nap too.

She nodded but kept seated, holding onto the empty glass as if Teddy might try to snatch it from her. "Paul was talking about hearing things in that building . . . a piano playing, scratching in the walls."

"He thinks it's haunted?"

"He said Satan keeps showing up." Annie stared at the glass and considered asking for another. "When I opened my eyes and saw that man standing there I thought it was the devil." She glanced over at Camel. "I've never been more scared in my . . . then this morning I couldn't think what to do, who to go to for help . . ." A strange stricken look came over Annie's face just before she turned sideways in the booth, lowered her head to the level of the tabletop, and vomited on the floor.

Teddy's shoes got splattered, he went around to Annie who was apologizing even before she stopped throwing up.

"Come on, I'll take you to my place," he said, helping her stand.

"I'm sorry."

"Forget it."

When Eddie came over, Annie said, "I'll clean it up."

He told her same as Camel did, forget it.

But she kept apologizing. On the way out she looked back at the people who were looking at her and just as Annie and Camel got to the door she said to the last person at the bar, "It's morning sickness."

By the elevator she leaned against Camel and kept her eyes on the floor. "All over your shoes," she said.

"Not a problem."

"I'm so sorry."

"Annie, forget it."

When the elevator came she told him, "I don't know why I said that about morning sickness, I'm not pregnant."

"I know."

"How would you—"

Then the elevator arrived and they got in. It was empty but stopped every few floors to pick up passengers, Annie holding onto Teddy as if she expected the ride to turn bumpy.

Half a dozen people were in there with them when Annie said, "I had my first orgasm with you, in your sleeping bag." She was speaking softly against his neck but in the close space of that elevator everyone heard her plainly. "Only ten years old but I felt so grown-up that night."

Camel stood stoically looking at his shoes.

The elevator stopped at the twelfth floor where two women got out, turning to get a good look at Camel so maybe they could pass on his description to the police. Up on Fourteen when Camel helped Annie from the elevator the other four people gave them plenty of room to exit.

Annie clung to him tightly, they made a clumsy time of it walking down the corridor to his office. While Camel was getting out his keys she raised up on her toes and whispered in his ear, "I'm sorry."

"It's nothing, forget—"

"No I mean our baby."

He stopped fumbling with the keys.

"I'm sorry about our baby," Annie said just before collapsing like she'd been shot, falling so suddenly and heavily that Camel dropped the keys to free up his hands and barely managed to grab Annie's shoulders before her head hit the hard tile floor.

10

BEFORE PUTTING HER TO BED CAMEL REMOVED ANNIE'S SHOES AND helped her lift off the blue dress . . . she had on no underwear and seeing her naked aroused him with such urgency that he felt foolish, quickly covering Annie with a blanket. She said the room was spinning, he promised it would stop. Within seconds she either passed out or fell hard to sleep and Camel went into the adjoining office where he conducted business, Camel Investigations.

Mainly he worked for lawyers, collected evidence for divorce cases, checked on people to see if they were who and what they claimed to be. Camel also did a little business off the books, he'd hire out to go have a talk with someone, encourage the person to be reasonable. Maybe it was someone who'd been jilted then started harassing the ex and the ex's new lover . . . Camel would go over and talk to the jilted party about self-respect, getting on with your life. Or maybe there's a feud in the family and this guy won't return some property belonging to his brother-in-law who then hires Camel to go over and talk with the guy, urge him to be reasonable and do the right thing.

In these endeavors Camel was himself eminently reasonable, he didn't threaten violence or embarrass people in front of others . . . and neither was he always successful, though more often than not he was. Something about Camel, his face, his demeanor, made people pay attention to him, encouraged them to comply with what he was asking them to do. His ex-partner Alfred Bodine used to say that when Camel talked to you in a serious way it was like the Voice of God, Old Testament.

His singular ambition had always been to be taken seriously. The highest compliment Camel's father could give anyone was to say he was a serious man. Didn't matter if the guy was a big shot or one of the grooms who hot-walked horses at the track where Camel's father lost money on a regular basis . . . if the old man thought someone was worthy he'd tell Teddy, "Now that's a serious man."

Being a serious man meant you could be relied upon, your word had value, you knew your business. Crooks could be serious men, so could drunks and people the world might consider losers . . . if they followed the rules. A serious man didn't claim more knowledge than he owned, he wasn't a loudmouth or bully, and even if he was poor he always carried a few hundred dollars cash on his person because cash is serious in a way checks and credit cards and promises to pay you later never can be. When a serious man picks up a restaurant tab he goes over to the waiter and pays it discreetly, he doesn't make a show of grabbing the check. If a serious man helps you out with a loan, he doesn't mention it around. And if he has a low opinion of you he either keeps it to himself or tells you to your face.

Camel tried always to follow these and other rules, what he would or wouldn't do . . . as complicated as chivalry, with Camel keeping the book on what was wrong, what was right.

Going back into the other room and slipping under the covers with Annie would be wrong, Camel knew this instinctively . . . though if Annie came through the connecting door right now and took him by the hand and led him back to bed, he would accompany her joyously, without second thought. He wasn't sure what the difference was, why going to her uninvited struck him as the act of a man who couldn't be taken seriously, yet *following* her to bed wouldn't break any of his rules. All this was tied up with what happened between them fourteen years ago and had very little to do with the legal fact that Annie was married.

Camel used to have affairs with married women, though not for several years now . . . not since his affair with a woman who would make love to him only in the bed she and her husband used. As soon as the husband left for a business trip the woman would contact Camel. When Camel arrived at her house she'd always make a point of mentioning, her eyes flashing when she spoke, "I didn't change the sheets." As if this should arouse him the way it did her.

One evening the husband called while Camel and the woman were in coitus. She picked up the bedside phone and carried on a conversation with her husband. She talked about ordinary things, she asked the husband how his flight was, did he have a nice room, the meeting go okay . . . and all the while she's on top of Camel, moving back and forth on him, rubbing her breasts for him to watch, pulling on a nipple harder than he would've dared, keeping her eyes locked on his.

Toward the end of the conversation she leaned forward and placed her left hand on the pillow next to Camel's head, her right hand still holding the phone, breasts hanging just above Camel's chest . . . then she brought her face close to his so that her lips were almost touching his mouth, the woman wide-eyed when she told her husband on the phone, "I love you."

After hanging up she fucked Camel the way a man sometimes will a woman, hard and fast to reach a conclusion . . . and Camel knew he was incidental, whatever was going on here existed between the woman and her husband.

Camel never saw her again after that, made excuses why he couldn't come over the next time her husband was out of town. The woman didn't seem brokenhearted but the incident continued to fill Camel with a sense of wrongness . . . not regret or guilt but a sense that what had happened simply wasn't right. Camel couldn't explain even to himself the difference between fucking the guy's wife while he's out of town and unaware of it *or* fucking the guy's wife while he's out of town and unaware of it and on the phone with her . . . but he knew in ways he couldn't articulate that the incident had crossed some line he didn't want to be over. Just as he was instinctively sure that getting into bed with Annie would turn out wrong, would not be the act of a serious man.

He hadn't met with much success in his life, didn't have a good marriage and his career went bad there toward the end when it really counts, he was estranged from his daughter, he was broke and had sold his car . . . but if you asked anyone who knew him even those who didn't particularly like him, to a person they'd tell you he was a serious man.

To ensure Annie wouldn't be disturbed by the calls he'd be making Camel closed the door between his two offices. The door had frosted glass in its top half so Camel could see if Annie woke up and turned on a light.

First call was to Michael Neffering, Eddie's boy who's a real estate broker . . . Camel asking Michael if he could research a piece of property called Cul-De-Sac, find out its history and if the property had ever been connected to anything criminal. Michael said he'd call back within the hour.

After several other calls Camel returned to check on Annie who still slept soundly. He wondered what she would think of the way he lived . . . in this room with daybed, hotplate, TV, microwave, half-size refrigerator, sink, cutting-board countertop, bookshelves, table and two chairs, recliner with footrest in front of it and a floor lamp behind, one corner of the room drywalled in to enclose the commode and shower. Maybe she'd think he'd mastered the art of low overhead.

Annie's face was plain in repose, it was animation that sparked whatever beauty she owned, the way she worked a smile up and down like window shades letting in sunlight, the way she flashed those blue green eyes like headlights going on and off high beams . . . that's how Camel had always thought of her, light to his dark.

When the telephone rang he slipped out of the room and softly shut the door . . . it was Michael Neffering calling back to tell Camel the Cul-De-Sac property had been in and out of the courts for as far back as he could trace. One entanglement over owner-ship came about because a person who would've inherited a one-third interest in Cul-De-Sac was convicted of murder.

Camel started taking notes.

"The victim," Michael continued, "was a minor, Hope Penner, who owned one-third of Cul-De-Sac, an interest that would've gone to her cousin, Donald Growler, except he's the one who killed her."

"What's that name again?"

"It's spelled *G-r-o-w-l-e-r*, I don't know if that's pronounced Grow-ler or Growl-er. The way it ended up, the girl's share went to J. L. Penner who owned the other two-thirds of the property and who was the uncle to both the victim and the killer."

"You said this Hope Penner was a minor."

"Yes . . . seventeen when she was killed. The uncle, J. L. Penner, died last year, his estate has been in probate ever since but I guess it got settled recently because it says here that Cul-De-Sac was sold a month ago to a couple from North Carolina, Paul and Ann Mil-ton."

Camel asked Michael if he had any details on the murder . . . where it occurred or what the motive was.

"No, nothing like that in these files. A few other names are men-tioned though. Lawrence Rainey and Judith Rainey, a married couple who worked for J. L. Penner and were left a small sum in his will. Elizabeth Rockwell was executrix."

Camel asked if he had phone numbers and addresses, Michael said he was sorry but no.

"Mikey does anything in your files mention *elephant*."

"Mention what?"

"Elephant."

"As in Dumbo or pink or what?"

"As in I don't know. A reference to elephant came up, I'm not sure how it connects to anything."

"What're you working on?"

"Mikey, Mikey."

"I should know better than to ask?"

"Right."

"No elephants, Teddy."

"Okay."

"You see the old man today?"

"Every day."

"He and mom are coming over for dinner tonight, why don't you come with them?"

"Love to Mikey but I can't, not tonight."

"Soon then."

"Absolutely. Thanks for the information."

Camel got on the phone to people he knew and three hours later had pieced it together: Seven years ago J. L. Penner, his niece Hope Penner, and his nephew Donald Growler were living at Cul-De-Sac. The niece was seventeen, a young lady who liked to party hard. The nephew was twenty-six, a handsome (his teeth were normal) but strange young man who kept a collection of severed animal heads in his room. Apparently the cousins were having an affair that turned bad, Donald Growler killing Hope Penner and using an axe to cut off her head which he then placed on a shelf in his room at Cul-De-Sac.

Camel went back to check on Annie who was still asleep. The blanket had slipped off her shoulders revealing an abundance of freckles, Camel remembering some of them individually. He gently pulled back that dark red hair to see if her ears still stuck out the way they did when he first met her and Camel was twenty-five years old and Annie Locken was ten.

11

"DROMEDARY OR BACTRIAN?" SHE DEMANDED UPON BEING INTRODUCED to Mr. Camel. Her mother said be nice but the precocious girl was already launching a bubbly lecture on what she'd learned in school about the one-humped dromedary camel and the two-humped Bactrian camel, how they store fat not water in their humps, "bet you didn't know that," and have a double row of eyelashes to protect their eyes from sandstorms and they can also close their nostrils completely shut, "I bet you can't."

Camel considered this a moment then squeezed his nostrils with forefinger and thumb.

"Without using your hands!" she squealed, bending forward to laugh, covering her mouth, going red in the face . . . Annie's mother telling her with little effect to settle down.

Camel was out of the army and recently hired by the D.C. police force as a uniformed patrolman. Friends had invited him down to their beach house on Cape Hatteras along with other of their friends, people he didn't know, everyone assembling for a four-day weekend . . . eleven in all, six adults and five children (four boys and one Annie Locken).

She was buoyant, funny, curious, and self-aware, bouncing between arrogance and vulnerability, trying out varieties and possibilitics of who she wanted to be. At age ten Annie was all arms and legs, monkeylike and coltish, she had a long neck, she had little ears that stuck straight out and proved useful to keep her hair away from her face, finger-hooking dark red tresses behind those protruding ears which then held as securely as barrettes. Her eyes were blue and green, she was liberally freckled.

No one who knew Annie as a child would claim innocence on her behalf, at least not an innocence that means free from guile, unaware of effect. Rather, her considerable charm arose from what often is mistaken for innocence: a lack of complication. When she was happy she bounced up and down and laughed with big eyes and snorted through her little nose, she clapped her hands. Hurt, Annie wept openly and with a depth of feeling that made it seem she would never stop weeping . . . until it didn't hurt anymore, then tears were gone, forgotten, traceless. Angry, her face clouded and her brows knit and her thin lips drew tight . . . Annie could've been modeling for an illustration in an anthropological text on classic human facial expressions. Asked a tough question, she would scrunch up her face and from the corner of her mouth a tongue tip would peak.

When the beach-house children played games that weekend Annie was guardian of the rules, chooser of sides, arbiter of out and safe. She was famous for making the boys cry . . . she'd get them down in the sand and force them to say uncle. Perhaps out of character for such a tomboy she preferred wearing dresses and in fact Camel never saw her in jeans or shorts. But she was always coming back to the beach house with those dresses torn and dirty, her hands and face looking as though she'd been working with coal. Annie's mother would send her from the dinner table to wash, Annie returning to fall wide-eyed upon barbecued chicken as if she were more than hungry for it, she was enraged that food was out there on a plate instead of in her belly where it clearly belonged. As she ate, barbecue sauce stained her mouth then up around her cheeks until she resembled a vampire well fed.

The day's play would scuff Annie's knees and palms, when her mother immersed her in the evening bath you could hear Annie throughout the house screeching from the effect of water and soap on cut and scrape . . . but after that bath Annie would come out clean and flanneled to sit among the adults, usually close to Teddy Camel, and apply a fresh set of Band-Aids in a performance of care and self-admiration to match any woman adorning herself with jewelry.

She had a crush on him, Camel was a policeman and also there was about the man some dark gravity that tugged at a girl so full of light and bounce. She would come loping up from the beach and spot Teddy in the group of adults and beeline for him to throw herself salt-wet upon his lap, draping an orangutany arm around his neck.

Her mother would tell her to stop pestering him.

"He doesn't mind," Annie would say . . . then look hard with predator-narrowed eyes at Camel and demand, "Do you?"

He would reply that her mother was right, she was a pest, and Annie would stick her tongue out, then run away to terrorize the boys who always stood when she came around, junior officers in the presence of their superior.

Her mother would say to Camel, "She's in love with you."

"I'm in love with her too," he'd reply.

No one took it wrong and Camel's actions with the girl were always correct. They went together for seashore walks and one evening they sat on the beach as the sun set behind them, Camel and Annie watching the sea change its mind from bright invitation to dark warning. On these times alone with her he never spoke to Annie or touched her in ways he wouldn't have done in her mother's presence, or her father's had he been alive, yet Camel felt strangely on guard whenever he was with Annie as if one part of himself sat in watchful judgment of another part.

Early in his career as a D.C. patrolman he had aided in the arrest of a man in his mid-thirties, a long-necked hillbilly being charged with having sexual intercourse with a girl of twelve. Camel kept an eye on him at the station house while paperwork was being assembled. The man lined up words in his head . . . and when he finally got them straight, he said, "I didn't exactly rape her you know."

Camel told him to save it for the detectives.

"You don't understand how it was. She's always coming out of the bathroom wearing a towel that don't quite reach, always running around in her underwear . . . wanting to wrestle with me." He pronounced it *rassle*. "I even told her, 'Hey, I'm your mom's boyfriend, not yours.' Didn't do no good, she'd come in my bedroom in the morning, her mother already off to work, and she'd ask me could I do up the back of her dress and she—"

Camel told him he didn't want to hear it.

The man nodded in total agreement. "Ain't nobody going to want to hear it, I know that . . . I *know* it."

Camel held the man in utter, violent contempt as he continued his pathetic plea: "Ain't nobody . . . no cop, no judge, no jury . . . nobody going to want to hear how that innocent little girl would come crawling into my bed when her mom wasn't at home, wearing nothing but panties and little training bra, asking me to rub her back. Twelve years old, okay . . . but she's got titties and she gets her period and—"

"Listen, asshole," Camel finally told him. "She's a child, you're an adult. Doesn't matter what she does, you're the one responsible."

He was nodding. "I know that, yessir I know that. I know what I did was wrong in the eyes of the law but—"

Wrong in Camel's eyes too. "While you're in prison I hope you get fucked up the ass on a regular basis."

This fairly took the man's breath away. When he finally was able to speak he told Camel, "You're a hard man."

People were always saying that about him.

The summer Camel first met Annie when she was a girl and he was a man, the eleven people staying at the beach house slept on cots and couches, in bedrooms and sleeping bags. Married couples were granted bedrooms, the three older boys tripled up, Annie shared a bed with the youngest boy who was hardly more than a toddler, and Camel took a sleeping bag and mosquito netting out onto the porch.

The last night of the long weekend, three A.M. and Annie was suddenly all elbows and knees next to him.

"What're you doing?" he asked.

"Charlie has stinky feet."

Camel laughed.

"He does! I hate stinky feet. I told him to wash his feet before he came to bed but he didn't and now the whole bed stinks like his feet, I'm not sleeping there."

"You're not sleeping here either."

"You got stinky feet too?"

Camel laughed again and started pushing her out of the sleeping bag but his hand slipped to grasp by accident a breast bud, hard and small like a golf ball. Annie reacted by locking her legs around him and becoming very still, waiting for what came next . . . Camel's voice turning cold: "Get out of here."

"What?"

"Go back to bed with Charlie or find somewhere else to sleep, you can't stay here."

"Why not?"

"Go on now," he insisted, demonstrating with stony voice that he didn't intend to make this into a game.

"You didn't kiss me goodnight."

"Get out of here."

"You kissed me goodnight last night, in front of everybody . . . why can't you now?"

"Go on, get out of here."

"Give me a kiss and I'll leave."

He tossed aside the sleeping bag and stood.

"You afraid of me?" she asked.

In a way he was. "I'm going to find your mother, let her deal with you."

"Okay, *okay.*" Annie got to her feet too.

Camel was holding the mosquito netting aside for her when,

passing in front of him, she went up on tiptoes to kiss him quickly on the lips. And said, "I love you."

"Go to bed."

"I know what that is," she said, touching him.

He pulled on the netting to make it come down between them. "I hear or see you again tonight," he warned, "and I'm waking up your mother."

"Tattletale."

"Get out of here."

"Grouch."

He listened to her bare feet padding across the porch and into the house, then Camel lit a cigarette and thought assiduously of older women he'd known, women who rouged their faces and drew their eyebrows as arches not found in nature, who laughed cigarette-husky and drank whiskey neat, women with slack bellies and breasts that sagged from weight and time, whose brambles grew thick-black from thigh to heavy thigh.

The next morning as everyone was getting ready to leave he debated telling Annie's mother what had happened but Annie and her mother were already in their car . . . Annie rolling down a window and throwing him a big kiss the way Dinah Shore did at the end of her television show. He didn't throw one back, he just waved.

Although Camel remained friends with the people who owned the beach house he didn't accept any of their subsequent invitations and eventually forgot about the girl.

Eleven years later she called. He couldn't place her name. She repeated it several times then became so angry she hung up on him. But called right back. "*Annie Locken* goddamn it I had a crush on you."

Then he remembered.

Annie explained she was in charge of inviting people down to the beach house this summer . . . would Teddy come? He begged off. She persisted: teasing, flirting, assuring him there'd be lots of people there for protection.

"Protection?" he asked.

"In case I try to crawl in bed with you again, I'm twenty-one now," she pointedly informed him.

"Which still makes me fifteen years older." He was speaking to a grown-up voice but picturing a ten-year-old girl.

"Things have changed."

Camel didn't realized how much until he arrived at the beach house and discovered he was the only person Annie had invited.

12

CLOUDS CAME IN LOW, DARK, THICK ENOUGH TO AWAKEN HUNDREDS OF sodium-vapor lamps well before their usual hour, Teddy Camel standing at the window of his office looking out across those acres of ugly yellow orange illumination. When he heard Annie in the other room he went to the connecting door, knocked, gave her time to collect herself, then went in.

She'd put the blue dress back on but not her shoes, Annie sitting on the edge of the bed looking embarrassed like a woman who'd gone home drunk with a man whose name she couldn't recall.

Camel asked how she was feeling, she said fine but she spoke in a very small voice.

Going over to sit next to her he almost asked what she meant when she said, right before passing out, that she was sorry about their baby . . . Annie had gotten pregnant that summer they spent together fourteen years ago when she was twenty-one and he was thirty-six? And never told him? That's what all those phone calls were about, the calls he never returned? But instead of going into any of that he said he had some information on Cul-De-Sac. "You feel like talking just yet?"

She slipped off the bed and walked to the sink, washed her

hands and face, dried off with paper towels, then turned around. "I have to call Paul, see if he's okay . . . tell him where I am."

"Why don't I borrow your truck, drive to Cul-De-Sac, get your husband, bring him back here, maybe we can thrash it out what he and that other guy are up to."

"Thrash it out?"

"Talk it out."

"No I think you meant what you said the first time, you can thrash the truth out of anyone can't you?"

Why was she mad at him? "I could try to get to the bottom of it, yeah."

Annie checked her watch. "It feels a lot later than five."

"Overcast. So what do you think, bringing your husband here?"

"I'm not sure how to explain you to Paul."

"Is he jealous?"

"He's a man."

"I meant—"

"He gets jealous, yes. When we were first married he wanted to hear about my old boyfriends." Paul would actually get sick to his stomach listening to her but still kept insisting Annie tell him everything.

Teddy wondered what she had told her husband about that summer fourteen years ago.

"I have to call him right now."

"The phone's in the other office."

Annie went to make the call but returned almost immediately, the line was busy. She sat next to Camel as he laid out what he'd learned about the homicide at Cul-De-Sac seven years ago. Camel asked her how long she'd known her husband.

"It's our third wedding anniversary, I met him about a year before we were married."

"Do you know where he was living seven years ago, what he was doing?"

"Paul wasn't connected with any murder if that's what you're getting at."

"Your husband—"

"His name is Paul."

Camel stood. "Well you think Paul is involved in something criminal . . . but you also think he's not the kind of man who'd break the law, that's what you said, a super-straight arrow—"

"Don't interrogate me."

He looked surprised then nodded . . . Annie was right, without noticing it he'd slipped into his old role as homicide detective, ferreting lies.

"The only criminals Paul has ever met are the ones he worked with in a prison program called Our Brothers' Keepers." She explained what she knew about the program, run by a religious organization and dedicated to helping former convicts make a fresh start.

Camel said it could be a connection. "Say he meets a prisoner who knows the Cul-De-Sac killer, finds out something was stashed in the building and—"

"That man last night, could he be the killer?"

"I don't think so, Growler's still in prison and according to the description I got there was nothing unusual about his teeth."

"Who?"

"Donald Growler." Camel pronounced it Grow-ler. "He's the one who killed his cousin in Cul-De-Sac, you ever hear your husband mention that name?"

"No."

A knock on the hallway door, Annie coming off the bed to stand behind Camel who was sufficiently roused by her frightened reaction that he drew a .357 magnum revolver from the holster on his belt. "Yeah?"

"Teddy it's me."

Camel put the revolver away and turned to Annie. "Ed Neffering . . . from downstairs."

She said she remembered.

Camel opened the door, Neffering giving Annie a big smile. "How you feeling honey?"

"Embarrassed."

"Don't be silly." Then to Camel, "I didn't know your friend was still here, I was going to ask you to take the stakeout tonight." He looked back at Annie. "We got a flasher bothering women in our parking garage, I've been working on a pattern when he hits and I think he might be due again tonight. The stakeout wouldn't take but an hour."

"Teddy could do that while I do some shopping."

Camel started to say no but Eddie spoke first, "It's all right, we'll catch him next time. I'd do the stakeout myself except—"

"You and Mary are having dinner with Mike and Kathy."

Eddie asked Camel how he knew but Camel just smiled that strange, pained smile of his . . . Eddie finally shrugging. "It's up to you about the stakeout, if you decide to do it you know the drill." Then to Annie, "Hope to see you again honey."

After Neffering left, Camel relocked the door.

"You go do your stakeout," Annie said. "I need some time anyway. I have to buy a few things, a change of clothes, maybe when I get back we'll have a chance to eat something too, then you can go get Paul. I'll keep calling Cul-De-Sac so I can explain to him you're coming. I'll pass you off as an old friend of my mother's."

"Yeah."

"Teddy? Telling him about all my old boyfriends? That didn't include you, I keep you in a separate room . . . no one else gets to go in there."

Camel nodded.

Annie smiled for the first time since awakening. "Did I hurt your feelings when I said I could pass you off as an old friend of my mother's?"

He shook his head.

"Teddy."

"A little."

"Good."

13

FOR HALF AN HOUR NOW STATE POLICE ASSOCIATE SUPERINTENDENT Parker Gray and his ex-partner Gerald McCleany, retired, had been sitting in a car parked across the street from a bungalow owned by Lawrence and Judith Rainey. Gray wore a dark suit, the pants showing a powdered sugar stain above the left pocket, Mc-Cleany dressed like he was heading for the golf course.

"Maybe they're taking a nap," McCleany said, producing a cigar, taking off the cellophane, sticking the cigar three-quarters in his mouth then drawing it out between fat wet lips in a manner both loving and obscene.

When the match struck, Parker Gray who'd been making a point of not looking at his old partner finally glanced over. "This car has never been smoked in."

McCleany held the match just in front of the cigar and sucked in with rapid puffs until the tip of the cigar itself began spouting flame. "Has now." Then laughed like it was a great joke.

Gray rolled down his window. He genuinely hated McCleany . . . was embarrassed by him when they worked together, had avoided him since McCleany was forced into retirement, and hated him all over again now that Growler's release from prison had thrown them back together.

"Tell me again about this asshole got Growler out," McCleany said puffing thoughtfully on the cigar.

"Paul Milton, belongs to a prison ministry group called Our Brothers' Keepers, they work with the parole board and when a prisoner is identified as a likely candidate he's paroled to the care of someone from this program who's supposed to be responsible for—"

"Jesus Parker I don't need to hear the whole goddamn annual report . . . what's Milton's *angle?*"

"I don't know, he might be legitimate except—"

"Yeah and I might be number one on the seniors tour this year . . . but I seriously fucking doubt it. Milton's from where?"

"North Carolina. Growler is supposed to be down there with him so Milton can keep an eye on—"

"Supposed to be my ass. Growler's back here, I can feel it in my nuts."

Gray rubbed his eyes. "You and Kenny Norton."

"What?"

"I told you, Norton is convinced it's Growler who's been asking around about him, trying to find out where he lives—"

"Norton . . . skinny Kenny Norton getting all squishy how we owe him protection, I should go over and pop one in that artsy-fartsy fucking fairy's head."

Crude bastard, Gray thought . . . I wish to God I'd never met you.

"Raineys' number in the phone book?" McCleany asked while puffing on the cigar, producing enough smoke to fog the car's interior.

"Yes."

"But Norton's unlisted?"

Gray nodded. "He said he keeps a low profile, moves around a lot, never leaves a forwarding address—"

"If you were half the detective I tried to teach you to be you'd figure it out . . . Growler comes back here to knock off everybody who testified at his trial, he has to go around looking for Norton but to find the Raineys all he has to do is open the fucking phone book."

"You think he's already got to them huh?"

"And Norton'll be next."

"Then us," Gray said.

"Yeah I hope that bastard shows up at my door some night."

"No I mean this whole thing we did, it's going to come back and bite us in the ass after all these years isn't it?"

"Not if I bump into Growler first." Saying this, McCleany got out of the car without waiting for Gray or explaining where he was going . . . just like the old days when Gray was always being forced to second-guess his senior partner.

The afternoon was darkly overcast, the air wet and feeling a lot colder than it said on the thermometer. McCleany and Gray went to the front door and knocked, rang the bell, waited for a response that never came. Again without saying anything to Gray, McCleany left the front porch and headed around back. Following in Mc-Cleany's smoky wake as they walked to the side of the house Gray remembered all over again how McCleany delighted in bullying people, breaking rules, feeding his various appetites, wanting Gray to join in on bouts of drinking and whoring, calling him a weak sister when he wouldn't . . . but of course Gray never informed on his partner, eating cheese was taboo even for an ambitious young trooper who otherwise believed in conducting himself by the book.

McCleany dropped his cigar, still lit, on the ground. "Remind me to get that on the way back." He went down a flight of concrete steps and stood by the basement door, when Gray got there Mc-Cleany was holding out a hand. "You got the gloves?"

Gray gave him a pair of latex gloves, put on a pair himself. They'd discussed this. If the Raineys couldn't be contacted by phone and didn't answer their door, McCleany and Gray would break into the house to see if Growler had been there.

"Look at this shit," McCleany said, indicating marks on the door jamb.

"Jimmied."

Still unlocked too. They went into the basement, McCleany pulling out a stainless steel snub-nosed .38. "Smells funny."

Gray sniffed . . . something like food that'd been left on the stove. "What're we going to do if they're just sitting upstairs huh?"

"In the dark?"

"How we going to explain being here?"

"We'll say we're burglars."

"Come on I'm serious, they could be napping or something."

McCleany's broad shoulders sagged in exasperation, something else Gray remembered from when they were partners.

"Listen if we walk in on the old farts *you* make up some story about what we're doing here, you're the associate superintendent . . . I'm just this old stumblefuck forced out of a job because my partner wouldn't go to bat for me."

"Wouldn't go to bat for you? For chrissakes—"

Again with the shoulder sag. "You want to discuss this *now?*"

Gray walked past him and went up the basement steps to the first floor . . . using a small flashlight he spotted the red-splattered couch and had no doubts about what the staining agent was.

Coming to stand next to him McCleany sounded almost delighted. "Growler."

Gray nodded . . . the bodies would probably be in one of the bedrooms. With everything unraveling, Gray was experiencing the same panic of the soul he suffered seven years ago . . . this was going to dog him until the day he died.

Except the bodies weren't in a bedroom, they were stuffed in a hallway closet and they were headless. As Gray looked at them he felt strangely unaffected, as if the bodies were mannequins.

"Our lucky day," McCleany said.

Gray didn't feel lucky, he felt doomed.

"Not only does our boy Growler kill the Raineys," McCleany was saying, "but he accommodates us by doing it with his signature style, beheadings."

"I got to call this in."

McCleany grabbed him by the upper arm. "Don't be a sap, we're going to give Growler a chance to knock off Kenny Norton before we start pulling any alarms."

"What the hell you talking about huh?"

"Will you listen to your old partner for once. If this case gets re-opened three people can testify we encouraged them to lie on the stand, Growler's already killed these two, that leaves Kenny Norton. With him dead there's nobody in this world can say we committed or abetted perjury."

"Elizabeth Rockwell—"

"We didn't tell her to lie, she testified she found the victim's head in Growler's room—the truth. She testified that once upon a time in some storage room Growler grabbed her tit and she was afraid he was going to rape her—the truth. That Rockwell broad can't hurt us."

"I mean what if Growler goes after her too?"

"As long as he nails Norton before the party's over I don't care who else gets it."

"Jesus that's cold."

"Yeah well if we get sent to prison, that make you feel any warmer?"

"Too many loose ends," Gray said. "Somebody from a religious program gets Growler out of prison then *buys* Cul-De-Sac, you got to wonder what that's about huh?"

"I told you, the guy's got an angle."

"And something else too . . . just before I left to pick you up I find out a retired homicide detective is making all kinds of calls about Cul-De-Sac—"

"Who?"

"Teddy Camel, used to be—"

"I heard of him, Teddy Camel . . . a real hard-on, the Human Lie Detector they called him."

Gray muttered it again, "Too many loose ends."

McCleany got right into Gray's face. "Not as many as there were seven years ago and we tied those up didn't we?"

"Obviously not, else we wouldn't be standing here." Gray looked again at the bodies . . . their being headless actually made them less horrible to him, no eyes to stare back.

"We'll go out the basement," McCleany said. "If our luck holds nobody'll stumble on what's happened here until *after* Growler has had his way with Norton."

"This is stupid."

"I'll take care of the loose ends," McCleany continued as they went through the living room. "I'll find out what Camel's interest is, go have a talk with what's-his-name, that asshole brother-keeper."

"Paul Milton."

"Yeah, why he got Growler out of prison, why he bought Cul-De-Sac . . . I can handle this just like I did the first time, the only thing that can bite us in the ass now is somebody suddenly coming up with those pictures."

Gray stopped on the steps to the basement. "I thought J.L. burned them."

"That's what I always thought too but you know J.L., he was a cagey old bastard and—"

"Jesus."

"Don't let your bowels start leaking, Parker, all I'm saying is we got to face the possibility that J.L. kept the pictures in spite of what he promised us about burning them, you know how he was, liked to have leverage over people."

"Jesus."

"What the fuck's wrong with you?"

"You been sitting on this all these years, the possibility those photographs are still floating around somewhere?"

"I didn't see any reason to give my old partner any more sleepless nights than you were already having . . . I figured the pictures would either show up or not. And they haven't. And maybe I'm wrong about it, maybe J.L. destroyed them like he said."

They were in the basement now, McCleany acting amazingly jaunty, taking a few practice golf swings, talking about getting to the driving range before it closed. Then he noticed something by the washer and dryer. McCleany walked over there and shined his light on the bloodstains. When he lifted the lids to the washing machine and dryer McCleany laughed out loud. "Hey come here Parker you'll get a kick out of this."

14

AT SIX P.M. ON APRIL 15 TEDDY CAMEL WAS COLD, BLOWING WARM BREATH into cupped hands, hiding in the shadows of a corner on level 3 of his building's parking garage, waiting to catch the geek who'd been exposing himself to women . . . Camel just then remembering he hadn't mailed his tax forms, they were still in the office. He took a moment to think what he should do . . . give this stakeout one hour like Eddie said, go up and have dinner with Annie, drop the tax forms off on the way to Cul-De-Sac to pick up her husband. With that straight in his mind he relaxed a little but felt cold again.

Camel wondered if he should've gone to the store with Annie instead of pulling this stakeout, she still seemed shaky . . . but she also acted like she wanted some time by herself, away from Camel. They could talk at dinner, it'd be their last chance before the husband comes on the scene . . . maybe they'd talk about what Annie said, our baby.

His feet hurt. Blood pooled in his lower legs. He should've put a coat on over the sports jacket. Checked his watch, one hour maximum he told himself.

Twenty or thirty people had walked by on the way to their cars, no one had spotted Camel back here in his dark corner. Most of the men were on their own but the women clustered in groups of three or four. The word was out on the pervert. He was short, five and a half feet tall, he picked on women who were even shorter, he usually struck on the third level but a couple times up on 4. Camel hadn't seen anyone suspicious.

Around half past six a black guy came walking up the ramp from level 2, taking his time, stopping every few steps . . . obviously not the flasher but this guy wasn't just looking for his car either.

When he got closer Camel saw the man's Air Force blue jacket, saw he was wearing a service belt heavy with flashlight and pepper spray and cuffs and radio, Camel finally recognizing him . . . Jake Kempis who worked for the shopping mall's private security firm.

Camel stepped out of the corner and Kempis turned quickly.

"Teddy?"

"Yeah."

Kempis's shoulders relaxed, he came over. "Eddie said you were up here somewhere."

"Eddie's still around?"

"Just getting ready to leave, I think he's bringing you coffee."

"Good."

"Staking out the flasher?"

"Yeah."

"Hiding in the shadows, that's work for a brother ain't it?"

"Spadework." Camel laughed.

"What'd you say?" Kempis asked, bristling.

"My old man. He wouldn't abide racial slurs, if he was with guys who started talking about 'niggers' and 'spics' the old man would just walk away. But to the day he died he'd call a black man a spade. I'd say, 'Pop that's a slur too.' But he'd insist it wasn't, said it was simply descriptive."

"As in 'black as the ace of . . .' "

"The old man a product of his time, like we all are."

"Like my dad was," Kempis said with no trace of wistfulness. "Too easy on white people. 'They have their ways, we have ours.' " Kempis started to say something more but didn't, instead he asked Camel, "Will you give me a call if you catch the flasher, let me turn him in?"

"You still trying to get that appointment to the state police academy?"

"Yeah, might be too old though." Too black, Kempis thought . . . then looked at Camel and smiled. "Except maybe you don't plan to turn the pervert over to anyone, maybe you're planning to lay a little vigilante justice on his nervous ass."

"No I don't operate that way."

"Anymore you mean." Kempis smiled. "I heard stories about you, back when you worked homicide."

"Yeah?"

He nodded, relaxed now. "Hey Teddy, I came here looking for you 'cause I got something to tell you just between us girls."

Camel waited to hear it.

"Boss calls me a few minutes ago, wants to know if I got anything on you."

"Anything like what?"

"My question too. He says anything *negative*. Like did I think you were the kind of guy who'd run scams."

"Scams?"

"He specifically mentioned shakedowns . . . but he acted like he might be happy hearing *anything* negative, like have I ever seen you falling-down drunk, had any complaints about you from people working on your floor, traffic accidents . . . the man was seriously hoping for bad news."

"I wonder why."

"My question again. He says it's a police agency interested in you. I say which one, he dances around without answering me so I say well fax me over the sheet. He says there ain't no sheet."

"Somebody keeping it unofficial."

"My thought exactly."

"But why?"

"My question to you."

Camel said he had no idea and Kempis glanced over like he didn't believe him. "I thought maybe something you're working on, making people nervous you might be screwing up an active investigation."

"No."

Kempis again with that disbelieving look.

"I'm telling you Jake the stuff I work on nobody would be interested."

"Well you're making *somebody* nervous. My boss hinting like a bitch it would do us all some good if I could suddenly remember something bad about Teddy Camel."

Camel wondered if it was connected to the calls he made this afternoon about Cul-De-Sac . . . he also wondered how much Kempis knew and how much he was fishing. "Hey Jake."

"Yeah?"

Camel positioned himself for a good look at Kempis's face to see if the man was going to lie to him. "This have anything to do with the elephant?"

"The *what?*"

Satisfied Kempis's confusion was genuine, Camel told him, "Never mind."

"Did you say elephant?"

"Nothing, forget it."

Kempis scratched under his chin with the backs of his fingernails. "I want that appointment to the academy . . . if you're working on something that's going to lead to arrests, maybe you could—"

But Camel was already saying no. "I take pictures of women checking into motel rooms at noon, I talk with guys who owe five hundred bucks on an old Buick . . . nothing anybody's going to get excited over."

"Yeah." Kempis still thought Camel was hiding something. "I hear anything else I'll let you know."

"Appreciate it."

After the security guard left, Camel returned to the dark corner just as a large form stepped off the elevator, shoulders leading, a big Styrofoam cup in each mitt . . . Eddie bringing the coffee. He walked about twenty paces from the elevator, stopped, listened, then just stood there . . . figuring Camel should've spotted him by now and made himself known.

But Camel kept to the shadows. Eddie walked up the ramp to the top level, wandered around there awhile, walked back down to the third level where Camel was supposed to be.

"All right asshole," Eddie finally said in a conversational tone.

Camel stepped out.

Eddie came over and handed him a coffee. "Ha, ha."

Camel smiled that peculiar grimace of his.

"Okay, you going to tell me now . . . how'd you know Mary and me were having dinner over at Mike and Kathy's tonight?"

Camel explained about calling Michael to get information on Cul-De-Sac . . . he also told Eddie about the homicide that occurred there seven years ago, the trouble Annie ran into when she showed up at the place last night to surprise her husband for their third wedding anniversary. After he got done talking Camel thumbed off the plastic lid on the Styrofoam cup, spilling hot coffee on his fingers and cursing softly under his breath.

"See this little cutout," Eddie said, indicating the plastic lid he had left on his cup. "You break it loose, drink through the lid and that way what just happened won't happen."

Camel told Eddie he knew about the little cutout but refused on principle to suck coffee through plastic slits.

"I suppose a man's got to take a stand somewhere," Eddie said.

"You need to work on this weenie wagger's pattern."

"He'll hit before seven, he'll pick on a short woman, five-two or so, it'll happen here on 3 or maybe up on 4, that's a pattern, not a guarantee . . . pattern means tendency."

"I have a tendency to get paid for this kind of work."

"Consider it your civic duty."

"Jake Kempis was here—"

"Yeah he came into The Ground Floor asking where you were."

"Wants us to give him a call if we catch this flasher."

"You could do that but first you could put the fear of God in the little pervert. Give him that look you got, you know the look I mean. Tell him, 'Never again.' A man sees that dead-eyed look of yours he knows the only way to stop Teddy Camel, cut off your head and bury it in a separate hole."

"Am I blushing?"

"You know what I'm talking about." Neffering drank some coffee, remembering things. "Without ever raising your voice you could get angrier than any man I've ever met."

"I'm not like that anymore."

"To put the fear of God in this pervert you could fake it."

Camel didn't tell him that the kind of rage he used to carry around, you can't fake it. He had to sip carefully at the coffee, it was too hot. "I wish I still smoked."

"I'm putting in a smoking section over in that far corner where no one sits anyway, separating it with etched-glass partitions, commercial-grade exhaust system. It'll be real nice."

Camel kept trying to drink the coffee.

"Not very many of my customers smoke but those who do aren't allowed to smoke at their desks, they feel like lepers standing outside . . . this way they'll come in my place and buy stuff, have a nice place to smoke."

"Happy as cancerous little clams."

Eddie sucked at his coffee. "That woman, Annie . . . I thought she made you happy but now I see she didn't exactly put you in a good mood."

"I'm in a great mood . . . freezing my ass off 'cause some guy can't keep his dick holstered."

"When she first came up behind you, the way she was standing there, beaming and grinning, waiting for you to turn around and see who it was . . . I thought she might be your daughter."

Camel gave him a lingering look.

"She's young," Eddie said defensively.

"Eddie, you want to know something, ask . . . stop nibbling around the edges."

"You two were an item once upon a time?"

"None of your business."

"I figured you weren't going to tell me."

"She's somebody I knew a long time ago, now she's married and's having trouble with her husband like I told you." Camel checked his watch. "You go to dinner, I'm giving this another twenty minutes."

"Yeah." Then Eddie remembered. "I came out here to tell you how I'm impressed, suddenly you're such a popular guy."

Camel waited for the explanation.

"Not only does a pretty young lady show up today looking for you, not only does Jake Kempis come in wanting to know where you are, a few minutes ago I get a call from some guy used to work Investigations Unit with the state police, retired now. He asks after you, asks what kind of cases you handle. I say oh you know the usual stuff, divorces, skip tracing, nothing very exciting . . . why you asking. He said no big reason, Camel's name came up in conversation and he was just curious what become of you."

"Who's the guy?"

"Gerald McCleany. I didn't know him very well, this wasn't like a call from an old buddy . . . more like a call from out of the blue. Curious huh?"

"Curiouser and curiouser." Camel told him about unofficial inquiries being made through the security firm Kempis worked for. "Only thing I can figure is someone's upset over those calls I made this afternoon about that homicide at Cul-De-Sac . . . but if it's a closed case with the killer in prison who should care?"

"Somebody."

Camel nodded agreement. "And I bet Annie's husband is right in the middle of it. You got a lot of friends still carrying shields, maybe you could ask around, find out if something about that case is hanging fire."

Eddie's reply was interrupted by a woman shouting on the parking level above where they were standing . . . both men dropping their coffees and taking off at a run, except Camel didn't drop his cup far enough away and since it didn't have a lid, coffee splashed all over his pants.

"You take the ramp!" Eddie called. "I'll cover the stairs, he won't use the elevator!"

Camel ran up the ramp full speed not realizing how long it'd been since he ran anywhere full speed much less uphill . . . by the time he got to the top level he was sucking oxygen through an open mouth.

A woman, five feet maybe, was trying to pull away from a guy only a few inches taller, he was actually wearing a London Fog raincoat, amazing someone still cared enough to bother with classic attire . . . he had one hand holding tight to the woman's cloth coat, his other hand down at his crotch.

Taking the concrete steps two at a time had winded Eddie too, he was doing a slow stiff lope toward the action looking exactly like what he was, sixty years old and overweight, Camel closing in none too fast from the other direction. The pervert heard them coming and released the woman as he desperately tried to put his dick away, the woman taking that opportunity to haul off and bash him from behind with her purse.

Eddie wheezed out, "Freeze!" The pervert ran right for him and Camel who came together thinking they were both going to grab the guy at the same time but he dashed between them leaving Eddie and Camel grabbing air . . . except the pervert ran for the railing that kept cars from falling off and crashing four floors down and by the time he realized his mistake Eddie and Camel had regrouped enough to sort of trap the flasher against the railing.

Sort of because the little guy was quick and the two bigger men weren't. Eddie's walrus mustache drooped with sweat, Camel was still mouth-breathing.

The pervert had short thinning hair and a ferret's nervous brown eyes over a big honker and a small rodentlike mouth, he looked a little like that nasty lawyer Roy Cohn and you could tell by the way his eyes darted back and forth that any moment now he was going to head-fake one way, dash the other way, and end up once again squirting between the two men.

To forestall that, Eddie told Camel, "Draw down on him."

Camel reached under his jacket and touched the grip of the .357 magnum revolver he carried . . . but like some people believe in God was how Camel believed in the old rule about never leveling a weapon at someone you're not fully prepared to kill and he had no intention of killing this flasher so when Camel's hand came out from his jacket the only pistol showing was the one he formed with his finger and thumb.

"Hands up," Camel said quietly.

The pervert gave a disbelieving look first at Camel's finger-thumb gun, then up at Camel's eyes, then back down at the finger-thumb gun . . . then he executed the head-fake Camel and Eddie both knew was coming but were nonetheless too slow to counter-act . . . the pervert slanting to the right and taking off at a dead run.

"Stop or I'll shoot," Camel said in the same quiet voice as he went into a shooter's crouch, raised his finger-thumb pistol, and took careful aim. "Pow."

Eddie stood there like he was watching a magic show.

Camel straightened up. "I missed."

"You're not taking this all that serious, are you?"

Camel put the finger-thumb back under his coat.

"Not only are you suddenly popular, suddenly you're a come-dian?"

He squinted a smile.

Watching the last of the pervert run down the ramp, Eddie wiped perspiration from his mustache and said, "I never much cared for little guys."

"They live longer."

"They do?"

"You ever see a ninety-year-old guy six-four?" Camel asked.

"None comes to mind."

"I read about it, the taller you are, the shorter you live."

"That weenie wagger's going to outlive both of us." Eddie looked at Camel. "Especially if you keep using your fingers to shoot at him."

They'd forgotten about the woman who'd been assaulted, the only one of them who'd done any damage to the pervert . . . she was standing off by her car watching all of this and finally asked them warily, "Are you police officers?"

Eddie said they were, he was about to add that there'd been a lot of budget cutbacks, that's why they had to shoot at fleeing suspects with fingers, but the woman spoke first in a voice that turned out to be a lot louder than necessary, "He was uncircumcised!"

Camel looked at Eddie. "Better make a note of that, Sergeant."

Eddie started patting his pockets, the woman already hurrying to her car. When she drove past them, Camel and Eddie offered at-your-service-ma'am salutes which she didn't acknowledge.

They stood there until her car was gone from sight though you could still hear it screeching corners. Eddie looked down at Camel's coffee-stained trousers and told him, "If you'd left the lid on like I said, that wouldn't have happened."

After a moment's pause Camel laughed harder and louder than he had in a very long time.

15

IT WAS HOT IN CUL-DE-SAC, FAT BLACK FLIES BUZZING AROUND LIKE August not April. Growler had taken his shirt off and being bare to waist showed how well muscled he had become in prison . . . his skin pale as if never touched by the sun, very little body hair, a scattering of pimples across his upper back, on his left shoulder a tattoo of a cartoon character, the Tasmanian Devil, and on his right bicep a heart with a crack in it and tears leaking out. He walked around the room scratching at his upper arms like he had a rash, he would repeatedly smooth back his black hair with both hands then obsessively wipe at his mouth and nose as if he thought they were still powdered white. He stopped in front of a kneeling Paul Milton. "St. Paul the one they crucified upside down?"

"No," Milton said, "that was St. Peter."

"What?"

Milton didn't repeat it or try to look up, he didn't want to see Satan's eyes staring at him or see those big teeth either.

"What did you say?" Growler demanded.

"St. Peter."

He heard it that time, Growler laughing and then hugging himself like he was suddenly cold in spite of the room's stifling heat. He returned to pacing and scratching at his arms . . . he was seriously wired as if the cocaine had been a live electric cord shoved up his nose into his brain. He stopped long enough to kick Annie's husband in the ass.

An easy target because Paul was buck naked on his knees, forehead forced to the floor, wrists pulled back and tied to his ankles, bare ass up . . . a contortion of supplication and humiliation and aching vulnerability.

"I know you got that goddamn elephant," Growler said. "You double-crossed me just like everybody else, didn't you, St. Paul . . . didn't you?"

"St. Paul was betrayed by a coppersmith."

"What?" With Milton's face shoved to the floor, Growler had a hard time understanding him.

"St. Paul from the Bible, he was betrayed by a coppersmith."

"Did you say coppersmith?" Growler leaned down to listen.

"Yes."

"I got backstabbed by my best friend who's a sculptor, who works in metal . . . how's that for a coincidence?"

"St. Paul was beheaded."

"No way!" Growler was surprised, genuinely delighted by this information.

"His head bounced three times."

"Get out of here!"

"And a fountain appeared at each of those three spots."

"I'll be damned."

"Yes you will."

Growler straightened up.

"I didn't take your elephant," Milton told him. "I was with you when we opened the shaft."

"Yeah and you were snooping around three weeks before I got here . . . you think I didn't notice how you'd been tearing into things, lifting floorboards and— Did you find any photographs?"

Paul said something Growler didn't understand.

"Listen to me asshole . . . *hey.*" He nudged Paul with his boot and spoke in a more conciliatory voice. "If you found those pictures I might let you keep the elephant."

Paul began reciting the Lord's Prayer.

Growler kicked him in the ass again. "You lied to me about having a wife . . . everybody lying to me, lying about me, lies, lies, *lies*." And kicked him again.

Paul grunted, that last kick really hurt. "I didn't lie about Annie, I just didn't mention her."

"What?"

He didn't bother repeating the distinction.

"You found the elephant, called your wife up here, gave it to her, that's why she ran out last night . . . taking the elephant with her."

"No."

Growler came around by Paul's bowed head. "Where is she?"

"I don't know."

"You were planning to meet her someplace, have a good laugh how you pulled one over on Old Scratch."

"Satan."

"Where's your wife!" He began rubbing his face again, felt close to tears . . . so frustrating, so goddamn infuriating, that beetle in his brain, everyone betraying him. "After I find Kenny Norton and Elizabeth, your wife's next on the list. I'll bugger her little ass until—"

"Get thee behind me Satan."

Growler heard that and it made him laugh. "Good idea," he said walking behind Milton and straddling his legs.

Paul was praying hard.

"Give you a taste of what Old Scratch has in store for Mrs. Milton."

Paul's prayers were interrupted by the sound of a belt being undone.

16

ANNIE PUT DOWN THE SHOPPING BAGS—NEW CLOTHES, SOME FOOD, A bottle of red wine—and let herself into Teddy's place with the key he'd given her. She looked around the room where he lived and considered opening drawers and flipping through his mail and checking under the sink for the cleaning products he used . . . she'd been fascinated with this man for twenty-five years. But Annie did none of those things, she knew he would immediately sense she'd been snooping and she couldn't bear his disapproval.

Except for the dismal reality of living in one room his quarters were as she expected . . . neat and clean, as unadorned as a barracks. Only two framed photographs on the wall, Annie assumed they were of Teddy's daughter and grandson. Disappointed with how little this room revealed, Annie opened the connecting door to Teddy's office . . . and stopped short.

"Oh," the man said. "Didn't know anyone was home." He was standing behind Camel's desk and had an unlit cigar in his mouth.

"Teddy'll be back in a minute."

"Sure." He was about sixty, average height, big belly, broad red face, thinning gray hair showing around the edges of his golf cap. He wore lime-green pants, a short-sleeved pink shirt, white shoes . . . and as Annie watched, he gripped an imaginary golf club and took a few practice swings. He seemed harmless, a pear-shaped man with thick arms and a fat ass.

"Are you a friend of Teddy's?" she asked.

"That's right."

"I'm Annie Milton." She held out her hand and he came from around the desk to shake it but didn't offer his own name in exchange. Instead he said, "Annie *Milton* . . . yeah Teddy's told me all about you."

That's a lie she thought . . . if Teddy had mentioned her at all he would've used her maiden name, Annie Locken. "And you're . . ." she asked.

"Late for a date," he said pleasantly except that his smile was more leering than friendly. "You got Teddy working on Cul-De-Sac for you isn't that right little lady?"

The reference to Cul-De-Sac started her heart beating fast, her palms sweating . . . Annie making a point of checking her watch. "He'll be back any second now."

Which also amused the man. "I'll catch him next time." He waved and winked and left the office . . . Annie locking the door after him.

She was still feeling anxious when she went over and stood by the phone to try Paul again. I'm staying with Teddy Camel, she rehearsed . . . he's an old friend of the family, a former policeman, I came to him because I'm scared about what happened last night and frightened of you too Paul, the way you denied that man was even there.

Paul will be suspicious, he'll ask, now who did you say this Teddy Camel was.

I told you, a friend of the family, an old friend of my mother's . . . and then there would follow other lies and half-truths, Annie using them as stepping-stones to get through this minefield.

Because she can't of course tell Paul about the Teddy Camel she's been in love with since she was ten years old, can't tell Paul how she tricked Teddy Camel into joining her at the beach house when she was twenty-one and Teddy was thirty-six . . . certainly couldn't tell Paul any details of that summer, how she walked around sore between the legs and sore in her heart too, crying over Teddy Camel and wearing his shirts, and if he'd said let's knock over a convenience store and kill some clerks she would've said yes and if he had wanted to tie her down and fuck her in places she'd never been fucked before, she would've done that too, she might even have been the one who suggested it . . . she practiced writing her first name next to his last name and all during that summer when she was twenty-one and saw him walking toward her she experienced an elation like being bitterly cold then drinking something warm and sticky sweet, his gestures endeared him to her and she kept looking at his face when he was looking elsewhere and, if she could have, she would've spread her body over his like an ointment . . . you can't tell something like that to a husband even if it is tucked away fourteen years in the past.

■　■　■

WHEN HE GOT to the beach house those fourteen years ago and discovered no other guests in attendance, Camel knew she wasn't telling the truth about all the other people canceling out at the last minute. She hadn't expected him to believe her, what surprised Annie was how angry he became. "Don't ever lie to me," he told her in a voice so chilling that she was physically afraid of him and almost called the whole thing off . . . then took a chance and said, "Stay with me anyway."

No he said he wouldn't do that . . . but he'd spend the night because it was too late to find a room.

Which meant she had the night. Annie was twenty-one and this time when she slipped into bed with him his protests were feeble and although they didn't make love that first night, neither did Teddy demand that she find somewhere else to sleep.

She made him breakfast.

She walked around in cotton underwear.

It wasn't that difficult.

So that by the third day they were in almost constant coitus, during recesses Annie would take him out along the shore and say, "Oh look, Teddy, the insatiable sea." He would hold her hand as they walked but only at night; in public, during the day, he wouldn't let her touch him.

She fell into talking jags which wasn't like her at all, not like her to cry for no reason either, she told Teddy Camel things that, hearing them today, would make her cringe . . . for every woman there is one man, for every man, one woman, and although you don't always end up with your soul mate and in fact can be perfectly happy with someone who isn't your soul mate . . . you're mine, Annie declared, and I'm yours.

He'd listen to all this while drinking expensive gin and smoking unfiltered cigarettes and making no replies but when Annie told him she had the beach house for all summer, Teddy surprised her by saying he'd accumulated almost two months leave and could go back to work for a week, make arrangements, then return here and the two of them could spend what's left of summer together.

That week he was gone Annie pined for him in ways that would strike you as pathetic if you've never been in love the way Annie was . . . and when Teddy returned they fucked so much that her genitals turned swollen and her nipples ached from his mouth and she bore his bruises.

Her jaws were sore, for the first time in her life she tasted semen and biting a shoulder she tasted blood . . . Annie swallowed both.

Her emotions shrink-wrapped to him so tightly that circuitry on occasion went haywire flipping Annie from laughter to tears or the other way around . . . Teddy watched without asking what any other man would ask, what's wrong? Sometimes she wanted to hurt him, he'd have to yank her by the hair to stop her biting him and once she slapped him across the face as hard as she could apropos of nothing except the delirium of love, it brought a glaze of tears to his eyes but not from emotion, just an automatic response to being slapped hard in the face . . . then he walked away, poured a gin, sat down to drink it, never asking why'd you do that, either he knew or didn't care.

They drank beer for breakfast and formed a conspiracy it didn't count as alcohol.

She read to him passages from books she loved and quoted

poems she knew by heart. Listening carefully, Teddy often said nothing.

"Oh listen to this Teddybear, right up your dark alley. 'J'ai appelé les bourreaux pour, en périssant, mordre la crosse de leurs fusils. J'ai appelé les fléaux, pour m'étouffer avec le sable, le sang. Le malheur a été mon dieu. Je me suis allongé dans la boue. Je me suis séché à l'air du crime. Et j'ai joué de bons tours à la folie.' "

Trying so very hard to impress him, I'm a senior in college, I can speak French . . . making him wait patiently for the translation.

" 'I called to the executioners that I might gnaw their rifle-butts while dying. I called to the plagues to smother me in blood, in sand. Misfortune was my God. I laid myself down in the mud. I dried myself in the air of crime. I played sly tricks on madness.' "

She looked up from the text and pronounced the author's name carefully for Teddy: "Rimbaud."

"*A Season in Hell,*" he replied . . . astonishing her.

He didn't like massages, giving or receiving, but allowed her to shampoo his hair.

She watched when he shaved and one time in the shower together she said he could pee on her if he wanted to but he didn't want to.

He bathed her, touching Annie more tenderly than any supplicant ever touched any queen . . . then fucked her like a whore on the bathroom floor.

She was always showing off for him, posing provocatively, raising a skirt to reveal her bare ass.

One night she dressed in a red skirt that barely covered that ass, wearing a tight tube top then in vogue, she balanced on red high heels with straps that wrapped around her ankles, she put on too much red lipstick and piled her red hair on top of her head and, emerging from the bathroom, demanded with theatrical bitchiness, "I'm bored, take me dancing." He told her he didn't dance and in any case wouldn't take her out looking like that, he'd be getting in fights all night long. She threatened, "You don't take me dancing, I'm going alone." Leaving the implication hanging like his cigarette smoke in the air between them, she demanded,

"Well?" Don't let the door hit you in the ass on the way out, he conveyed through gesture, posture. Annie left, Teddy didn't call to her or ask her to reconsider, neither did he follow after her or say, when she returned at midnight, where have you been I was worried sick. She told him, "I just went out and sat on the beach, in case you were wondering." He said, "I wasn't."

They shot pool, they played miniature golf . . . Teddy was serious in these endeavors, having fun without smiling unless you counted the way he squinted.

Unprecedented in her adult life she begged for attention, debased herself and felt ennobled doing it . . . pouted, played a little girl, cried on purpose, went all kittenish and coy.

One time she pulled a knife on him. He slapped it out of her hand and neither spoke of the incident again.

She said things a person seriously in love will say, linking the concept of love with the word forever, getting giddy over the moon . . . he never laughed at her and never hurt her physically except as an unintended consequence of vigorous intercourse.

Teddy was always surprising Annie by what he knew, whom he had read, he surprised her by being good at crossword puzzles, they got preferred service at restaurants and bars maybe because of the way she gazed at him with adoration and the way he looked noble and this combination elevated the spirits of waiters and bartenders and even passersby who'd turn around for another look at Annie Locken walking with Teddy Camel.

If she'd kept a diary that summer she would've capitalized his pronouns.

Annie wasn't on the pill, she'd lied to him about that and for some reason the Human Lie Detector didn't detect this particular lie. He was however aware that she wasn't nearly as sexually experienced as she wanted him to believe, much of what she did in bed with Teddy that summer she'd never done before . . . like getting pregnant.

Annie didn't tell him.

Fourteen years ago she was in love with him as deeply as a person can be in love, as deep as the sea she might've said at the time

. . . once she masturbated him as they stood in that ocean and Annie told him, salt to salt.

Each time they'd walk down to the shore she'd say, "Oh look, Teddy, the insatiable sea."

Until finally on the last day of that summer he asked the question she'd been angling for: why do you keep saying that?

"Because I'm the insatiable sea," she answered.

He didn't comment.

"Now you're supposed to ask, 'If you're the insatiable sea, then who am I?' "

"Okay."

"Ask it."

"Consider it asked."

"You're those rocks there, see how they're getting worn down."

He looked at the rocks, then at Annie, then he said, "Takes a long time."

"I got all the time in the world."

He said he didn't.

"Let's get married."

He didn't say no, he just looked seaward his blue eyes squinting in a way she found almost unbearably attractive.

"I'm serious." And she was, Annie already knew she was pregnant. "Let's go get a license right now today, we'll stay here whatever waiting period there is, then we'll get married and I'll go back to Washington with you."

That's when he said no.

"I can make you happy, I love you . . . marry me."

"No."

She kicked him hard in the leg and demanded it: "Marry me goddamn you!"

"No."

"*Yes.* Marry me or I'll fucking kill you."

"I doubt it."

"If you don't marry me I'll kill myself."

"Yeah well . . ."

Annie performed all the tricks she knew, pouting and crying

and cajoling and promising what she'd do for and to him on their wedding night and every night of their marriage after that, debasing herself and begging him and then threatening to go off and fuck every man she meets . . . nothing worked.

"Do you love me, can you at least say you love me?" she asked.

"No."

Jesus he was a hard man.

"Then it's over?" Her mind would not compute such a sentence. "The summer, us . . . everything?"

When he didn't deny it she felt claws at her heart.

"Teddy . . ."

He waited.

"And so, sir, how would you sum up this past summer?" she asked, her voice playful, mocking the weight on her heart. "How would you characterize the young lady?"

He looked her right in the eye. "The sweetest little piece of ass I ever had."

Annie choked on it but willed herself to be tough . . . tough like Teddy Camel, telling him, "Or ever will have."

"Probably."

"Or ever will have."

"Yes."

None of which Annie Milton could tell her husband so when Paul finally answered the phone at Cul-De-Sac she told him lies and half-truths, committing those sins of omission to which marriages are docked like little boats too fragile for the open sea.

17

PAUL PUT THE PHONE DOWN AND TOUCHED HIS FACE. EVERYTHING HURT. His nose had been freshly broken, a tooth knocked out, the older injuries along the left side of his face still being heard from . . . but it was Growler's final violation that hurt the worst, both physically and mentally, causing Paul Milton's already fragile hold on sanity to slip. I did this for Annie, he told himself. I lost all her money, I did this for Annie. Telling himself these things didn't help.

He wished he could sleep or, failing that, could simply and peacefully die, Paul no longer cared if Annie went to the police. Is that where she was? On the phone just now she said she was with a policeman . . . Paul couldn't remember everything she'd told him, something about a policeman coming out later this evening to . . . what, to *what?*

"What?" he asked aloud. He was lying on his side on that big black leather couch in the middle of the old library he'd made into his workshop . . . finding it difficult to concentrate because of all the whispering from the chimney, that girl, those men. What were they whispering? *"What?"* he asked again.

"You talking to me?"

When Paul sat up everything hurt.

"Jesus buddy what happened to you?"

Paul looked to the doorway of the workshop and saw a golfer standing there . . . wearing green pants, pink shirt, white shoes, white golfing cap. He was smoking a cigar and holding a club. Considering the mysteries of Cul-De-Sac this apparition didn't surprise Paul as much as one might think.

"You want me to take you to the hospital?" the golfer asked, removing the cigar from his mouth.

Paul touched his swollen lips and misshapen nose . . . and thought, he can't see where it hurts the worst.

"I'll run you to the hospital," the golfer offered again.

Was this the policeman Annie had mentioned on the phone, an old friend of her mother's she'd said.

McCleany came into the room and stood in front of the couch. He looked at Paul for a long time then addressed an imaginary ball, aimed down an imaginary fairway, taking a real swing . . . then held up the club for Paul to see and said, "Three-wood."

But there wasn't any wood on the club, the grips were plastic, the shaft was graphite, the head was metal . . . Paul knew there was a parable in this if he could just figure it out.

"He's been pretty rough on you?" the golfer asked as he walked to the fireplace and threw his cigar in.

Paul said nothing.

The golfer came back to stand very close to him. "Where is he?"

Paul shook his head.

"You ain't telling or you don't know?"

The question struck Paul as incredibly difficult to answer.

"You sure you don't need to see a doctor?" McCleany asked.

Another tough question.

"He won't let you sleep will he?"

"No he won't." There was an assumption between the men, who they were talking about.

"I know what the two of you are looking for, where is he?"

"I . . ." Paul wasn't sure how much he should tell this man.

"Yeah?"

Paul thought if he could just close his eyes and go to sleep, maybe when he woke up the golfer would be gone.

"I'm waiting."

Paul reached up to see if his glasses were on . . . they were but then why couldn't he focus?

"Photographs," the golfer said.

"What?"

"That's what the two of you are hunting."

"We're hunting elephants," Paul said.

McCleany's turn to be confused. "Elephants?"

"I would like to confess now." Paul found the golfer vaguely re-assuring, he was squat and waddly and grandfatherly . . . but was this a golfer from God or was he from Satan?

"Ever hear of Moe Norman?" McCleany asked, swinging the club again.

Paul hadn't.

"Greatest natural ball striker the game has ever seen."

Paul listened carefully.

"Set forty course records, so accurate they called him the Pipeline, could put a ball in a bushel basket at two hundred yards, weird-ass swing though. Canadian."

It was like a story in the Bible, you had to listen carefully and then pray for understanding.

"You find those pictures or not?"

"Elusive," Paul said.

"What?"

"More elusive than any elephant."

"Jesus buddy you're—"

"Jesus *is* my buddy."

"Where's Growler?"

"Who?"

McCleany put the head of the club on Paul's neck. "I don't care if you *are* beat up, I'll finish the job you get cute with me . . . now where's Growler?" He was pronouncing the name Grow-ler, Paul had been told it was Growl-er. McCleany pushed on the club until Paul choked. "Donald Growler goddamn you."

"Goddamn me," Paul readily agreed, making no effort to re-move the club head from his neck.

"You're weird," McCleany said, withdrawing the club and taking a casual half-swing.

Paul agreed with that assessment too.

"Give me the photographs or tell me if Growler's found them yet, you do either of those things for me and I'm out of your life . . . now ain't that simple?"

"Simple?"

"Yeah. You know what I'm talking about don't you . . . dirty pictures."

"Filthy," Paul concurred.

"You see them?"

"Did I see them?"

McCleany's shoulders sagged. "I'm going to fucking shoot you."

"Okay."

While studying Paul, trying to figure out what to do with him, McCleany leaned on the three-wood like it was a cane.

"Sometimes I hear a piano playing," Paul said.

"Hope played a piano."

Paul thought about that for a moment then declared with great emotion, "What a beautiful thing to say." Tears filled his tired, itching eyes. *"Hope played a piano."*

"I met your wife."

"Annie doesn't play the piano."

"She plays the flute."

"She does?" Paul genuinely surprised by this bulletin.

"I caught her playing Camel's flute."

He didn't understand.

"Your wife's a sexy woman . . . red hair, cute little caboose. Know where she is right now?"

"With the police?"

As McCleany laughed he used thumb and forefinger to press the bridge of his fat nose. "I guess that's one way of looking at it. She's staying with an ex-cop, I walked in on them . . . there's no polite way of putting this, son, she was giving him a blow job."

Paul's heart squeezed tight in his chest.

"Oh yeah," McCleany said, examining his club. "They were

going at it hot and heavy." He looked at Paul. "Sorry to be the bearer of bad news."

"I saw Satan, he has genitals hanging from his face."

"Jesus kid you are seriously fucked up."

"Yes," Paul agreed. "I seriously am."

McCleany regripped the three-wood. "Moe Norman holds the club the way you would a hammer, stands way back from the ball. He's still around you know, didn't have the temperament for the pro tour. I can't get the hang of his swing."

In response Paul told him, "Crazy people don't hear voices inside their heads, they hear the voices talking to them from outside . . . if it was just a voice inside your head, you could ignore it . . . more or less."

McCleany stared at him.

Paul asked, "Are you the policeman Annie sent to pick me up?"

"She's sending a cop over to take you in?"

"She said something about a camel."

McCleany laughed. "This particular Camel is the guy whose dick your wife was trying real hard to swallow."

"Oh." It was a lament.

"Come on I'll give you a ride to Camel's office, let you sort him and your wife out . . . but first you level with me about those pictures. Growler found them yet?"

"No."

"You telling me the truth?"

"Yes."

"Okay good, now we're making some progress. Where's Growler?"

"He's looking for . . . a friend?"

"A friend?"

"What a friend we have in Jesus."

McCleany raised the club. "Don't start."

"Kenny?"

"Growler's out looking for Kenny Norton?" This pleased McCleany enormously.

"Can't find him though."

"Shit, if all he needs is an address, I can help him there."

"You said Annie is . . . committing adultery?"

This question also cheered McCleany, he hadn't been sure that his lie about Annie had registered.

"Is she?" Paul asked in anguished voice.

"She's fucking Teddy Camel, yeah."

"Please don't say it that way."

"It hurt less if I say she's 'committing adultery'?"

How can you tell what hurts less or more when everything hurts?

The golfer was speaking to him, asking something about how long does it take Paul to recover.

"From what?"

"A blow job."

"Oh."

"Me, my age, takes twenty-four hours to reload, ain't that a kick in the ass . . . in my day I could fuck them on an assembly line but no more. A young guy like you, what . . . half an hour and you're ready to go again? The question is, how about Teddy Camel?"

Paul was almost sure that's the name Annie mentioned, she said he was an old friend of the family.

"Hey buddy."

"Yes?"

"If we hurry up and get to Camel's place maybe you can prevent a doubleheader."

Baseball? Paul's mind was such a muddle.

The golfer asked him if he had a gun.

"A gun?"

"Don't repeat every goddamn thing I say!"

"Okay."

"Now do you own or have access to a firearm?"

Paul thought carefully before answering, he didn't want the golfer to get mad at him again. Finally he said, "No."

"I sure as hell can't loan you mine . . . how are you with a knife?"

"A knife?"

McCleany jammed him hard in the gut with that three-wood. "I saw some butcher knives down in your kitchen, we'll grab one on the way out."

Holding his stomach Paul leaned over on his side, putting both feet up on the couch. "I'd like to sleep now."

"Jesus Christ—"

"Our Lord and Saviour," Paul said dreamily.

McCleany grabbed an ankle and pulled him from the couch, when Paul landed on his ass he cried out in pain.

McCleany helped him to his feet, brushed him off a little, put an arm around Paul's shoulder. "Got something for you." The golfer held out a meaty hand, centered in the palm was a key.

Another parable, Paul thought . . . a *key*.

"The key to Camel's office," the golfer said. "Got it from a security guard. Go ahead, *take it*."

Paul did, sensing inevitability.

18

"YOU'RE BACK." ANNIE GOT OUT OF TEDDY'S RECLINER AND CAME TO HIM but then wasn't sure what to do when she got there, a kiss on the cheek, a friendly hug? She'd been in love with the idea of Teddy Camel for twenty-five years but they'd been together only two times, once when she was ten and then that summer when she was twenty-one . . . in some ways he was a stranger. And now that she was no longer immediately terrified about what had happened at Cul-De-Sac, no longer emboldened by vodka, Annie felt awkwardly shy around Teddy . . . ended up speaking too loudly and cheerfully, "Hey how'd that stakeout go, you catch the guy?"

Camel's reply came as always in cool understatement. "No." He didn't tell her about it. "You ready for dinner?"

She made those exaggerated facial expressions a woman will use when seeking empathy. "Well I bought some food and a bottle of wine so we could eat here . . ."

"Good."

Her big smile was followed by a broad look of concern. "But I finally got through to Paul and he sounds really disturbed, I'm not even sure he understood what I was telling him . . . I'm feeling guilty about what he's going through so maybe we shouldn't take the time to have dinner, maybe you should just go out to Cul-De-Sac and get him right now."

"Okay."

That's what's so maddening about this man, she thought . . . he won't try to talk me into having dinner with him, won't say he's disappointed we're not going to have some time together, doesn't even act ticked off, just says *okay*.

"You got the keys to your truck?"

"Sometimes I could just slap you."

"You've done that."

"Don't you want to know why you infuriate me?"

"Not really."

She made a growling sound, wanted to shake him.

"Maybe we have time for a glass of that wine you bought," he said.

She almost asked, And now I'm supposed to be grateful? . . . but knew it would sound bitchy. "Paul's been out there at Cul-De-Sac for a month on his own, I suppose he can survive another half hour . . . I'll get the wine."

Camel accepted the bottle from her without looking at the label and while he was pulling the cork he told Annie, "You look pretty."

Which caught her by surprise . . . not that she hadn't given thought to the clothes she'd bought: a simple white cotton dress that went down to her ankles, the bodice closed with a white cord that Annie had tied in a bow. She'd put on makeup, used a brand of lipstick called Red Abandon, wore dangly earrings. Annie was barefoot. She was also in the middle of her cycle.

Last month she read a magazine article that said women, married or single, more often than not initiate affairs at a time in their cycle when they'd normally be most fertile . . . and this holds true even if the women are using birth control measures, which of course Annie was not.

Being in the middle of her cycle was one reason Annie traveled from North Carolina to surprise Paul, hoping to get pregnant on their wedding anniversary . . . except now she was with the man who made her pregnant fourteen years ago, is it any wonder that clear-eyed people claim there are no accidents, no coincidences.

When he handed her the glass of wine, Annie took note of two things . . . one, the glasses he'd brought out were expensive crystal and, two, age had bent him over a little.

"Cheers," he said.

"Cheers," she replied, then talked a little about the wine.

He listened, adding nothing.

"Before I forget," she said, "there was a guy in your office earlier . . . I found him standing behind your desk, he wouldn't tell me his name."

"What'd he look like?"

"About sixty, dressed like someone on the way to or from the golf course . . . said he was a friend of yours but I think he was lying about that."

"Don't know any golfers. You leave a door unlocked?"

"No. He knew why I came to you, he knew about Cul-De-Sac."

Camel told Annie about his conversation with Jake Kempis, about the call Eddie got from the retired state police investigator. She asked if he thought any of that was connected to Cul-De-Sac, Camel said he didn't know. They sipped at the wine and purposely didn't catch each other's eye, then Annie said, "In some ways you *have* changed."

"Fourteen years."

"You don't seem angry anymore, your anger used to frighten me. Remember that fight you got in with that big red-faced guy on the beach?"

"Yeah."

"Pow, pow, pow," she said, throwing a flurry of blows with her left hand that caused the glass in her other hand to spill a little wine on the floor. "Sorry," she said, looking around for a towel.

"Leave it."

She stopped looking for the towel and told him, "That fight was over before it got started."

"Stupid of me."

"He was a jerk."

"Yeah but all we had to do was move on down the beach. He was there with his wife and kid, remember? I ask him to turn down the radio, he's got to show the wife and kid how he's their protector. It wouldn't have hurt us none to move on down the beach."

"You were showing off for me."

"And he was showing off for his family . . . ends up with a busted nose, humiliated in front of his wife and kid. To what point?"

"Prove you were the baddest dog on the beach."

"Yeah well . . ."

"What?"

"Mostly now I stay up on the porch."

"Just stopped being pissed off at the world?"

"I guess." He poured them each another glass of wine. "I used to wake up in the morning, like you said, pissed off at the world, I was mad before anything happened to make me mad, by the time I got out there among people I was loaded and cocked, I don't know why, never did figure it out, not like I had some trauma in childhood to make me angry all the time . . . but it was there, I could feel it like a knot in my stomach."

"And it just went away?"

"Right here in this room, or at least that's the first time I knew it was gone. A crew had been sent by the building manager to paint the place before I moved in, I specified that I wanted the walls white. All my working life I'd been looking at institutional green, I wanted plain white walls. I come in, the crew's just finishing up . . . every wall here was painted green.

"I said to the crew chief the walls are supposed to be white. He didn't take it very well. I guess he'd had a rough day, everybody on his ass, it's Friday afternoon and he didn't have room enough for one more complaint. So he said to me, 'Well, pal, they're not white, they're green.' He told me I'd have to put in another work order, they'd catch me next cycle through, six months maybe. Then he told his guys start wrapping it up. Ignoring me. Daring me to say anything.

"In the old days that's when the knot in my gut would've started twisting. I never had to work up an anger, never had to summon it

. . . it just came on its own. So I stood there staring at that crew chief, waiting for the anger to hit, like waiting for a drug to take effect . . . any second now I'm going to shove his face against those wet walls, tell him he'd better start licking that green off. And either he would fight back or he wouldn't. Guy probably could've beat the shit out of me, not that that ever stopped me before.

"But it never arrived. The anger. I just wasn't mad. I didn't feel twisted up inside, had no desire to fight the guy. I don't know. Maybe you really do get wiser as you get older, maybe it's just a lower hormone level.

"This crew chief, seeing that I'm not going to do anything, he decides to exploit the situation, tells me, 'You got any problem with my work, keep in mind I could turn you in for setting up an apartment here.' Because the building is supposed to be commercial space only, no residential.

"I showed him the work order that specified white walls and I said, 'I had to look at green walls in the army, green walls all the time I was a cop . . . I was just hoping to get away from green walls, that's all.'

"He asked me what I did in the army, I told him I was an MP and he said yeah I might've been one of the MPs hauling him out of the cathouses he used to frequent back when he was in the Army, and I asked him where he served, he said he did a tour in Nam, so I told him, 'Welcome home.' Because most of the guys never got a parade, never got welcomed back . . . and his whole attitude changed, he said he had a brother-in-law who was a cop and we talked about that for a while, then he took the work order, looked at it, looked at me . . . says he and his crew would be back Monday morning to repaint the whole place white. Said he knew where some carpet was left over from a big job, he'd arrange for it to be delivered after the painting was done, have it laid for me too . . . no charge. Apologized for the screwup with the paint. We went down to The Ground Floor and had a couple beers together.

"And afterwards I'm thinking, Jesus Christ, *it's that easy?* I wanted to call people, tell them I was sorry for being such a hard case, I hadn't realized there was an option. Wanted to call bars where I'd been in fights, apologize to guys I'd beaten up for no good reason—"

"Did you want to call me?"

Camel didn't answer right away, he was unaccustomed to talking so much and finally settled for telling her, "I thought about you a lot over the years."

"Not enough to write back, return any of my calls."

"I guess not."

"Did you keep my letters?"

"No."

"Paul's kept everything I ever wrote to him, even notes I left for him in the first apartment we rented."

"There's a better grade of man around now."

"You think men like Paul are weak sisters."

"No."

Annie ran a fingertip around the rim of her glass. "I wanted to marry you so bad, I was going to show up one day on your doorstep and slit my wrists in front of you just so you'd have to take care of me."

"It wouldn't have worked."

"You would've let me bleed to death?"

"No I mean us getting married."

"Why?"

He poured more wine, finishing the bottle. "You got pregnant that summer?" The question caught Annie off guard but of course Camel already knew the answer. "I'm sorry I wasn't there for you."

She was afraid if she tried to speak right now she'd start crying.

"You were the best thing that ever happened in my life," Camel told her.

Now she couldn't even look at him or she'd start bawling.

There was a long silence but it didn't make either of them feel particularly awkward, almost as if they were soaking up each other's presence, reacquainting themselves by osmosis.

"I better have some coffee before I drive out there," Camel finally said. "Would you like a cup?"

"No thanks." Her voice seemed to be okay. "A cup of tea would be nice."

Camel went to the counter by the sink, Annie watching him from behind. "Do you like living here?"

"It's convenient." The truth was, living here made Camel crazy, especially at night when he couldn't sleep and had nowhere to roam. He surprised himself by confessing to her, "I wish I had a house."

"Really?"

"When I was married I had a great house, two-story Victorian with a double set of stairways . . . I loved walking around at night when everyone else was asleep, checking on things, going out into the yard, coming back in." It struck him as a novel idea now, to have grass under his feet anytime he wanted. "I used to end up down in the basement, putter around with my tools." He remembered how, when the circular saw came on, the light bulb hanging from its wire over the workbench would dim like it was wincing from the power draw. Living here in this single room the only night-roaming options open to him were crossing over to his one-room office and standing in there or taking to the building's hallways and stalking those empty corridors, getting bored stares from the guard who walked from one box to the next putting in a key to prove he was there.

While Teddy stood at the counter getting the tea ready, Annie came up behind him and slipped an arm casually around his waist, her hand resting on his hip where she felt the big revolver. "Armed and dangerous."

He grimaced a smile.

"That summer we spent together you kept your guns locked in the trunk."

"I was afraid you'd shoot me."

"I might've." She tugged on the revolver's grips. "Let's see it."

Camel dried his hands and brought out the .357 magnum revolver but wouldn't let Annie hold it.

She asked him if his work was dangerous.

"No."

"Then why—"

"I've been armed my entire adult life, I wouldn't feel right without them."

"Them?"

From an ankle holster he brought out a five-shot .38 special revolver, from the pocket of his sports coat he produced a five-shot .22 magnum revolver . . . laid all three of them on the counter like evidence of a crime.

"Jesus Teddy."

"I know. It's . . . strange. When I'm cleaning one pistol, I always keep another nearby, loaded and ready. This little twenty-two magnum? In the shower I put it in a sandwich bag and keep it on the soap dish."

"What in the world are you armed *against*?"

"I don't ask that question anymore, I stay armed on faith."

"Scary."

He agreed it was. "You take lemon with your tea right?"

"You remember."

He remembered from their summer together that Annie put a wedge of lemon in everything she drank . . . the gin, the soda, the water, the tea, even the coffee they brewed at three A.M. so they could stay up to see sunrise over seawater and then drink beer on the beach, Annie pushing a wedge of lemon down the beer bottle's long neck.

He remembered Annie naked and in bed, the sheets twisted on her legs, sheets that stayed damp with sweat and humidity, Annie did too . . . her small breasts topped with swollen red nipples, her white freckled skin betraying with purple bruised accusations everywhere he had squeezed too tightly, sucked too hard. He remembered that everything of her also tasted of him. Camel would haul himself from bed and drink a quart of water straight down, dehydrated from loss of sweat and spit and semen.

"If you don't have lemon . . ." she said as he continued standing there, staring off.

"Bought a nice one yesterday."

Camel found the lemon and placed it on a cutting board admiring its yellow perfection, at the end opposite the stem stuck out a nipple almost exactly the size and hardness of Annie's as he remembered them. Camel took knife in hand, anticipating the smell. The lemon did not disappoint: summer childhood lemonade memories came with the juice that ran out over his fingertips and onto the cutting board. The high sharp odor of lemon soaked sinus deep and made his jaw hinge pucker, made him salivate.

He looked at Annie. "All the shit I've been through, I brought it on myself. Divorce, keeping people at arm's length, getting kicked off the force, not being there for you when you needed me, general hard-ass alienation . . . I read a phrase once that described it perfectly: tragedy without drama."

She stayed close to him. "You probably realize now what a mistake you made turning me down . . . in fact you're going to ask me to leave Paul and marry you, aren't you?"

He waited a beat then said, "Yeah, why don't you leave your husband and marry me?"

"No . . . I can't."

Camel squinted and turned back to the counter to cut another wedge of lemon. "Fair enough." Raising lemon-wet fingers to his mouth, he anticipated sourness before tasting it.

"Me too," Annie begged, offering her open mouth.

When he put those fingers to her tongue, she shuddered.

19

EITHER IT WAS THE COCAINE AND PILLS OR GROWLER REALLY WAS clinically paranoid, absolutely convinced that a conspiracy had not only framed him for Hope's murder seven years ago but was also manipulating him now that he was out of prison. How else to explain Kenny Norton's address? Growler had left Cul-De-Sac to score some additional pharmaceuticals, came back to find a sheet of paper taped to the door: Norton's address. Too excited to bother checking on St. Paul, Growler got back into the rental car and started driving. But he'd been away from the area a long time and got lost, couldn't find the address and began suspecting it was bogus, became convinced again he was being manipulated, anonymously given this address just to set him off on a wild goose chase . . . but why, he never knew *why*.

Just after eight P.M. Growler stopped at a convenience store to get directions. When he stepped up to the elevated checkout counter a pimply clerk pointed him to the back of the line.

Growler asked his question anyway, "How do you get to Lee Street?"

The clerk was already turning away, ringing up a quart of skim milk for some old fart fumbling for exact change.

Growler burned a dead-eyed stare at the clerk, a white kid with

a big nose and a large gulping Adam's apple . . . one of those per-
petual adolescents who could've been seventeen or twenty-seven,
long hair and a face full of scabby old pimples fighting for space
with a fresh crop of juicy red ones, the kind of kid you'd suspect as
a chronic nose-picker.

"Where's Lee Street?" Growler asked again.

Ignoring him the clerk raised a set of bored brown eyes to the
next person in line, a working mom holding an oversized package
of disposable diapers in her right hand, balancing a crying baby
on her left hip.

Growler tried hard to keep his anger tamped down, safely coiled
. . . but working just as hard against this good intention was the cocaine he'd snuffled on the way here, twisting knots in his paranoia,
putting a flame to the same rage that led him to kill the Raineys.
Growler couldn't keep his hands from jangling, like he was trying
to shake them dry. The mom sat her brat and the diapers up on
the counter, went searching in her purse for money.

Growler losing it. Ever since Lawrence Rainey said he'd found
Hope's photographs, Growler had been thinking of little else . . .
the photographs and the elephant. And of course how everyone
was always betraying him, telling lies, son-of-a-bitch anyway, dirty
bastard liars . . . mumbling all this under his breath.

No other customers in the store now, the mom had left in a
hurry, Growler barely able to control his voice as he demanded to
the clerk, "Where's Lee Street?"

"We sell maps, down there to your left," the kid said, indicating
a rack in front of the counter.

"You don't know where Lee Street is?"

"Maps down there to your left," the clerk repeated, avoiding eye
contact like a practiced bureaucrat.

Growler sweating in his leather jacket, feeling the red flannel
shirt he wore turning wet under the arms . . . trying his best to hold
on to his composure long enough to get out of here without
killing the pimple king up there on his elevated platform. "I understand you sell maps but I remember Lee Street being right
around here—"

"Maps down there to your left."

Growler started to raise his voice but then smiled showing those oversized teeth. He used to be vain about his good looks, Hope said he was sleek like an otter and Growler had taken great pride in that assessment, but young and handsome were the qualities that got him so heartily fucked in prison, Growler then wishing he was old and fat and repellantly ugly . . . having these horse teeth installed was a step in that direction.

Blinking in genuine surprise at those big choppers the clerk was thinking what a laugh his buddies would get when he told them about *this guy*.

Finding the rack of maps, Growler grabbed one then came around to the swinging door that gave access to the platform behind the counter.

"Customers not allowed back here," the clerk said, apathy in his voice replaced by a suddenly sharpened anxiety.

Growler kept coming, swinging his left hand up to cup the young man's groin, squeezing his balls . . . the clerk yelling out, "Next block take a left, Lee Street's two blocks over!"

"Could've told me that when I came in," Growler said, releasing his grip and tossing the map to the kid. "Now stick that up your ass."

The kid nodded as if saying okay you made your point.

But Growler repeated the command. "Stick it up your ass."

The clerk turning to the phone, telling Growler, "Welcome to nine-one-one, asshole."

He jerked the receiver away and kicked the kid in the left knee, Growler wearing heavy work boots with steel toes, hurting the young man enough that he fell to the floor cursing . . . Growler kicked him again, in the ribs. "Drop your pants and stick that map up your ass."

The clerk tried to scoot away, Growler stepping on his leg. "Either I see that map disappear up your ass or I break your fucking neck . . . now take off your pants and *do it!*"

For the first time since starting to work here the young man actually prayed for customers but none came into the store so he stayed on the floor hoping this crazy fuck would just get bored and leave, surely he wasn't serious about the map . . .

Growler put a leg back to kick the kid in the head, then caught himself . . . what am I doing, going to get sent back to prison before I ever see Kenny or Elizabeth . . . Jesus Christ get a grip he told himself, reaching down and picking up the map. "I'll take this, how much is it?"

The clerk gawked in disbelief.

"How much!"

"You can have it mister."

"No I want to pay for it."

"A dollar?"

Growler dropped the bill on the floor next to the clerk. "Thank you."

"You're welcome." First time he'd ever said that to a customer.

"I wouldn't call the cops if I were you."

"No sir."

Although Growler's nerves felt like they were juicing 220 he made a point of strolling unhurriedly from the store.

■   ■   ■

"HELLO KEN."

"Donald."

A moment's pause between the two men as Ken Norton tried to compute the magnitude of the nightmare arriving here at his apartment, Donald Growler standing there drinking in his old friend's abject horror.

Too late Norton tried to close the door on Growler who, prepared for this maneuver, had jammed his boot in place and now pushed back with his shoulder. After a three-second struggling stalemate Growler forced his way into Norton's apartment and slammed the door behind him.

Norton was already running for the telephone, Growler pacing right behind him. Before Norton could lift the receiver to his ear, Growler slapped that ear with his open hand, slapped it hard enough to injure Norton's eardrum . . . proof of which came in the form of a straw-thick trickle of viscous blood.

Norton pressed both hands to his damaged ear, Growler kicked him in the shin and hung up the phone.

Ken Norton was on the floor now, Growler kicking him randomly though not hard enough to rupture internal organs or break bones, not yet . . . Norton begging for him to stop.

Growler did. "Why'd you lie about me at the trial?"

"The cops *told* me to!"

"Bullshit."

"No they did."

"They were that desperate to make their case?"

"I don't know."

"You going to tell me the cops stole our elephant too?"

"I thought you hid it."

"It's not there."

"Donny—"

"Don't call me that. Remember I told you what I was going to do to you if I ever got out of prison."

Norton remembered.

Growler paused, trying to balance a need for information against seven years of rage . . . don't kill him yet, don't kill him yet. He took a deep breath and modulated his voice. "Smells nice in here."

Norton had been burning fragrant candles.

"Done real well for yourself," Growler said, looking around. "Financed it all with the elephant, did you?"

"*No.*"

"Did you get the full three million for it?"

"I never saw the elephant after you made the switch—"

"Liar."

"I swear to you—"

"Turn over."

"Don, please—"

"Turn around goddamn it."

Norton did. He'd answered the door wearing only a blue velour robe that tied loosely in front with a sash and hung down to just above his knees . . . now that he was on the floor facing away from Growler, the robe having ridden up to his waist, Norton's bare ass was exposed to Growler who took his time aiming the steel toe of his right boot, driving it hard into Kenny who grunted like an ox being poleaxed.

"Feel like you're going to shit?" Growler asked standing over him.

"I think . . . Don, I think you really hurt something down there."

"You call that hurt? Ever pull a train, Kenny?"

When Growler resumed the kicking, Norton began crabbing across the carpet into a corner of the living room. Friends told him he was crazy for putting in a white carpet but he kept his apartment the way he kept himself, neat and clean, and the white carpet had never been stained. It set off the flowered sofa just as the pristinely white walls set off the various paintings that Norton had done, each ornately framed, each lit by a small lamp affixed to the bottom frame. Also distributed around the apartment were pieces of Norton's sculpture, most of it representational wildlife, wolves and bears, but some free-form pieces too. Like the paintings, the sculptures were discreetly lighted. He'd been selling some pieces in Washington stores, a few galleries were interested. Kenny's life had been good these past few years and he loved this new apartment, though he wished now he'd made more of an effort to befriend neighbors . . . if he started screaming would they come to his rescue before Growler kicked him to death?

Norton held up his hands and feet to ward off the heavy boot, Growler content to kick whatever came within range . . . a wrist, the bottom of a foot, an elbow, calf. He was sweating again and his black slicked-back hair had become wildly dislodged to hang over his ears in a way that made him look particularly thuggish.

"I asked you if you ever pulled a train." Growler spoke without interrupting his kicking spree.

"Oh God, stop . . . Jesus God please . . ."

To give his right leg a rest Growler switched to the left.

In spite of all this abuse Norton hadn't yet ruined the white carpet, his blood vessels were rupturing internally to spill out into surrounding tissue, forming bruises.

Thirty-nine years old, he frequently introduced himself by saying, "I'm Ken Norton . . . but not the boxer." It often got a laugh because this Ken Norton was skinny and white and decidedly unathletic, so gentle in appearance and disposition that you got the impression he might faint away if you startled him by clapping your hands too loudly. He had gentle Bambi brown eyes, his long brown hair pulled back in a ponytail, he wore one looped earring the size of a penny.

Growler stopped kicking and asked again, "You ever pull a train, Kenny?"

"What I did to you was unforgivable Donny—"

"Son-of-a-bitch," Growler muttered as he kicked again and again. Norton turned his face to the wall, receiving the boot to his back, his kidneys.

"Seven years I pulled that fucking train," Growler continued muttering as he kicked. He wanted to make his old friend understand the full measure of hell that Growler had suffered, tell the whole story from the very beginning when five men jerked his pants down and bent him over a rolled-up mattress and held his arms and legs as they took turns . . .

"I wanted to die, I wanted to die," Growler kept saying as he kept kicking, leaning both hands against the wall to brace himself for better leverage. Growler stomped straight down on arms and legs, wherever the boot landed on bare skin it left angry tread signatures . . . Growler in the grips of so powerful a wrath that although the horror of the last seven years ran as a narrative in his mind, what came out of his mouth were only phrases spat and growled.

". . . holds me on his lap and hugs me and tells me . . ." Growler still stomping Norton who had started screaming like a woman.

". . . then another half-dozen line up and I have to pull that train too . . ."

Norton squirming around trying to stand.

". . . in the hospital with cotton wadding stuffed up my ass . . ."

Norton screaming, "HELP! HELP!"

". . . my ass sold for cigarettes, sent like a goddamn delivery boy to give blow jobs . . . shut the fuck up Kenny!"

But Norton wouldn't shut up, Growler kicking him in the legs to keep him on the floor.

Norton pleading, "I'm sorry, oh God *I'm sorry!*"

Growler took a rest. "You're not sorry—"

"I am."

"Who was in on it with you?"

"In on what?"

"Framing me! You and the Raineys, Uncle Penny and Elizabeth—Where does she live now? You got her address?"

"Yes but she didn't—"

Growler kicked him. "Where's the elephant, where's Hope's pictures, why'd you lie about me!"

Norton wept pitifully.

"Larry Rainey told me he'd seen those pictures Hope took, I know they exist goddamn it."

"I'm sorry, I'm sorry Donny—"

Growler kicked him in the mouth.

"I had my teeth knocked out too," Growler said, resting again. "Filthy fucking guy didn't like the blow job, hit my front teeth with a pipe . . . see the new ones I had put in?" Growler grimaced to show off his unnaturally large teeth but Norton, over on hands and knees trying to throw up, didn't look. "Cost me a fucking fortune . . . and every pack of cigarettes I paid, every dollar of scrip . . . earned with my ass . . . good strong teeth, they're screwed right into the bone."

Norton spat stuff from his mouth. When he saw all that red-white-pink shit on the precious white carpet his instinct was to clean it but wiping at the mess with his hand succeeded only in spreading it around.

"Thought these fucking monster teeth might discourage attention but of course it didn't work, first time back on the block . . ." Which triggered some memory, Growler clenching those teeth, screaming through them: *"WHY DID YOU LIE ABOUT ME!"* He kicked Norton in the side of the head, squarely on the temple, causing him to make an oafish sound then slide forward into the wall and collapse over on his side.

Growler looked down with disappointment. "You dead cocksucker?"

20

CAMEL'S BED WAS NO MORE THAN TEN FEET FROM WHERE HE AND ANNIE stood exchanging a lemony kiss, and as he thought about making that ten-foot trip she had already decided neither to offer herself nor resist whatever overtures he made, Annie fully aware this was moral abdication but that's the decision she'd made, to let Teddy decide.

After the kiss he embraced her and looked at the freckles spilt down the back of her neck. That summer fourteen years ago he played connect-the-dots on Annie with a ballpoint pen and promised he'd count them all before the summer was out but of course the count kept getting interrupted, and now Camel's mind perversely flashed an image of Annie on all fours with her little white ass up in the air, that *look* she gave him when she turned back over one slender shoulder to watch what he was doing, he'd remember that look forever.

They were kissing a second time when the door from the hallway opened.

The silence was so heavily strained that the air in the room seemed to undergo a severe drop in pressure, then Annie spoke the man's name with an almost insupportable sadness, *"Paul,"* while Camel's attention snagged in two places, the first being Paul's hand which held a butcher knife, the second was the countertop right next to where Paul stood . . . and upon which Camel had left all three of his side arms.

21

SCRATCHING AT THE INSIDES OF HIS FOREARMS AS HE WATCHED KENNY Norton's battered ribcage for signs of movement Growler desperately needed another few lines to stop himself from completely unraveling . . . *Norton's at peace now but what about me?* Growler was still suffering, still didn't know why he was betrayed, who had the elephant, the pictures, really it was too massively unfair. Growler's addled mind trying to figure what he should do next, find Elizabeth's address, Kenny said he had it, then go back to Cul-De-Sac and take a shower, change into some nice clothes, impress Elizabeth before I do everything to her I intended to do to Kenny here if the sissy hadn't just given up and died on me.

Which was when Norton took a sudden big gasp as if just then remembering to breathe, Growler witnessing this with big teeth smiling. "Come on Kenny, let's go to the kitchen." He tried to drag his old friend by the ponytail but Norton was like dead weight and as Growler continued pulling it seemed the ponytail might actually break away . . . Growler finally changing tactics, holding Norton under the arms to pull-drag him through the living room, trailing red on white carpet, then across the dining alcove and into the small kitchen where blood leaked onto the surgically clean white tile floor . . . Norton all the while making little sounds from deep within his chest cavity: low groans, groggy moans, soft growling.

Going through Norton's kitchen drawers Growler found a new clothesline still in the package but no heavy meat cleaver like the one the Raineys had in their kitchen.

"Where do you keep the knives?" Growler asked of the supine Norton who didn't respond and earned a light kick in the back of the head which made him say, "Ohh," like a gentle exclamation from a troubling dream.

Growler found an aluminum-bladed butcher knife and used it to cut the clothesline.

Bringing in a straightbacked chair from the alcove Growler stripped the blood-stained robe from Norton then lifted him onto the chair and steadied him there with one hand while with the other he looped line around Norton's neck, tying the free end to the handle of the false drawer in front of the kitchen sink. Growler fastened Norton's ankles and wrists to the chair, also tied cord around the man's waist and cinched it tightly to the back of the chair to keep him from sliding off.

After filling a four-quart stainless-steel pot Growler threw cold water in Norton's face causing a sharp intake of breath that also inhaled blood, Norton gagging and choking until Growler raised the back of the chair and tipped him forward. When Norton stopped coughing, Growler poured another gallon of cold water over him, Norton's blood diluted into pink streams that ran down his chin and neck, his chest and belly, into his furry groin.

"Why'd you lie at my trial?"

Norton's head lolled as if lacking muscle tone to keep it upright. Growler slapped him until he came around, head up and eyes open to see what horror came next . . . Growler screaming about elephants and betrayals.

Norton coughed, spat out another tooth . . . when his tongue went exploring alien spaces that familiar teeth had so recently occupied he made a face like a man tasting something rank in his dinner.

Growler scratched at one forearm then the other, trying to keep his mind straight. "Kenny, did you see the pictures Hope took . . . who was in them?"

Norton shook his head slowly back and forth.

"Did she take pictures the day she was killed?"

Norton at a loss for words.

"Unless you give me some answers I'm going to cut off your head, is that clear?"

Norton indicated it was, then tried to form words with his mangled mouth. "Gopth . . . the gopth toll me to lie."

"Why?" Lawrence Rainey also claimed he'd been instructed to lie at the trial but *why* . . . were the cops protecting Growler's uncle, had J.L. killed Hope? It made sense . . . Growler being convicted of Hope's murder is what enabled J. L. Penner to inherit Hope's share of Cul-De-Sac. But Growler had run through this conspiracy theory in prison, and while Uncle Penny could've bribed the cops, could've leaned on the Raineys to perjure themselves, how did he coerce Kenny . . . Kenny hated J.L., Kenny was not only Growler's best friend but also his partner in a scam that could've netted them three million dollars. Kenny's betrayal was the part that *didn't* make sense.

"How'd they get to you?" Growler asked as he stepped behind the chair and pulled on the rope loop around Norton's neck causing the man's hands to try jerking upward in protection but those hands were tied down and all Norton could do was struggle wildly in the chair as Growler pulled more and more tightly, the rope cutting off supplies to lungs and brain.

He finally let go leaving Norton gasping for air as Growler came around in front of the chair. "I want you to see something." He kept the leather jacket and red shirt on but dropped his pants.

Norton gasped from having been choked and from what Growler was showing him.

Satisfied with this reaction Growler pulled up his pants. "Now you know who you're dealing with." He went searching again through the kitchen drawers coming up with a pair of pliers that he carried over to Norton and clamped onto that gold-loop earring. "You still play the guitar?" When he didn't get an answer Growler jerked lightly on the earring and Norton nodded yes, yes. "Where?"

Norton looked to his left.

"*Where* asshole?" Jerking the earring again.

"Claw-thet, claw-thet!"

"Closet?"

Norton nodded. With one quick downward tug Growler ripped the earring out, tearing Norton's earlobe in half and producing from the man a high keening wail that was more an expression of wretchedness than pain.

In the utility closet Growler removed the guitar's high E string, then used a little saw that was hanging on the wall to cut off two eight-inch pieces of broom handle. He wrapped each end of the guitar string around the middle of each length of broom handle . . . he'd seen this done in prison and it made a good garrote—you formed a loop in the wire, slipped it over someone's head, then pulled real hard in opposite directions.

He came out of the closet and held the garrote in front of Kenny Norton's ruined face. "Might be a tight fit." Growler stepped behind him. "As the actress said to the bishop."

The loop went around Norton's neck just above the clothesline still in place.

"You were my best friend," Growler said as he got a good grip on the two sections of broomhandle.

Norton nodded an enthusiastic agreement. "I wahth, I wahth Donny."

Growler went into a crouch to improve leverage. "And you know I didn't kill Hope because I was with you when she was murdered."

"I know."

Growler flexed his biceps, readying himself. "And you sold me out."

"They were going to arreth me!"

"For what?"

"A boy . . ."

"What?"

Norton's face twisted into contorted expressions, he wanted to explain but ended up mewling pleas for mercy.

Growler cursed him then jerked hard in opposite directions on the lengths of broomhandle, Norton trying to scream but unable to force sound past his constricting throat, Growler pulling harder, arm muscles straining as the tightening wire sliced flesh like a blade.

Norton's tongue expanded like a grotesque fat slug that had been stuffed into his mouth but was now sticking out from his lips to escape.

Growler pulled harder, the wire sinking out of sight into Norton's neck, terrified eyes bulging, their threadlike blood vessels bursting.

Growler spread his legs, bent his head, pulled all the harder.

Norton's face turned a dark violent red as he thrashed around so hysterically that he and the chair would've fallen over had Growler not been keeping them upright. Norton's neck produced a collar of bright blood, the skin below the wire almost normal in color but above the wire his flesh had turned a deep purple approaching black.

Growler kept pulling, a stream of urine suddenly shooting straight up from Norton's penis, the abnormally high pressure driving that urine stream all the way to the kitchen ceiling.

The wire had cut carotid arteries and jugular veins, blood everywhere, the kitchen a slaughterhouse, the floor slick. As Growler looked down over Norton's bare shoulder he saw the man's penis twitch in spasms before ejecting a single stringlike length of semen that twisted in flight before landing curled like a question mark in the blood, piss, and water on the kitchen floor.

By the time Norton shit himself, his head was already leaning lazily to the side, the wire cutting its way through to spine.

With the lengths of broomhandle farther apart Growler found it difficult to keep up the pressure but when the wire slipped into the cartilage disk between two vertebrae, when Growler braced himself and jerked hard one last time, the spine and its cord were neatly severed and Norton's head rolled down one shoulder before going into a free fall hitting the kitchen floor with a heavy thump-thud like a ponytailed bowling ball.

Face up.

Incredibly, Norton's mouth slowly opened, getting wider and wider. Growler watched fascinated . . . as if that decapitated head were about to tell him secrets of elephants and betrayals . . . but when the mouth opened wide enough for a scream it just stayed like that, silent and gaping.

Standing there sweating, breathing hard, looking down at Norton's open-mouthed, open-eyed expression staring back up from the floor Growler submerged deep inside himself searching for regret or guilt . . . finding none, he unzipped his pants but then suffered a paralyzing case of bladder shyness and had to concentrate very hard to overcome it.

22

PAUL MILTON SAW THE GUNS TOO AND BEFORE CAMEL COULD REACT Milton exchanged his butcher knife for the pistol closest to him, that little five-shot .22 magnum, a revolver barely larger than a derringer but deadly enough at close range. He pointed it at Annie, at Camel, then back at Annie . . . the worst type of person in the world you want pointing a weapon at you, someone who's frantic, confused, hurt . . . Paul's face battered like he'd been in a car wreck, Annie more shocked by her husband's condition than embarrassed to have been caught by him. "What's happened to you?" she asked.

"Something terrible," he said. Unspeakable, he meant.

Camel felt sick to his stomach from the stupidity of what he'd done, leaving his weapons on the counter like that . . . so totally out of character for him to be careless with firearms, showing off like a teenager for Annie.

And now he faced a man with a gun. Camel knew the standard operating procedure . . . talk to the guy, put him at ease, ask what he wants, show you're not a threat. But Camel thought it might be more effective simply to walk over there and gently take the gun away, do it now before the guy gets a taste of control and starts liking it . . . he obviously isn't familiar with firearms, Camel could tell by the way he gripped that .22 like he was worried it might explode on its own . . . just walk over there and take it out of his hand, he'll probably feel relieved to be rid of it. Of course if Camel's wrong he gets shot.

Without announcing his intention or looking at the man directly, Camel started in Paul's direction.

"Stop."

Camel didn't.

"STOP!" Paul raised the .22 and squeezed on the trigger causing the hammer to pull back.

Camel stopped. "That's a double-action revolver," he said. "No spur on the hammer, no safety . . . it fires just by pulling back far enough on the trigger."

Paul had no idea what he was talking about, still holding the trigger in that about-to-fire position.

"All I'm saying is, you want to shoot me, that's one thing . . . but if you haven't made up your mind yet, well then you're about to shoot me by accident if you don't ease off on that trigger."

After a torturous pause the trigger finger relaxed allowing the hammer to reseat itself and Camel to take a breath he hadn't realized he was holding.

"I'm her husband," Paul said more nervous than indignant.

Camel had already figured that part out.

"Paul," Annie asked again, "what in God's name happened to you?"

He raised his left hand to his face, blackened, bruised, broken. "You should've said what in *hell* happened to me," Paul corrected her before looking again at Camel and repeating, this time with emphasis, *"I'm her husband."*

Camel thought it odd Annie had married a man so slight and young . . . maybe Paul looked more substantial before he was injured and when he's not suffering from lack of sleep and jealousy and rage. His white pants were dirty, work shirt heavily stained, the lenses of his rimless glasses filthy and the earpieces bent wildly out of shape, the right one didn't even touch his ear, it pointed up and away from Paul's head.

"I was afraid after last night," Annie was saying to her husband. "I called you earlier remember? Explained I was here with Teddy? He used to be a policeman, Teddy's an old friend of the family."

Camel wished she wouldn't use his first name . . . put some distance between us, refer to me by pronouns: this man, he, that guy there.

"You were kissing him," Paul pointed out to his wife.

Annie said she could explain that though in fact she couldn't, not to a husband.

"You gave him a *blow job.*" He wasn't accustomed to using the words, saying them like a little boy practicing curses.

"No," Annie insisted.

Paul swung the gun in her direction and pulled on the trigger.

"Hey," Camel said quietly, causing the .22's muzzle to come back toward him as he ran a set of calculations . . . someone unfamiliar with firearms and shooting a two-inch barrel could easily miss even at this close range, then the concussion and recoil might surprise him enough he wouldn't be able to get off a quick second shot. Camel was about to rush Paul when Annie stepped toward her husband.

"Stay away from me," Paul told her. "You just don't care who you sleep with . . . *fuck* . . . do you . . . all a guy's got to do is ask, isn't that right?"

"I've never been unfaithful to you."

His ruined eyes opened wide. "Giving this guy a blow job, that doesn't count?"

"I didn't—"

"LIES!" He was shaking now, a real case of the shivers, a shattered man, and although cuckold horns weren't sprouting from his head you could tell by looking at him that he felt those horny roots spreading out through his brain like hot, living cancer.

"Paul," Annie said, "whatever's happened to you out at Cul-De-Sac is affecting your thinking, you're imagining—"

"Imagining I came in here and found you hugging and kissing him!" He turned toward Camel and spoke with funereal regret. "She gave you a *blow job.*"

"No," Camel quietly replied, "that didn't happen."

"I *know* it did!"

"*How* do you know?" Annie asked. "Your friend with the horse teeth tell you?"

Paul started to explain about the golfer but instead he told Camel, "You know what my ambition was, before I met her, my ambition was to serve God . . . that's right, go ahead and laugh."

"I'm not going to laugh," Camel said.

"You know what she called me once, she said I was hapless."

Annie frowned, she didn't remember it.

"*Hapless,*" Paul repeated . . . like a death sentence.

"Oh Paul—"

"Shut up!" His head shook so wildly the eyeglasses were dislodged and seemed about to fly from his face. "Too bad you didn't come home tonight instead of giving out blow jobs, I could've made us rich . . . I sold my soul to make us rich."

"What are you talking about?"

"The elephant."

"The—"

"I found the elephant!"

"What *is* it?"

"It's an *elephant.*"

She tossed her head, Annie was now more angry and frustrated than afraid. "Paul, what are you involved in?"

"I'm not involved in *adultery.*" When his glasses slipped again, he tried to push them up, then in a fit threw them to the floor. "I'll kill everybody here!"

"You're not going to kill anybody," she told him.

"Why, because I'm *hapless?*"

"Oh Paul . . ."

He again aimed the muzzle at her face, again squeezed on the trigger . . . and each time Camel saw that hammer move it was like his heart stopped in anticipation. "I'm coming over there and getting my revolver back," he said in an even voice, starting to do exactly that.

Sensing finally that Camel was serious, realizing a conclusion was about to be reached, Paul looked at Annie. "I don't think I ever really told you how very sorry I am for losing all your money."

"Paul—"

"Remember what I asked you to remember."

"What?"

"Remember what I asked you to remember," he repeated before lowering the pistol and relaxing his shoulders. Paul even managed a sly grin that revealed a blood-ugly space where a tooth had been knocked out.

Days later Camel would recall thinking at the time that Paul was about to say he was sorry, he never intended to shoot anyone. But what he actually did, he suddenly raised the pistol and turned its muzzle up to his own mouth . . . Camel rushing those last few steps, getting a hand on the revolver's cylinder but not in time to stop Paul from squeezing the trigger all the way this time, the bullet blowing out his remaining front teeth, exploding into his mouth, exiting the back of his neck in a showy spray of blood, tissue, and bone.

ELIZABETH ROCKWELL LIVED IN A MODERN ONE-STORY BRICK HOUSE OF
the type commonly seen abutting golf courses though this one
didn't. A garage was attached, shrubbery hugged all four sides of
the house, and though it was only April the yard grass had already
been forced by chemicals to be nice. Large sandstone rocks were
placed in a manner thought to be artful here and there on the
front lawn. Designed for easy living, insulated like a thermos,
clean and efficient, Elizabeth Rockwell's house was without charm
or eccentricity.

Not so its owner, a tall big-boned woman of fifty-four . . . if you
saw her astride a horse you'd consider her strapping. She was
dressed this Monday evening in black silk slacks and a white silk
blouse and open-toed sandals. She wore a lot of jewelry and her
grayish blond hair was expensively coiffed . . . Elizabeth one of
those distinguished women who didn't leave the bedroom without
looking her best.

She came from old money which her parents frittered away before she was of an age to appreciate it . . . forcing Elizabeth to live
like a commoner on talents and scramble. She made money in real
estate.

Many years ago she also carried on a liaison with a local squire,

J. L. Penner, and assumed he would eventually make her mistress of Cul-De-Sac. But when J.L.'s niece Hope showed up, Elizabeth was displaced by the teenage girl who possessed an almost supernatural ability to charm men . . . Hope also played chess brilliantly, the piano beautifully, and fucked like the proverbial. Elizabeth didn't reconcile with J.L. until after the niece was murdered.

Hope's death broke something in the old man who spent his remaining years selling land and accumulating money, never again sponsoring any of the political fundraisers or elaborate theme parties or late-night, closed-door, special invitation-only sessions for which Cul-De-Sac had once been alternately famous and infamous.

Elizabeth earned a percentage of the Cul-De-Sac estate when she served as executrix of J.L.'s will but the only thing she inherited from him directly was a minor chess set from the large collection he had amassed to please and impress his niece.

Hope and J.L. played chess together very nearly every day, she always said she played best on the most expensive sets . . . J.L. eventually spent millions of dollars buying sets from all over the world. After Hope was murdered, J. L. Penner never played another game of chess and, to Elizabeth's knowledge, did not even look at his collection of sets, eventually bequeathed to the Humane Society.

Elizabeth Rockwell was thinking of none of this, hadn't thought of it in years, when the kitchen doorbell rang the first few notes of "Some Enchanted Evening." She got up from the table where she'd been drinking coffee. Wondering who was calling this late in the evening, seeing no one standing outside the door, Elizabeth opened that door . . . Growler stepping from the side where he'd been hiding to put one booted foot on her threshhold.

"Elizabeth . . . how kind the years have been to you."

He had expected her to be as terrified as the others but after registering an initial surprise Elizabeth Rockwell smiled and spoke his name with complete composure, "Donald."

"Shall I come in?" he asked, smiling but showing no teeth. Back at Cul-De-Sac he had primped for her and changed clothes . . .

dark suit, white shirt, red tie . . . and now like a suitor he looked both hopeful and nervous. His black hair was greased back and although his eyes were bloodshot and weary he otherwise made an elegant presentation not counting those heavy steel-toed boots.

"Are you escaped?" she asked.

"Released."

"Surely not."

"Afraid so."

"I'll have to write the governor and express my dismay with our penal policies."

"I have some penile policies that would dismay the shit out of you."

"Donald you always were common, shall I call the police or will you leave?"

"I told you, I didn't escape—"

"But now you're trespassing so please leave."

When she started to close the door Growler pushed his way in.

"Oh dear, you *are* going to force me to call the police." Elizabeth's voice was softly mocking.

He remembered that voice with a special poignancy. When Growler stayed at Cul-De-Sac and Elizabeth was the tall sexy lady squired by Uncle Penny, Growler lusted for her with the fervor of an adolescent. Instead of ignoring him or putting him off gently she would mock him exactly as she was doing now. She once followed him into a storage room at the back of Cul-De-Sac and, reaching past Donald as if he weren't there, pressed her bosom to him as she stretched to get something from a shelf . . . the young Donald gripped by such hormonal frenzy that he impulsively grabbed a breast. Elizabeth didn't deign to remove his hand, she just looked him in the eye and threatened to tell his uncle . . . as she was now threatening to call the police.

He glanced around the kitchen. "Nice digs."

"You know how it is for the modern woman, we have to make our way in the world."

"How would I know anything about modern women, I've been in prison."

"Society does frown upon murder."

He flashed those large black eyes. "Think about me a lot have you?"

"Never."

"Come on."

"Yours is an acquaintance I don't dwell on, believe me."

"Well fuck you very much."

She appraised him cooly. "If you really have been released I assume you're on probation. One phone call and I'll have you back in prison before morning . . . if you don't leave this house immediately."

"Such a fucking dragon lady."

"You've coarsened even beyond what you were as a boy."

"Seven years in hell will do that."

"What do you want Donald?"

"You ever see the Raineys, good old Judy and Lawrence?"

"No."

"How about Kenny Norton, I got your address from his book, the two of you must've kept in contact."

"No."

"Well if you're expecting to hear from them, the Raineys or Kenny, I wouldn't hold my breath."

"What do you mean?"

This time when he grinned, those big teeth were revealed.

"Good Lord, Donald, what have you done to yourself?"

He quickly brought his lips together and muttered something.

"Pardon me?"

Shaking his head he looked at her with an expression absent any playfulness. "I thought maybe you and the Raineys and Kenny got together occasionally to gloat."

"No dear . . . I haven't seen them since your trial."

"How much did Uncle Penny pay you to frame me . . . is that how you financed this house, that Cadillac in the driveway?"

"Listen darling the hour is late and talking with you is proving tedious as always. I wasn't compensated for testifying against you . . . I would've paid for the privilege."

He was surprised she continued being so haughty considering what he had in store for her, couldn't she guess his intentions?

"Hope might've been a little slut," Elizabeth continued, "but no one deserves to die like that."

"I didn't kill her."

Elizabeth laughed at him. "This was all covered at the trial."

"I was framed."

"We wuz robbed," she said mockingly.

He stepped close enough she could smell his breath when he spoke. "I'm going to kill you right here in this kitchen . . . make a joke out of that why don't you."

When she turned to leave, Growler corraled her against the big bronze refrigerator. "You know about the elephant don't you?"

Elizabeth feigned a bewildered expression but Growler caught the truth in her eyes. "Where is it?" he asked.

"Where's what?"

His turn to smile mockingly, pressing Elizabeth to the refrigerator's double doors. "Tonight you're going to treat me like you did Uncle Penny . . . I remember how you'd look at J.L. when the two of you were having dinner together, locking onto his face like every word out of his mouth was a gold coin . . . a snake watching a rat . . . Jesus I wanted you to look at me with that kind of fascination, just once. Maybe we can arrange it tonight." He brought a hand down to cover her breast.

She didn't remove his hand this time either. "I pity you."

"You're the one going to need pity," he promised.

"Donald—"

"I want you to do to me whatever it was you did to Uncle Penny *after* the two of you finished dinner and went upstairs to the library, closed the door, locked it . . . I used to stand out in the hallway listening, what did you do for him Elizabeth, spank his bare butt with a hairbrush, there was a lot of whimpering coming from that room."

"Is that what you want Donald, someone to spank you?"

"No I want you to get down on your knees and blow me, that's what I want."

"People in hell want ice water."

He laughed, squeezed her breast.

"You're hurting me."

"Tell me about the elephant."

"Donald—"

Tearing at the blouse until all the buttons popped, he pressed a forearm to her neck and held Elizabeth hard against the refrigerator.

"Donald please . . ."

He clicked his teeth together right in her face. "Where's the elephant?"

"When we—" Growler's forearm nearly crushing her throat, Elizabeth was unable to continue until he eased off. "When we inventoried J.L.'s collection, during the appraisals, that's when we discovered it had been switched."

"Where's the real one?"

"We never found it."

He looked at her and was surprised to see she was telling the truth.

"You stole it?" she asked.

"I would've thought Kenny and I would've been prime suspects."

"The fake wasn't discovered until after your uncle died last year, you'd been in prison for six years by that time . . . no one made the connection."

"Maybe you didn't *want* the connection made, 'cause you found the elephant, the real one and—"

"No."

He continued looking at her intently, their faces only a few inches apart. "Will you kiss me?" He was totally, pathetically serious.

Elizabeth considered the request and then, like a bidder at an art auction, used a subtle expression to indicate consent.

He actually closed his eyes, which was when Elizabeth lunged forward and bit him hard on the right cheek.

He jumped back more from surprise than pain, covering his cheek with a hand as Elizabeth ran from the kitchen.

He caught up in a carpeted hallway, bringing her down then sitting on her stomach, pinning both hands to the floor . . . she could see her teethmarks like a set of parentheses high on his right cheek.

"It's going to be a terrible night for you," he promised. "Scared?"

"Of course I'm scared, I know what you're capable of Donald . . . I saw what you did to Hope."

"I didn't do that!"

"Then who?"

"Goddamn it Elizabeth you were part of the conspiracy—"

"There was no conspiracy, at least I wasn't part of one. I testified to the truth . . . I *did* find Hope's head in your room, you *did* assault me that time in the—"

"Assault you? I grabbed your tit because you were pushing it in my face—"

"The Raineys saw you going into Hope's room the day she was killed and Ken Norton testified that—"

"THEY LIED!"

"Well I didn't lie at your trial Donald, you have no reason to be doing this to me."

He released her arms and sat upright. "Did you see those photographs Hope took?"

"No."

He slapped her.

"I *didn't.* Your uncle mentioned them once, this was after he got sick . . . he indicated something about having Hope's photographs, keeping them as insurance, that's what J.L. said but I never—"

"Whoever's in those pictures with Hope, that's who killed her."

"I never saw them."

He slapped her again. "Goddamn it who was in those pictures?"

"Murray!"

Which completely bewildered Growler. *"Who?"*

"Murray!"

But now he saw where Elizabeth's hazel eyes were looking and he heard footsteps and he realized too late she hadn't been referring to the photographs, she'd been calling to the blond giant who was just then descending upon Growler.

Picked him up by the shoulders, threw him on the floor, stood over him in muscled glory . . . six-two, 210 pounds of perfectly proportioned, twenty-five-year-old manhood, a hard-bodied, rippled-stomached young specimen with long blond hair tied in the back with a red ribbon. He wore a tight white T-shirt that stretched tightly to cover his pecs, baggy gray shorts reaching below his knees. Murray was barefoot.

Elizabeth got off the floor and backed away, pulling the white blouse together and holding it closed with one hand.

From the floor under this colossus's legs Growler laughed. "Hired yourself a hot young stud, have you, Elizabeth?"

She was still too shaken to speak.

"Personal trainer," Murray said.

Growler laughed again. "This time of night, what kind of training you call that?"

Murray looked over at his mistress. "What's going on, Beth?" The young man's slack-jawed duh-diction revealed that his superb training had been limited to the physical.

"Beth?" Growler rolled his eyes. "Tell me, Murray . . . Beth pay you by the hour or the inch?"

"Huh?"

Having regained a degree of composure Elizabeth said, "Donald if you're telling the truth, if you really didn't kill Hope, then I'm truly sorry—"

"*Sorry?* Sorry doesn't cut it you rotten bitch—"

"Hey," Murray grunted, putting a bare foot on Growler's neck and pressing down.

"What was I to think?" Elizabeth asked. She stayed well back from the two men. "All that testimony against you, those animal heads you kept in your room."

"I didn't kill Hope!" Growler knocked Murray's foot away and sat up.

"What's he talking about Beth?" Murray whined as he stepped back and held himself like a wrestler ready to grapple.

"Something that happened a long time ago dear."

"You want me to beat him up?"

She came to stand close behind her big boyfriend, laid a long-fingered, age-spotted hand on his massive shoulder. "We're going to hold him for the police."

Growler was still sitting on the floor. "When you helped send me away to prison Elizabeth I might've been a sissy . . . but seven years in hell made me one mean cocksucker."

"Really," she said.

"It's going to take more than Baby Huey there to hold me for the police."

"Hey buddy," Murray said, "anytime you feel froggy . . ."

"Yeah?" Growler asked getting to his feet.

Murray couldn't remember the rest of it.

"This is for you Elizabeth," Growler said, pulling from his suit coat pocket the garrote made from guitar string and broomsticks.

"Go through me first buddy," Murray said.

Elizabeth patted him on the back. "You keep Donald here, I'll call the police."

She went to the kitchen and was just picking up the phone when she heard them fighting in the hallway. Worried Murray might be getting the worst of it Elizabeth left the phone and walked quickly to a cabinet drawer where she kept her little silver .32 semiautomatic.

When she returned to the hallway Murray was on his stomach, Growler kneeling on the young man's broad back, the garrote around Murray's neck . . . and the only reason he hadn't already been decapitated, Murray had managed to slip his right forearm between the wire and his neck.

"Let him up," Elizabeth said leveling the automatic at Growler.

He looked at her, gauged her seriousness, then slowly got off Murray. The defeated Adonis stayed on the floor and rubbed his neck. Growler still held onto one broomstick handle, the garrote dangling from his left hand.

"Whatever that nasty thing is, put it down," Elizabeth commanded.

But Growler didn't, he simply turned his back on Elizabeth and her fallen knight, walked the length of the hallway, and exited her front door.

"Ain't you going to shoot him?" Murray asked as he regained his feet.

"I guess not," she replied, lowering the .32. "Are you okay?"

His feelings were hurt. "Beth, he fights dirty."

She comforted him with the hand that wasn't holding the pistol. "I know he does, sugar . . . I know he does."

24

CAMEL HAD BEEN IN ROOMS LIKE THIS HUNDREDS OF TIMES . . . TEN BY twelve feet, furnished with a wooden chair and a sturdy metal-legged table covered with some kind of gray linoleum vinyl soft enough you could make an impression with your thumbnail, from the looks of it a lot of people had done exactly that. A video camera on a tripod stood in the corner and one wall carried a panel of smoky, reflective glass that hadn't fooled anyone since *Dragnet*. The other three walls were painted light green from the floor to halfway up, the top half was white, the line between the two colors wavered. The beige carpeting was napped as thin as hope, the ceiling was acoustical tile. In periods of long silence the fluorescent lighting produced an incessant hum so faint you could start thinking it came from inside your head. The room smelled of air that had been used and reused too many times, breathed in and out of hundreds of lungs, you could also smell stale smoke, though ashtrays weren't in evidence, and old sweat and the general stink of anxiety left behind by troubled people. All these odors were overlayed with Lysol and you kept wanting to open a window but of course there were no windows, no views, no fresh air. Camel's memories of these rooms from his days as a homicide detective were made sharp and new this early A.M. hour, his debut as a suspect.

■   ■   ■

PAUL MILTON HAD died more or less instantly, he landed on the floor like a puppet would, you cut its strings. People with fatal gunshot wounds to the head mostly just drop, they don't get blown back against walls with arms and legs spread out, they don't twirl or dance or call out for loved ones . . . they fall without sound or ceremony, most of them. Paul did.

Annie went to him and got blood all over her white dress while holding Paul's head . . . Camel didn't see any point telling her not to move the body, he didn't bother checking for a pulse either. A man drops like that, he's dead.

Camel washed the blood off Annie's hands and arms, then called the state police. He also telephoned his lawyer because the idea you don't need a lawyer if you haven't done anything wrong, Camel had been disabused of that his first year on the job.

Waiting for the police Camel asked Annie if she had anyone in the area she could stay with, of course she didn't . . . newly arrived up here from North Carolina knowing no one is why she came to Camel in the first place. He said he'd call Eddie Neffering, reminding Annie that Neffering was the owner of The Ground Floor, the big guy with the bushy mustache. Annie said she remembered but her eyes were glazed and Camel wasn't sure anything he said registered with her. Eddie will be waiting when the detectives finish questioning you, Camel explained . . . you go home with him. What about you, she asked. He said the police would probably take a little longer with him. *Why?* Because that's the way things work, though Camel knew the exact two reasons he'd be held for interrogation . . . one, Annie's husband killed himself with Camel's gun and, two, Camel had powder burns on his right hand.

■   ■   ■

IT WAS TOO hot in this room probably on purpose, Camel felt greasy-skinned and tired-eyed, wishing he could shower and change clothes. He needed to take a piss and became self-conscious about his posture and facial expressions, whether he stood or sat, how he carried himself when he walked around the room . . . knowing he was being watched and how his watchers were analyzing him.

He'd be a fool not to worry. Even putting aside the suspicious setting of Paul Milton's death (comes in to find his wife kissing another man), Camel was aware that grabbing for the .22 magnum just as Milton fired it had put powder marks on Camel's hand which could be interpreted as evidence that *he* had done the shooting.

A lot depends on the detective who's assigned the case . . . if he believes me, Camel thought, I'll be out of here before dawn. He checked his wrist having forgotten they'd taken his watch, no clock in this room of course, Camel estimating the hour at three A.M.

It was in fact one-thirty Tuesday morning when the associate superintendent for criminal investigations entered the interrogation room . . . Camel surprised that a guy so high up on the state police food chain would bother with a case like this.

Parker Gray carried in his own chair. "Mr. Camel, I'm Parker Gray—"

"I know who you are."

They'd met a long time ago. Gray was thirty-six, Camel recognized in this man something of himself when he was Gray's age, the same kind of hard-on anger Camel used carry, a lack of appreciation for the art of compromise, a tendency to roll over people with the iron certainty of always being right.

When Gray asked Camel for his version of what happened, Camel didn't say well gosh I already told the other officers, I already gave a statement . . . he knew the drill and recounted for Gray the events leading to Paul Milton's death.

"Your lawyer's with Mrs. Milton," Gray said. "Same lawyer representing both of you?"

"She didn't know anyone to call, Mark's helping her until—"

"But you knew to call a lawyer right away huh?"

"After I called the state police, yes."

"Call an ambulance?"

"He was dead, the state police would send out an ambulance anyway."

"You know the routine huh?"

"Yes." Camel also knew enough to wonder why Gray hadn't given him the usual explanations and warnings, hadn't reread him his rights, hadn't turned on the camera.

"Mrs. Milton an old friend of yours huh?" After he asked the question Gray who hadn't yet used the chair he brought in went around and stood behind Camel. Most suspects won't turn to look at their interrogator, they're glad not to have to face him, but Camel moved to maintain eye contact.

"Yes Annie's an old friend."

"I bet."

Even in his dark suit and striped tie Parker Gray looked like a trooper . . . you could easily picture him gazing out sternly from under a Smokey Bear hat, lecturing a speeder. He had a square jaw and a five o'clock shadow that came out at noon. His eyes were brown and unusually narrow, he had a petite nose that didn't seem to fit with the other features of his face . . . the overhanging brow, the big-knuckle cheekbones, the stone jaw. The man wasn't that tall, five-ten maybe, but the general impression you got was strength and a lot of testosterone.

"You and Mrs. Milton were having a sexual relationship huh?"

"No."

"Never had sex with the woman?"

Camel figured it was going to come out, Annie might have already told them about the summer they spent together. "We had a relationship fourteen years ago."

"A relationship?"

"An affair."

"Sexual?"

"Yes."

"So last night was like a reunion huh?"

"I told you why she came to me, her husband—"

"She hired you huh?"

"Yes."

"Give you a check, retainer, what?"

"We hadn't formalized—"

"Handle it off the books, old times' sake huh?"

"Something like that."

"Which is why she was in your bedroom huh, handling it off the books?"

"Cheap shot Parker."

"It wasn't your bedroom?"

"I live in one room so yeah it was my bedroom, my kitchen, my—"

"Her husband comes in catches the two of you having sex huh?"

"No."

"You and Mrs. Milton were what, sitting in separate chairs, looking at old photo albums, what?"

"I was holding her."

"Holding her in your arms huh?"

"Yes."

"But not kissing her?"

"I'm sure Annie has told you—"

"You *were* kissing her?"

"Yes."

Gray went back to the other side of the table, forcing Camel to move again. "Paul Milton comes in, finds you and his wife kissing or maybe you were doing more than just kissing, Milton lunges for you with a butcher knife he brought from his place, you pull a little twenty-two magnum and shoot the husband in the mouth."

"You forgot to say *huh*."

"What?"

"I didn't shoot Annie's husband."

"No?"

"He killed himself the way I told you."

"But you being an experienced homicide detective I bet you can see real clear how I could make a case for the way *I* told it huh?"

"Yes."

"Especially since you have powder marks on your right hand, you are right-handed aren't you?"

"I explained that, I grabbed for the revolver just as—"

"You're going to have a tough time selling it . . . guy comes in, catches you with his wife, grabs your gun which you conveniently left out on a counter for him but then he doesn't shoot you or his wife like you'd expect of an irate husband, decides instead he's so pissed off at catching his wife with another man that he's going to shoot *himself* in the mouth? And to top it all off you say you're the hero trying to save the husband's life by grabbing—"

"Charge me or release me."

Gray smiled like it was something he had to practice in front of a mirror.

"I'm making a formal request Parker, I want to talk with my lawyer."

Gray sat in the chair. "I remember when we met, I remember you were a good detective too . . . and I'm not unmindful of professional courtesy."

So that's why the camera's not on, Camel thought . . . Gray's warming to some sort of deal he wants to offer.

"What do you know about Cul-De-Sac huh?"

"Only what Annie told me."

"I hear you been calling around asking about a homicide case occurred there seven years ago."

Bingo. "How's that related to Milton killing himself?"

"You tell me huh?"

"Don't know."

"How'd he get a key to your place, we found it in Milton's pocket."

"Don't know that either."

"Milton was beat up bad, some of the wounds several days old . . . who was doing that to him huh?"

"Sorry don't know."

"Here's something else I bet you don't know, Paul Milton had been buggered."

"Buggered?"

"As in up the ass."

"You're right Parker I didn't know that."

"Not a friendly buggering either . . . so what was going on out there at Cul-De-Sac huh?"

"I don't—"

"Mrs. Milton hire you to find something?"

"You mean find something at Cul-De-Sac?"

Parker Gray nodded.

The elephant . . . Camel deciding to throw it out there and check Gray's reaction. "Are you referring to the elephant?"

"The what?" Complete miss, Gray totally baffled. "Did you say elephant?"

"Yeah."

"And?"

Camel didn't know what else to say.

"Teddy . . . come on, talk to me."

"The man Annie saw at Cul-De-Sac Sunday night, that's the reason she came to me, because she was scared, he said he was looking for an elephant and then tonight before Paul Milton killed himself he said he'd *found* the elephant."

"But you don't know what any of that means, what they're referring to?"

"No I don't."

"Did Paul Milton or his wife ever talk about finding photographs?"

Camel was about to say no one's mentioned photographs when he caught Gray's worried expression, the anxiety in his eyes. "I'd prefer not to discuss that."

Gray stood. "You son-of-a-bitch I'll have you indicted for shooting Milton, would you *prefer* that huh?"

"Did you work on the homicide at Cul-De-Sac seven years ago?"

"Don't question me—"

"Why's everyone worried about that old case, is the killer, Donald Growler, is he out of prison . . . or maybe he's got new lawyers—"

"You're not here to question me!" Gray started to say something else but then put a hold on his anger, crossing his arms and turning around, speaking with his back to Camel. "There'll be another detective coming in to record your statement."

"You're not even assigned to my case are you?"

Gray said nothing, his back still to Camel.

"Someone screwed up on that old Cul-De-Sac homicide didn't they . . . are Growler's lawyers reopening—"

"Goddamn you Camel."

"Hey Parker my only interest in this is protecting Annie."

"Then if I were you I'd take her back to North Carolina." When Gray turned around his eyes were sad not angry. "And stay away from Cul-De-Sac."

25

GROWLER CAME HOME TO CUL-DE-SAC IN A SERIES OF THREE CABS. A FEW
miles from Elizabeth Rockwell's house he'd fallen asleep at the
wheel and crashed the car that Paul had rented for him. Growler
wasn't hurt in the wreck but he acted so deranged that the first
cabbie chucked him out after two blocks, the second cabbie
wanted to take him to a hospital, and the third cabbie threatened
him with a tire iron all the way home. Growler finally arrived at
Cul-De-Sac more confused than ever because it seemed to him
that Elizabeth told the truth . . . that she had not taken part in a
conspiracy against him, that at the time of his trial she really believed he'd killed Hope, and that although she discovered the elephants had been switched she didn't in fact know where the real
one was.

Up in Paul's bathroom Growler looked in a mirror and touched
the bite mark Elizabeth had left high on his cheek . . . he still intended to kill her, that big corn-fed Murray too. But killing them
like killing the Raineys and Kenny would put him no closer to answering the questions that had gnawed those brain holes over the
years . . . who masterminded his betrayal, *why?*

Growler went looking for St. Paul. His workshop was locked
from the outside. Growler checked all the second-floor rooms and

was halfway through the third level when he realized the futility of searching further . . . the son-of-a-bitch had absconded.

When Growler went to the balcony and looked down three floors he experienced a powerful desire to lean forward and go headfirst over the railing, end all this maddening doubt.

At first he'd considered Paul Milton a loyal partner who had nothing to do with the elephant's disappearance, then Growler became convinced that St. Paul used the three weeks he was here alone, before Growler arrived from prison, to tear Cul-De-Sac apart until he *did* find the elephant . . . but *then*, after torturing Paul in the most terrible ways imaginable, Growler changed his mind again and accepted Milton's word that he hadn't taken the elephant.

Now, however . . . Growler gripping the balcony railing so tightly his muscles trembled from the pressure . . . *now,* now with Paul having left Cul-De-Sac after he'd *promised* to stay here until Growler's return, now Growler was reconvinced that Milton was the one who'd taken the elephant, that he passed it to his wife when she was here Sunday night, and now, *now* the two rotten lying ratfuck conspirators are probably back in North Carolina, getting a line on selling the elephant, laughing their smug asses off for pulling a fast one on Old Scratch.

This time when he leaned forward, the tread on his heavy boots slipped on the hardwood flooring, Growler catching himself at the last possible moment. Shaken, he stepped back from the railing . . . too many people needed killing for him to end it all just yet.

He had maybe twenty-four hours to finish what *they*, his betrayers, had started seven years ago because soon bodies would be found, the Raineys' and Kenny Norton's, and it wouldn't take long after that for the cops to trace Growler from prison to North Carolina to here. He had to find Paul Milton and his wife, he had to force them to turn over the elephant, then he'd kill them. And if they didn't have the elephant he'd kill them anyway. That was his philosophy now, kill them all anyway.

26

DAY WAS COMING DAWN ON APRIL 16, NOT THAT TEDDY CAMEL WOULD
notice in a windowless holding cell, sitting on a fold-down bench,
elbows on his knees as he stared at the floor. State police detectives
had questioned him for another hour or so after Parker Gray left,
Camel thought he was going to be released but instead found himself under arrest for manslaughter, charged with killing Paul Milton.

The way Parker Gray had outlined the case Camel could see how
he might be convicted. The prosecutor will say Milton came in
with a knife, found his wife with an old lover, Camel shot Milton in
the mouth. Another point not in Camel's favor . . . a man will commit suicide by placing a muzzle against his heart or his head or *inside* his mouth but the detectives who questioned and eventually
charged Camel said they'd never heard of a suicide where a man
shoots himself through his teeth. Neither had Camel. He knew
how it happened of course: Milton intended to get the muzzle in
his mouth before firing but he was once again pulling back on the
trigger not realizing how close the hammer was to striking. This
would be one more complication Camel's lawyer would have to explain to a jury . . . along with why Camel, a normally cautious man,
had left his firearms out on a counter . . . and why he was kissing

another man's wife. Juries didn't process complications very well, they preferred simple stories: husband catches man with wife, man kills husband. Camel didn't like juries.

He figured he had at least three things going for him. First but least compelling, he was innocent. Second, Annie was a witness though a prosecutor could say she was Camel's lover, her testimony tainted. Third, whatever Paul Milton was involved in at Cul-De-Sac, whoever had beaten and raped him . . . these elements could be assembled to show Milton's suicidal state of mind.

Camel was reviewing all of this when he heard breakfast call, surprised to realize how hungry he was . . . then surprised again when Eddie Neffering came in carrying the breakfast tray.

"I thought my lawyer was the only one who could get in to see me."

"Hey Teddy when I retired I left behind a lot of friends."

Another of Eddie's life lessons Camel thought as he accepted the tray, uncovered it, sat on the bench and began eating.

Eddie stayed standing.

"You want some of this?" Camel asked between bites.

"No I have a friend who's in jail, I'm too upset to be eating."

Camel squinted a smile as he continued with breakfast.

"I bet I could take your blood pressure and pulse, they wouldn't show any elevations would they?"

"How's Annie?"

"Shaken up pretty bad."

"Still at your house though."

"Yes, trying to get some sleep . . . she couldn't eat anything either."

"Yeah well . . ."

"I hear Parker Gray's got his ass in a sling."

"Really?"

"Broke the rule. You're supposed to charge someone at the end of an investigation, not the beginning."

Camel agreed. "Plus this wasn't even Gray's case."

"The way I hear it, Gray more or less ordered the detectives to charge you, then he held his breath and stamped his feet until the judge set bail high enough you'd have to stay in here. Why's Gray got a hard-on for you?"

"I don't know if he does, mostly it was like he was worried about something else and I was just in his way." Having finished the oatmeal and powdered eggs, Camel drank some of the coffee, hot and weak. "You found out anything about that Cul-De-Sac homicide?"

"Victim was seventeen-year-old Hope Penner, decapitated by her cousin Donald Growler who was convicted and sent—"

"I know all that. Is this Growler still in prison, does he have a lawyer who's reopening the case?"

"Don't know."

"I'd like to find the guy who scared Annie, the guy with the teeth . . . have a little talk with him."

"Why don't you go to Cul-De-Sac and see if he's still hanging around?"

Camel looked at Eddie. "Does it come as a surprise to you, I can't make bail?"

"I made it for you."

He didn't say anything.

"I put up The Ground Floor as collateral."

"Jesus Eddie."

"I think they're going to void bail anyway, maybe even dismiss charges . . . meanwhile you just have to stay on your best behavior so I don't lose my place of business."

"I would've never asked you—"

"Hey it's a done deal, they're processing the paperwork now. I need you out anyway, help me set another trap for that weenie wagger in the parking garage."

Camel stood. "Thanks." But didn't know what else to say.

"This ain't going to be one of those tender moments is it . . . we start hugging each other and talking about how we value our friendship?"

Camel assured him it wasn't. "They finish with my office or is it still sealed?"

"Don't know, haven't been up there . . . but here's a bulletin for you. The officer in charge of the investigation, Hope Penner's murder seven years ago? Gerald McCleany."

"The guy who called you out of the blue, asking about me?"

"That's the one."

"I know there's something about that case hanging fire, it's what's making Parker Gray so twitchy."

"I got some addresses." Eddie unfolded a sheet of paper. "Judith and Lawrence Rainey, worked for J. L. Penner, the victim's uncle, both testified they saw Donald Growler going up to Hope Penner's room the day she was killed. Kenneth Norton, friend of Growler's who originally gave him an alibi then changed his story. And an old girlfriend of J. L. Penner, Elizabeth Rockwell, she also testified against Growler."

Camel took the sheet and put it in his pocket.

"You're welcome," Eddie prompted.

"I guess I'll need a car."

"I tried to tell you when you sold yours there'd be times—"

"What're you driving?"

Eddie looked stricken. "You're not going to borrow my Ford." He owned a 1965 Ford Fairlane he'd been restoring over the years, a car he didn't love as much as his wife and children but close.

"Come on gimme the keys."

He said no again but Camel waited and eventually Eddie handed over the keys though with great reluctance. "There are certain things I have to explain about that car."

"Explain on the way. I'll drop you off at The Ground Floor . . . no, your house, that way I can check on Annie."

"Let her sleep."

"You sure she's—"

"Teddy she's in my daughter's old bedroom safe and sound, let her sleep."

27

SHE DIDN'T FEEL SAFE OR SOUND, SHE WASN'T ASLEEP IN EDDIE'S DAUGH-
ter's former bedroom either . . . Annie was on her way to Cul-De-
Sac.

The Nefferings, Eddie and his wife Mary, had been generous
and gentle with her but as the hours ground by, as she watched out
the bedroom window for signs of light, Annie felt like she would
explode if she didn't do something . . . take a long walk, run to ex-
haustion, scream, hurt herself, *something*. She departed the Neffering's house before dawn was even a bad promise, Eddie already
gone and Mary still asleep. Annie walked fast and without a desti-
nation in mind, the cold morning air making it easier for her eyes
to tear though she wasn't crying. After more than an hour of hard
walking, revelation came like one of those literary coincidences
no one really believes . . . at the exact moment Annie saw light
painting the eastern sky. She caught a cab to the shopping mall's
parking garage and found where she had left Paul's old pickup.
What had finally come to Annie with dawn was what Paul wanted
her to remember . . . now she was going to Cul-De-Sac to find out
why.

As Annie drove she thought about that man with the awful
teeth, what he might do to her if he was at Cul-De-Sac. She was

frightened of him of course but in a larger sense Annie believed she probably deserved whatever happened to her today . . . had she gone back to Cul-De-Sac and stayed with Paul instead of re-playing golden old memories with Teddy none of this would've happened, Paul wouldn't be dead and Teddy wouldn't be in jail.

Driving the truck, trying to remember how to get there, she felt guilt weighing her down like icy slush water that her heart had difficulty pumping, that made Annie heavy and cold . . . if the man was waiting for her out at Cul-De-Sac, if he killed her, the prospect wasn't entirely abhorrent, not this particular morning it wasn't.

Turning at the brick pillars marking the entrance to Cul-De-Sac's half-mile lane Annie felt her hands moisten on the truck's steering wheel. But seeing the building in full daylight for the first time surprised her, the setting was lovely . . . a gentle tree-covered knoll surrounded by grassy fields with heavily wooded ridges on three sides and not another building in sight. Neither was Cul-De-Sac itself as frightening as Annie remembered. A great square hulk of a building sorely in need of paint and repair, it still re-tained a certain shabby dignity.

No sign anyone was here, no vehicles, no man with monstrous teeth waiting for her on the colonnaded porch. She parked the truck to the side of the building but didn't get out, Annie locking both doors and keeping the engine running, her hands still grip-ping the steering wheel.

When she arrived here from North Carolina and finally got Paul to open the door to his workshop up on the second floor, he had put his hand on the brick chimney in that former library and told her several times to remember the chimney. Before he killed him-self last night he said, *Remember what I asked you to remember.* Annie was convinced he'd left something for her, left it in or near the chimney.

She still hadn't cried over his death and felt guilty about that too. Had she really called Paul hapless, Annie didn't remember the occasion. She never meant to hurt his feelings, Paul had been good to her.

After that summer with Teddy Camel she became involved with a series of men who mistreated her, lied to her, tough guys and sneaks, one of them browbeat her into a three-way with his old girl-friend and another cleaned out her apartment and sold every-thing to finance a drug habit. But she *chose* these men, they weren't forced on her by some higher power, it was Annie who was embarrassing herself . . . punishing herself, she eventually con-cluded, for not being good enough to marry Teddy.

She'd thought Paul Milton was her recovery, a genuinely gentle man who was always careful with her, but look how it turned out . . . he'd spent all her money just as those other men had, he'd in-volved himself in something illegal, gone partners with a man who was creepy. Maybe she was attracted to Paul because she instinc-tively recognized in him a potential for trouble, for extremes. And now he's done something so extreme he could no longer bear liv-ing . . . what is it, what's he done here at Cul-De-Sac?

When Annie finally released the steering wheel she left wet handprints. Turning off the engine and unlocking her door, Annie got out of the truck and into a day so piercingly clear that her vision seemed to have improved from normal. The sky was high and blue, clouds flawlessly white, air clean and sharp enough that she took conscious pleasure from the simple routine of breathing. This must be what it's like when the sun shines over Antarctica.

She walked to a side door but it was locked, she'd have to go in through that back window again. Annie went around there, the window open as it had been the night before last, she climbed in . . . easier this time because instead of a dress she was wearing jeans and a white blouse borrowed from Mary Neffering. Annie crept through the storage room and out into the corridor. As she made her way toward the front of Cul-De-Sac she felt like a child crank-ing a jack-in-the-box . . . any moment now something would jump out and scare her.

But nothing did. The building was quiet, no pianos playing, no wall-scratching. She threaded her way through overly warm corridors crowded with cardboard boxes and bundled newspapers and assorted junk. It struck Annie now that this building was sad rather than sinister, a building used, abused, and abandoned, reopened and patched up, then boarded over again and neglected . . . when it was a hospital, soldiers had died here of lingering wounds, when it was an asylum, women had gone steadily insane here. That girl was killed here seven years ago, Paul had lost his mind here. These walls had absorbed too much sadness, these floors have borne up too much pain . . . Annie wouldn't feel settled again until she'd left Cul-De-Sac never to return.

She went around to the front entrance, to that wide stairway at the edge of the atrium large and shadowy, hungry for light. She continued on up to the second floor, down the hallway-balcony, to the old library where Paul had set up his workshop.

The heavy hasp was open, the door unlocked. Annie pushed into the room bracing herself for whatever shocking discovery she was about to make . . . but the room looked as it had when she first saw it two nights ago. The fireplace on the far wall must've been magnificent at one time, almost large enough to stand in, but its mantelpiece had been torn out to leave bare brickwork around a gaping hole.

Annie walked by the big black leather couch Paul had been using as his bed, horsehair stuffing showing like wiry pubic hair in a dozen rips and splits. She noticed the leather was freshly stained, Paul's blood?

Seeing his tools lined up so neatly on the shelves made Annie sad for him, such an orderly man and she had made such a mess of his life. Cords to the power tools were neatly coiled, hammers and screwdrivers hung from brackets in order of size, saw blades were glossy with oil, boxes and cans of nails were meticulously organized on various shelves, everything clean, well-maintained, stored properly. Safety equipment was arranged in one section, glasses and shields and fire extinguishers . . . Annie thinking, Paul never took a chance on anything in his life except me.

She was at the fireplace now, examining the brickwork and the area around it for messages, clues, a diary, suicide note . . . finding nothing except a half-smoked cigar on the grate. Moving the fire-screen and bracing herself with one hand Annie bent down into the fireplace and looked up the chimney seeing a rectangle of blue sky way up there at the top . . . when clouds floated past she felt like she was moving.

If there's nothing here, why had Paul repeatedly urged her to remember this chimney? Annie was about to duck back out when she noticed a rag, the edge of a rag sticking up from the rear of the damper. Bending over more she got her hand up there and reached through the open damper into the smoke chamber . . . the rag, actually a cotton drop cloth, was wrapped around something. Contorting her body, getting soot on the white blouse and jeans, all over her hands and on her face too, Annie finally managed to grip the drop cloth, pulling it toward her, bringing it out of the fireplace.

It was bundled around a galvanized metal box two feet long, a foot deep and wide . . . closed with a padlock. She carried it into the middle of the room, the box heavy enough she needed both hands.

Annie tried to put the truck key in the padlock but of course it didn't fit, she tried sawing through the lock with a hacksaw but that didn't work either, and finally she tried banging on the lock with a variety of hammers, making a lot of noise but otherwise ac-complishing nothing.

She sat on the floor to think. The hasp was attached to the box with rivets, if she could drive them out . . . Annie found a can of spike nails and used them as punches, hammering a nailpoint into each rivet. It took a long time, she repeatedly missed with the ham-mer and hit her thumb or fingertip, got tired and had to switch arms, but she kept at it, obsessed with getting the box open. When she wiped sweat from her face, the fireplace soot smeared until she looked as if she'd been working the coal . . . Annie exhausted and filthy by the time the hasp broke free.

She took a breath before opening the chest, would it be full of

money, would it contain a letter from Paul explaining everything
. . . and which of the two would Annie rather find? She slowly
raised the lid, squinting in anticipation.

Two items lay inside the chest: a nine-by-twelve envelope and
something wrapped in a section of sheepskin. The envelope was
on top, Annie opened it and brought out papers dealing with Our
Brothers' Keepers, the religious program Paul belonged to, an organization dedicated to helping prisoners. One form carried
Paul's signature, he had pledged to help a parolee get a job and
find a place to live, had pledged personal responsibility for the
parolee's well-being, religious instruction, and lawful behavior.
Another paper named the parolee . . . Donald Growler.

That's the name of the man Teddy said killed the girl here in
Cul-De-Sac seven years ago.

After this surprise Annie pulled from the envelope an even
larger one, a copy of Growler's photograph: the man with the
teeth. Paul was in partnership with the man who killed his cousin
here in this very building . . . *why?*

Annie raised up on her knees, she wasn't even trying to make
sense of this, not yet . . . then something else from the envelope,
more photographs. She spread them around on the floor,
snapshot-size pictures of people having sex. Annie was totally baffled. Paul keeping a secret stash of pornography? It didn't make
sense. Are these photographs why he went crazy, why he killed
himself . . . is Paul *in* these pictures?

She examined each of the eleven black-and-white photographs,
they were grainy and taken in low light but Annie could clearly see
it was the same woman in each shot . . . a young woman, maybe
even a teenager, who had a cute face, small breasts, and long blond
hair. The setting was also the same in each picture, a bare mattress
on a floor.

Annie looked carefully at the men who were on top of the young
woman, beneath her, spooned in behind, receiving oral sex, giving
oral sex, their faces caught full or in profile or partly obscured between the girl's legs . . . eleven different men but Paul wasn't
among them. Maybe he had *taken* the photographs.

Annie went back to one of the pictures . . . something familiar about the man's face. She'd seen him before but couldn't remember where, couldn't place him. Looking at all eleven pictures again, something struck her as odd about the angle of the camera, it must've been on a ladder or even up near the ceiling. Each photograph covered the precise same area, the mattress squarely in the center of all the pictures even when the young woman and her various partners had rolled at least partially out of view. The camera was obviously in a fixed position, up on a wall or the ceiling, focused on the mattress.

Annie went through the photographs a third time. The girl *knows* these pictures are being taken but the men *don't*. See how in some of the shots she looks over a man's shoulder and stares up at the camera . . . here she's on her hands and knees with a man behind her, the man's head resting on her back, maybe he's just climaxed, and she's looking up, making a face the way a kid might mug for the camera. In this next picture she's smiling, this one she's sticking out her tongue, this one she's rolling her eyes . . . the young woman having a private dialogue with the camera, commenting on the men's performances. But in none of the photographs do any of the men look at the camera or in any way acknowledge its presence.

Where did Paul get these? Annie couldn't even guess at an answer. Finally she brought out the other item in the chest, whatever was bundled in that sheepskin. This was what made the chest so heavy . . . something as solid and weighty as a bowling ball. Unwrapping the sheepskin carefully so she wouldn't drop its contents Annie gasped, even more surprised by this than she had been by the photographs.

Still up on her knees, hammers and papers and spike nails scattered around her, Annie didn't sense another's presence there in the room with her, she didn't get that creepy feeling that someone was staring at her. In fact if she hadn't heard a floorboard creak and then turned . . .

Satan's blue face hovered there at Annie's eye level, a huge dark blue face with demonic eyes and hooked nose, horns and everything just like in illustrations except for one unique feature . . . Satan's impossibly large mouth, covered all over with curly black hair, was gashed wide open in a leering grin and from the very center of that mouth stuck a stiffening cock, Satan's own tongue.

28

"WHERE YOU GOING FIRST?" EDDIE ASKED AS HE AND CAMEL LEFT THE state police building.

Camel checked the sheet of addresses. "Probably this Elizabeth Rockwell, she's closest. You packing?"

Eddie looked at him like he was crazy.

"You don't carry?"

"Why would I?"

Camel's turn to look at Eddie like he was crazy.

Eddie said he had a .45 at home. "That sweet little officer's model I showed you, it's unregistered."

"All mine were taken in as evidence. Tell you what Eddie, can you call Mary and ask her to bring the forty-five to The Ground Floor, I'll swing by there after I talk with this Rockwell woman. And if Annie's up to it she can come in with Mary, we'll all have lunch together."

"You interested in food already again?"

Camel was. Being on this case had sharpened all his appetites, he'd been thinking a lot about how Annie looked as he helped her remove that blue dress.

When they reached the cherry red '65 Fairlane parked at the

curb Eddie said, "Why don't you rent a car, I could let you use my credit card."

"No I want this one, it's red."

"You could rent one that's red . . . why's red so important any-way?"

"Red cars go faster."

"Faster than what?"

"Than cars that aren't red."

"Red cars go faster than cars that aren't red," Eddie repeated like an astronaut reading from the Flat Earthers' handbook. "And this is the man I'm entrusting Lucille to?"

"You one of those guys names his car?"

"What's wrong with that?"

Camel grimaced. "You give your dick a name too?"

Eddie looked embarrassed, Camel took out the keys. He got behind the wheel, Eddie riding shotgun, but before Camel started the ignition Eddie started his lecture. "This is a nineteen-sixty-five Ford Fairlane Five Hundred two-door hardtop with a two-hundred and seventy-one horsepower high performance two-eighty-nine cubic inch vee-eight, the Ford two-eighty-nine being the prototype for all of Ford's better engines . . ."

"Eddie—"

"Other engines generate more horsepower of course but for durability and reliability and all-around performance the two-eighty-nine is probably the best engine ever manufactured in this country. The sixty-five Fairlane was never as popular as the sixty-six or even the sixty-four . . ."

"Eddie—"

". . . but I like the boxy old look and—"

"*Eddie.*"

"Yeah?"

"I ain't marrying it."

"Don't buy gas."

"No?"

"It takes a hundred-and-ten octane, you won't find any of that."

"What if I run low?"

"The tank's full, you drive enough to run low you bring Lucille home, hear me?"

"Feel like I'm dating your daughter." Camel started the engine, revving it gently.

"For crying out loud Teddy, never gun a cold engine, ninety-five percent of an engine's wear takes place in the first ten seconds after starting."

He revved it again, Eddie muttering under his breath.

"Love the way that ol' two-ninety-two sounds," Camel said.

"*Two-eighty-nine*. Dual exhaust, glasspacks. You know of course I've done a frame-off restoration of this car, took me—"

Camel interrupted him by dropping the transmission into first, Eddie reaching over to grab the steering wheel. "Wait. Remember that movie, *Thunder Road*?"

"Robert Mitchum."

"Yeah—don't even think about it."

Camel nodded, floored the accelerator, popped the clutch, left a screaming strip of rubber on the street . . . Eddie Neffering thrown back in the passenger seat and saying more to himself than to Camel, "Why am I not surprised?"

■　　■　　■

WHEN SHE OPENED the door Camel wished he had Eddie's .45 with him because Elizabeth Rockwell was holding a little silver semiautomatic down by her side. Camel showed his private investigator's license which had a hokey badge with it that sometimes fooled people.

"Took you long enough to get here," Elizabeth said, slipping the .32 into a pocket and ushering Camel into her kitchen.

"You were expecting me?"

"I called last night, was told a detective would be sent out as soon as possible . . . you consider this as soon as possible?"

Camel apologized, playing along with the misunderstanding.

"Would you like some coffee?"

"Yes ma'am."

She smiled at his good manners. Camel guessed her at mid-fifty, he liked her looks, a woman tall, straight, and strong who gave the impression she didn't suffer fools or tolerate lapses in proper be-havior . . . like your aunt who never got married but became a col-lege professor instead, the aunt who corrected your grammar and told you to keep your elbows off the table.

Elizabeth wore a long yellow skirt that matched her jacket which covered a white blouse with a big floppy bow at her neck. Yellow shoes with low heels, big diamonds on many of her fingers. Dressed well for morning. She had short gray blond hair and wore dark glasses . . . a little heavy on the makeup, Camel figuring it was to cover the bruises he could still see high on her cheeks and he guessed she probably had a black eye too which explained the dark glasses.

As Elizabeth prepared the coffee he looked around the kitchen, everything modern and clean with a lot of frilly, doily stuff . . . the toaster for example had its own knitted cover. In walked a broad-shouldered young man who stopped at the doorway as if to show how he could fill it. He wore tight black jeans and an even tighter blue T-shirt, he had long blond hair and he had an angry red line around his trunklike neck.

"Murray darling," Elizabeth said, "this is Teddy Camel, he's with the state police."

Murray didn't hurry over to shake hands, he leaned against a counter as if planning to stay right there like a brooding appliance . . . Camel wondering if Murray was in the habit of knocking women around.

When Elizabeth put the coffee cup on its matching saucer in front of Camel she said, "Murray doesn't do caffeine."

"I'm not a police officer," Camel confessed.

"Yeah then who the heck are you?" Murray from the counter de-manded.

Camel looked at him, Murray radiating a hard stare right back. Camel had read once that if two people stare at each other for more than five or six seconds it means they're going to fuck or fight . . . not interested in either activity with Murray, Camel looked at Elizabeth and said, "I'm a private investigator working—"

"Private?" she interrupted. "Why are the state police using private detectives?"

"They're not."

"Then who you working for buddy?" Murray wanted to know.

Elizabeth told him she'd handle this, then asked Camel, "Why haven't the state police sent anyone? I was instructed not to call any other agency, to wait for a state police detective."

"I don't know ma'am."

"You'd think the state police would be rather desperate for my information about Donald."

Donald Growler?

"Milk?" Elizabeth offered.

"No ma'am."

"Yes I thought you'd drink it black."

"Caffeine'll kill you," Murray offered from the counter.

"Ma'am—"

"You can probably ease up on the ma'ams now," she said.

"Okay. The Donald you referred to, is that Donald Growler?"

"Murray asked who you are working for, is that privileged information?"

"I don't mind telling you. Annie Milton hired me—"

"A couple named Milton bought Cul-De-Sac."

"Yes. Annie was worried her husband might be involved in something illegal with a man she'd never met until the night before last . . . a man in his early or mid-thirties, dark eyes, black hair, his most distinguishing characteristic is—"

"Huge teeth."

Camel surprised again.

"Donald Growler," she said.

And surprised *again*. "None of the descriptions I got said anything about Growler having unusual teeth"

"He obviously had them installed in prison, I can't imagine a government-run facility would do that to a person, even a convicted killer."

"Donald Growler is out of prison." Camel said this aloud to make sure he had it right.

Murray guffawed, Elizabeth smiled condescendingly. "Yes, Donald Growler is most assuredly out of prison, he said he'd been released . . . but released or escaped he's out and more dangerous than ever. He threatened to kill me and *would have* killed Murray if I hadn't had this pistol." She patted her pocket and said she still didn't understand what Camel was doing here.

"Paul Milton shot himself last night."

"Good Lord."

"Whatever he was involved in with Growler, it drove him to suicide. When did Growler show up—"

"Last night around ten."

"What'd he want?"

She hesitated, Murray from the counter advising her, "You don't have to tell him nothing Beth."

Elizabeth said, "Why don't you fix yourself a nice cup of Ovaltine dear."

"Yeah well I ain't leaving you alone with this guy."

"You don't have to sweetheart, the Ovaltine's right there in that cabinet." She turned her attention back to Camel. "How much do you know about Cul-De-Sac and Hope Penner's death?"

"Almost nothing."

"I love telling secrets."

"I love hearing them."

"Yin and Yang."

"Trains and tunnels." As soon as he said it Camel wondered, where the hell did that come from?

Elizabeth was surprised too. "Mr. Camel," she said coquettishly while Murray preparing his Ovaltine got the vague impression these two old farts were flirting with each other.

Camel was a little red in the face. "You were going to tell me Cul-De-Sac's secrets."

She asked how far back she should start, he said he had time.

"A quick history then. Cul-De-Sac was built in 1860 by Phillip Penner, a wealthy plantation owner from southern Virginia who sold his slaves and used the money to construct a hotel for travelers on their way to the District of Columbia. Those construction costs nearly broke him, by the time the hotel was finished Penner said he had reached the bottom of his figurative bag of gold, that's why he named the hotel Cul-De-Sac, the literal translation is 'bottom of the bag.' "

"French."

She offered Camel another condescending smile, Elizabeth Rockwell was good at that.

"During the Civil War Cul-De-Sac was used as a military hospital, after the war Penner reopened it as a hotel and when he died Cul-De-Sac was boarded up. The building and the land that went with it, two hundred and twenty acres, stayed in the Penner family. Through the years Cul-De-Sac was used for various purposes, a mental asylum for women, then during the Second World War it was leased by the federal government and opened to recuperating soldiers. Through much of the fifties Cul-De-Sac was boarded up again but meanwhile those two hundred and twenty acres were becoming very valuable."

The history lesson was making Camel itchy but he didn't want to offend her by saying get to the point. "Who owned the property seven years ago when—"

"We're almost there." She was a habitual interrupter who didn't like being interrupted. "In 1960, Cul-De-Sac's centennial, the property was owned by Phillip Penner's three living heirs . . . two brothers and a sister. One of the brothers, J. L. Penner, resided at Cul-De-Sac. His sister's son, that would be Donald, also came to live at Cul-De-Sac, then seven years ago J.L.'s brother died and the brother's daughter came to Cul-De-Sac . . . are you following this?"

Camel said he was. "The nephew is Donald Growler, the niece was Hope Penner."

"You *do* know something about this case."

"Not nearly enough."

"Hope was seventeen when she was killed, she and Donald had

developed a relationship more intimate than we normally like to see between first cousins even here in Virginia."

"And that relationship is what led to the murder?"

"So it seems." Elizabeth took off the dark glasses, Camel was right about the shiner. "With the death of his niece, J.L. became sole owner of Cul-De-Sac."

"Growler give you that eye?"

"Yes. Should I continue then?"

"Please."

"Only after J.L. inherited Hope's share was he able to start selling off land. In fact there was some vague speculation at the time . . . there's always vague speculation in these cases, as I'm sure you're aware, Mr. Camel . . . speculation that J.L. might have been involved in Hope's murder."

"That he killed her?"

"That he was involved. J.L. was able to consolidate his ownership of Cul-De-Sac *only* through the specific set of circumstances that occurred, Donald Growler murdering Hope Penner . . . if Hope had died under other circumstances her share would've gone to Donald. Even if Donald and Hope had died together, that remaining share of Cul-De-Sac would've gone to charity, not to J. L. Penner. He had bought out his sister's interest years before but J.L.'s brother hated him and set up a trust in such a way as to ensure J.L. never got that remaining one-third ownership. Of course the brother could not have foreseen what finally happened, who could've?"

"So Growler goes to prison, gets out, hooks up with Paul Milton who buys Cul-De-Sac . . . for what reason?"

She didn't answer.

"What were Growler and Milton looking for at Cul-De-Sac?"

"I don't know."

The lie surprised Camel, he hadn't been ready for it. He liked Elizabeth Rockwell, admired her style, a lady with a lot of class and brass . . . then she insults him by lying . . . it seemed so out of character, as if she had suddenly cleared her throat and spat on the floor.

"You're lying." Camel's voice was quiet but came with the authority of someone who wasn't wrong about these things.

"Hey buddy!" Murray warned from the counter. "Watch your mouth!"

"Drink your Ovaltine dear," Elizabeth said before turning back to Camel. "Murray has a point . . . you're a guest in my house, I'm providing you with information you've requested, I hardly think you should be calling me a liar."

"I didn't call you a liar, I said you were lying."

She looked amused. "There's a difference?"

"I sincerely hope so." Although references to an elephant had drawn blanks with everyone else, Camel decided to try one on Elizabeth. "Were Growler and Milton looking for an elephant?"

She hesitated, didn't want to be caught in another lie. "Are we playing games Mr. Camel?"

"I'm trying to investigate—"

"You're fishing."

"Sounds better when I call it investigating."

She smiled without the condescension. "Give the devil her due, Hope Penner was a brilliant young woman."

Camel waited to hear what this had to do with an elephant.

"Hope played the piano at concert level, she was an accomplished artist, spoke several languages, she could've been a chess master . . . J.L. fancied himself a good chess player but Hope beat him consistently, which delighted J.L. In his eyes Hope could do no wrong . . . like every man who ever met Hope he was totally infatuated with her."

"Did it go beyond infatuation?"

She gave Camel a look that made him regret the question.

"I don't think that's a subject on which I'd care to speculate."

He said fair enough.

"After Hope died J.L. went into both a mental and physical decline. Although he became very rich selling land he also became very reclusive and more than a little strange. By the end of his life he was barely in possession of his faculties."

"And at this time you were his—"

"Before Hope came to live at Cul-De-Sac, J.L. and I were engaged to be married. After her death he and I were simply friends."

"Her death unhinged him?"

"Her *life* unhinged him, Mr. Camel. He loved showing her off, J.L. would host a party for Hope every night for seven or eight nights in a row. He gave her cars, indulged her drug habits. When J.L. discovered what an excellent chess player Hope was, he began buying chess sets and very soon became a serious collector. He developed an obsession for the East India Chess Set, not the most famous chess set in the world but perhaps the most expensive. It had been broken up in the last century, its pieces sold and resold to buyers from all over the world. The entire set could never have been reassembled at any price but J.L. did manage to purchase almost all the black pieces and one white . . . the knight."

"The white knight?"

"He and Hope would have fondling sessions with it."

Camel again waited for her to explain.

"J.L. and Hope would creep hand-in-hand to the library where he kept his chess collection and they'd take out the East India white knight. Hope loved to hold it and she would say, 'Oh J.L. you're my white knight.' And he would promise Hope that someday the elephant would be hers. It was all rather pitiful."

"You said he promised Hope the *elephant* would be hers?"

Elizabeth looked at Camel as a teacher might regard a particularly dull scholar. "The East India Chess Set's black pieces were carved ebony, the white pieces were solid gold . . . and the white knight was an elephant."

"A solid-gold elephant."

"Encrusted with jewels."

"Worth?"

"Three million dollars. Why *Monsieur Chameau,* do you have something in your eye or are you actually smiling?"

"Smiling," Camel admitted. "Like a scoundrel."

LINDA KAY GRAY WAS SMILING TOO, IT WAS A TREAT FOR HER WHEN Parker came home in the middle of the day. She'd heard his car, heard him go into the kitchen . . . that's where she was hurrying now.

"Park?"

He was at the table with his back to her, when Linda came around to sit across from him she lost her smile . . . he looked terrible.

"What's wrong?"

Parker Gray stared across that table as if he didn't recognize his wife.

"Park?"

He shook his head.

"Something at work?"

"I . . ." He cleared his throat. "I've been suspended."

"Good Lord what for?"

"I came down too hard on a man brought in to be questioned about a shooting."

"What do you mean, came down too hard . . . you hit him?"

"No. I pushed for his arrest and—"

"They wouldn't suspend you for—"

"And I got into a shouting match with a couple of our detectives."

"Over what, arresting that man?"

Parker Gray held up a hand . . . how could he explain to his wife that their whole life together, their marriage, the success he's had with the state police, everything has been built on a convoluted conspiracy that grinds on him every night?

"I'll make some coffee."

Watching his wife work at the counter Gray felt a strangely powerful impulse to pull out his 9mm and shoot her in the back of the head . . . then kill himself. Allowing this apocalyptic fantasy to run a course Gray suddenly realized why so many men end everything with a murder-suicide . . . killing someone, especially someone you love, *requires* you to take your own life, it's what a man does when he can't summon the courage to commit suicide, he forces his own hand. That's what Paul Milton had been toying with, threatening to shoot his wife and Camel so that, seeing what he'd done, he would have no choice but to kill himself. Except Milton finally found the balls to do it on his own, without the motivation of murdering someone else first. Gray experienced a mixture of relief and regret when he finally put it out of his mind, the idea of shooting Linda in the back of the head.

He'd known all along of course that Milton's death was a suicide, Gray had to charge Camel to keep him bottled up until McCleany could finish what they'd started at Cul-De-Sac seven years ago. Goddamn McCleany anyway . . . and goddamn me.

"Take just a minute to drip through," Linda said as she sat again at the table. "You feel like talking about this now?"

No he would never feel like talking about it.

"Park?"

"What?"

"Is it something else, I mean beside the suspension?" She was thinking, he's having an affair.

While her husband was thinking, the only way out of this if I don't want more people to die . . . I'm going to have to kill myself and then go to hell.

30

"REFERENCES TO AN ELEPHANT KEPT POPPING UP," CAMEL TOLD ELIZA-
beth Rockwell. "I questioned people but no one tipped to it. Not
knowing what it was or what it referred to was starting to get under
my skin. Now I know, that's why I smiled."

"You *do* have a passion for secrets, don't you?"

He squinted another smile. "Tell me another one."

"As I said, the East India white knight is a solid-gold elephant . . .
approximately eight inches long and eight inches tall, trunk and
right foot raised in triumph, the entire piece heavily decorated
with various precious gems, diamonds and rubies and emeralds. I
saw it many times in J.L.'s collection and could never decide
whether it was beautiful or garish. But its monetary value was
never in dispute."

"Three million bucks."

"That's the value we settled on for insurance purposes. What it
would be worth on the open market I don't know . . . probably
more."

"Where is it?"

"The elephant was stolen."

"By—"

"I don't know."

"Can you—"

"After Hope was murdered, J.L. never looked at his collection of chess sets again, I guess they reminded him too much of her. I was executrix of his will which was tied up in probate for a long time, all his possessions held by a security company. When we finally got around to doing a complete appraisal we discovered that the elephant, the real East India Chess Set white knight, had been replaced by a copy cast from brass, studded with false gems made of colored and cut glass. A pretty good copy if you didn't examine it too closely."

"Who pulled the switch?"

"Pulled the switch." The phrase amused her. "We assumed someone connected with the security company, in fact we made a claim against that company's insurance. J.L. left most of his estate to charity, there weren't any greedy heirs to pursue the matter."

"Growler stole the elephant before he went to prison."

"So it seems. No one suspected Donald because the switch wasn't discovered until last year, after he'd been in prison for six years. But when he was here last night he was very intent on finding that elephant."

"Who's got it?"

"I don't know. Apparently Donald hid the real knight somewhere in Cul-De-Sac but while he was away someone found it and that has made Donald very, very angry. You see . . . is this starting to bore you?"

Camel assured her he remained fascinated with everything she was telling him.

Elizabeth smiled and touched her hair. "Obviously I've been giving this some thought since Donald's visit. His best friend, his former best friend, is an artist . . . maybe Kenneth is a sculptor also."

"Kenneth Norton?"

"Yes. If Donald and Kenneth, they were always up to something, if Kenneth sculpted a copy of the East India elephant . . . well don't you see, Donald lived at Cul-De-Sac and had access to J.L.'s collection and could've easily made, pulled the switch. Maybe Donald and Kenneth were planning to leave the country, the white knight financing their life in Europe, Donald was always talking about living in Europe."

"And the murder, its connection to—"

"Maybe Hope found out about the plot and threatened to tell J.L., although I think it's vastly more likely that she was in on the scheme from the very beginning."

"You didn't like her."

"I hated her."

"But not enough to kill her?"

Murray didn't warn Camel to watch his mouth because Murray had become bored with the conversation, was looking out a window, and failed to catch Camel's implied accusation.

Elizabeth didn't take offense either, it was too ludicrous. "No I didn't kill Hope."

Camel believed she was telling the truth.

"Until last night I was absolutely convinced Donald had killed her."

"Until last night?"

"He was enraged. Prison has changed him from a weird and rather delicate young man with a taste for the macabre . . . he kept severed animal heads in his room . . . to a well-muscled violent psychopath who's on a mission."

"A mission?"

"Revenge upon everyone who helped send him to prison. He was most vociferous in proclaiming his innocence. Of course at the trial he claimed he was innocent too but last night for some strange reason I believed him."

"Then who do you think killed Hope . . . J. L. Penner? You were saying before that he benefited by inheriting the girl's share of Cul-De-Sac."

"I could see J.L. arranging to frame Donald for the murder but no, J.L. didn't kill her, he was in love with Hope. Donald was too. In fact I don't think I can recall one man who was immune to Little Miss Hope Penner."

"She had a lot of lovers?"

Elizabeth laughed. "A lot? She had legions. A ludicrous number of lovers for a girl so young Mr. Camel. She was . . . well I can't think how to describe it forcefully enough without being crude. She was sexually active, promiscuous, perverted—"

"Perverted?"

"Do you know about the photographs?"

Camel knew only that Parker Gray had asked if photographs were found at Cul-De-Sac.

"Mr. Camel?"

"No I don't know about the photographs."

"We'd better have more coffee . . . Murray how's your Ovaltine?"

"I'm bored."

"I know you are darling, why don't you go upstairs and—"

"How long you going to be?"

"Mr. Camel and I are going to drink one more cup of coffee each, then we'll be done with our chat."

"Caffeine'll kill you."

"I know dear, but so very many things will."

"I'll wait for you upstairs . . . you okay here with *him?*"

"Yes darling, Mr. Camel means me no harm."

"Better not," Murray warned before bear-walking from the kitchen.

She watched his departure with obvious fondness, telling Camel, "He's such a dear . . . fun to be with, loyal, totally faithful—"

"Yeah I had a dog like that once."

Elizabeth started to protest the remark but laughed instead, laughed hard enough to wet her eyes . . . then looked at Camel and said, "Oddly enough I actually enjoy your company."

"You're okay too Beth."

She considered him for a moment then poured the coffee. "As with everything else Hope did, she was an accomplished photographer . . . won several awards, displayed in local galleries, I mean the girl really was too good to be true. Built her own darkroom, did her own developing. After her death it was discovered Hope had set up a secret camera in a room where she entertained her many lovers . . . the room where she was killed. Hope hid the camera up on the ceiling, pointed down at a mattress on the floor, rigged to snap pictures at certain intervals. Mr. Camel you can't imagine what a collection of photographs she must've had . . . riding instructors, soldiers, policemen, actually anyone in uniform, UPS men I'm sure, various samplings of Cul-De-Sac's political VIPs . . . J.L. was active in the Republican party . . . oh, Hope's list of conquests goes on and on, local boys, gardeners, visiting TV repairmen, a cousin, maybe an uncle, men she met in bars and dragged back to Cul-De-Sac."

"Did you see the photographs?"

"No."

"Then how do you—"

"I'm speculating. The apparatus for taking those photographs was discovered during the murder investigation but the police never found any pictures. At his trial Donald was adamant that the photographs would establish his innocence."

"Because—"

"I suppose he thought one of her lovers killed her or maybe he was hoping the murder itself had been caught on film."

"Elizabeth . . . do you know where the pictures are?"

She hesitated, then shook her head. "Just before J.L. died he mentioned Hope's photographs. Maybe he had them from the very beginning, keeping them hidden to ensure Donald would go to prison and then holding on to them over the years because some very prominent men must've been caught on film with that seventeen-year-old girl and J.L. liked having leverage over people, especially people with influence."

"And one of those influential men killed Hope."

"Entirely possible."

Camel finished the coffee, told Elizabeth he was grateful for the information.

"I'm just happy *someone* is investigating this, I find it incredible that Parker Gray—"

"Parker Gray?"

"Yes, he's an associate superintendent with the state police."

"I know but—"

"I find it incredible Parker hasn't sent a detective to talk with me as he promised when I called him last night, God knows what Donald will do to Kenneth Norton or the Raineys . . . in fact he might have already done something, he made a veiled reference to having harmed them, you should go over and make sure they're okay."

"They're next on my list to visit but why—"

"Good."

"Why did you call Parker Gray—"

"The obvious person to call since Gerald McCleany is retired."

"I still don't—"

"Mr. Camel you should've come to me straight off, I could've put all your ducks in a neat little row."

"You're right, I wish I had talked to you—"

"Gerald McCleany was the state police detective in charge of investigating Hope's death."

"Okay, that I knew."

"And young Parker Gray was his junior partner."

"I'll be damned."

"I certainly hope not, Teddy."

31

DONALD GROWLER WAS NAKED, UP ON TIPTOES, PROUDLY DISPLAYING A massive dark blue tattoo spreading from his abdomen down to his groin and across both upper thighs. This tattoo, the horned grinning visage of Satan, was positioned such that the devil's reptilian eyes were below Growler's navel, the hooked nose above his pubic hair, that huge mouth stretching across Growler's genitals and onto his thighs in a way that put Growler's dick at the very center of Satan's fat open lips.

Annie had been startled by Growler sneaking up behind her, now she was afraid of what he intended to do, rape her, but she also couldn't stop looking at the tattoo . . . fascinated that someone would mutilate himself like that. She didn't notice the other tattoos, the little broken heart on his right bicep or the Tasmanian Devil on his left shoulder.

"Old Scratch wants a kiss."

Annie looked up from the tattoo to Growler's own leering expression, dark eyes wide enough to show white all around, hair wet-sleek, big buck teeth in full grin . . . Growler's face as terrible as the one below. Someone had bitten him on the right cheek.

"Should warn you though, he's got a hell of a French kiss."

Annie was still on her knees as Growler's eyes switched back and forth from watching her to glancing down and admiring the tattoo himself.

"It must've hurt," she finally said.

The comment bewildered him . . . and when he replied his voice had softened. "Hurt like you wouldn't believe."

"Why did you do it?"

He shrugged, the wildness in his face gone. "I thought it would ward off attention, some of them are incredibly superstitious . . . but it worked about as well as these stupid teeth I had put in." When Growler came down off his toes he had assumed an air of vulnerability, you could hear the little boy in his voice. "Should've had Old Scratch tattooed on my ass is where I should've had him tattooed."

"Prison must've been horrible for you."

He nodded . . . then his posture stiffened and he got that hard look in his eyes again. "What do you know about me being in prison?"

"I just assumed it was a prison tattoo."

Suspicious now, Growler circled Annie and saw what she had taken from the chest, had unwrapped from the sheepskin. "You bitch I knew you had my elephant!" But he was more thrilled than angry, bending down to take the gold-and-jeweled elephant in his hands, turning it around and around as a mother might examine and admire her newborn child. Annie noticed he'd lost his erection.

"I found it in the chimney," she explained.

"That's why your face is so dirty," Growler said absently, his attention riveted to the elephant. "I'm as happy as . . ." But he was unable to think of equivalents for happy, all of his experience these past seven years had been in the opposite direction.

Meanwhile Annie was looking at her hands black with soot, trying to imagine what her face was like.

When Growler finally stopped admiring the elephant he told her, "I knew St. Paul stole this but give the bastard credit, he held out on me no matter what I did to him . . . and I did everything."

"He's dead."

"Paul?"

"My husband is dead, yes."

Growler laughed. "You greedy bitch, you killed St. Paulie for this elephant, Jesus what a pair you two turned out to be."

"No he shot himself."

"Why?"

Because he caught me with Teddy, Annie thought . . . but she told Growler it was because of him. "Paul went crazy from being here with you, from whatever it was you did to him."

Growler laughed again. "Good. He was supposed to be my partner, I'd already agreed to give him a cut of whatever the elephant brought, but your husband turned out to be greedy like you. I had this elephant hid in an old dumbwaiter shaft that was sealed up, St. Paulie must've got in from the basement, climbed the shaft like the rat he was. Did all this before I arrived here from prison, then when we opened the shaft on the second floor, where I stashed the elephant originally, it was gone and St. Paul was all innocent-like, actually had the balls to accuse *me* of lying, he said I made up the elephant story just so he'd get me out of prison. 'No, no,' I told him, 'there really is an elephant, someone stole it while I was in prison.' I promised him I'd find out who but of course it was St. Paul all along, he lied to me and I believed him like he was a man of God. Have to admire the bastard . . . I wish I'd killed him when I had the chance."

"Paul was a good—"

"Your husband was a rat bastard, supposed to be religious, turned out to be a lying thief instead . . . hiding my elephant in the chimney so you could come here and—"

"I didn't know anything about this!"

He kicked her shoulder with a bare foot. "How can you people lie the way you do, I catch you with the elephant and you still lie—"

"No!" Annie was desperate to explain. "Before Paul shot himself he said something about the chimney in this room but he didn't specifically tell me what was hidden there, never told me about his partnership with you . . . he denied you even existed."

Growler cursed her, again calling Annie a liar . . . when she started to stand he told her to stay on her knees. "Just the position I want you in." He returned to admiring the elephant. "Solid gold, baby. And some of these diamonds are worth a hundred thousand dollars just on their own. I got a buyer lined up in England, three million, no questions asked."

Annie looked again at the elephant . . . three million dollars, she had held *three million dollars* in her hands? Even with the danger she faced, Annie felt a sudden and powerful sense of possessiveness toward the golden sculpture. Paul had died to get it for her. It should be mine, she thought . . . it should be *mine*.

"Part of a set from India," Growler was saying. "I don't know if anyone ever played chess with it, obviously meant for display, everything oversized . . . all the white pieces were solid gold, this elephant is one of the knights."

"How did you and Paul get connected?"

"Through Our Brothers' Keepers. I couldn't get anybody to sponsor me for parole until I told Paul what was hidden here in Cul-De-Sac. This elephant came from my uncle's collection, a friend of mine cast a brass replica and I switched them, hid the real one . . . but then Hope was killed and I got framed—" Growler suddenly glowered at Annie. "Why you stringing me along, St. Paul must've told you all this."

"No I swear—"

"Doesn't matter, I got it, I got it now! And I've taken care of everybody but Elizabeth . . . and *you*."

"I won't say anything to anyone."

He carried the elephant over to the tool shelves and carefully placed it between a circular saw and an electric sander, then returned to Annie and told her, "I drove your husband in-fucking-sane." Laughing at a memory he began stroking himself. "I was in the tub when St. Paul walks into the bathroom, he hadn't seen my tattoo yet. St. Paulie's eyes got big as saucers when he spotted Old Scratch here floating just below the surface . . . freaked him out of his fucking gourd. I went with it, told him I was Satan, said I'd been imprisoned by the forces of good but his own greed for gold had freed me to roam the world once again, doing evil. I spread it on so thick I had a tough time keeping a straight face. But St. Paulie lapped it up. I think he was a little wobbly to start with don't you?"

Annie was finally crying . . . was it for Paul or for herself?

"Take off your clothes."

"Just let me leave, I won't—"

He kicked her in the side of the head, the blow disorienting Annie but not injuring her because Growler was barefoot.

"Take off your clothes, don't make me tell you again."

She began unbuttoning the blouse.

He bent down and rubbed a thumb along her cheek, smearing tears through the soot. "Ought to make you shower first. Hey look at me."

She did, Annie recognizing that ravenous expression, she'd seen it on too many men's faces, eyes glazed with sexual greed.

"Come on hurry up, you got Satan's tongue sticking straight out."

She removed the blouse, then her bra.

"Now take off your pants."

But Annie stayed on her knees. If she tried to run, if she picked up one of the tools scattered on the floor . . .

He made a fist. "I'm going to split your fucking nose open if you don't do exactly what I tell you. I ain't had nothing but whores since I been out, you're my first civilian ass . . . not counting St. Paul of course."

"I'm not going to let you do this to me," she said quietly.

"How you planning to stop me?"

She didn't know.

"Come on baby Old Scratch is hungry." He grasped her shoulders. "You can take those jeans off in a minute, first you're going to blow me."

"I won't," she said stubbornly.

He grabbed hair at both sides of her head, Annie could smell his musk. "I feel any teeth," Growler warned, "and I'll cripple you."

"I found some pictures!"

He let go of her. "Where?"

"In the chest with that elephant." She indicated the pho-tographs on the floor.

Growler went around to look. He'd been so taken with the ele-phant he hadn't even noticed the snapshots. Picking one up he said, "I'll be damned."

Annie turned on her knees, she knew she had to do it now. Growler gathered up the remaining photographs, he was standing there going through them, absolutely engrossed by what he was seeing . . . not noticing Annie as she took a spike nail in her left hand, grasping a hammer with her right.

I'll get only this one chance she thought. Annie quickly placed her left hand on top of Growler's foot, her fist steadying the nail, her other hand coming around with the hammer to hit as hard as she could. The nail entered his left foot just above the second toe but didn't go all the way through.

As matters turned out Annie got a second chance after all . . . Growler bellowing, stepping back, tripping, putting his foot back on the floor to stop from falling. She lunged forward and, holding the hammer in both hands this time, swinging hard, Annie hit the nailhead squarely, driving the spike completely through Growler's foot and into the wood floor beneath.

He was screaming, slapping her across the top of the head as Annie hit the nail again and again until only the head showed.

When she rolled away from Growler he sounded like an animal being butchered alive, filling the room with his rage and pain, cursing her worse than she'd ever heard as he tried to lift that left foot but of course couldn't, Annie had spike-nailed him to the floor.

32

IT WAS NOON ON TUESDAY, APRIL 16, AND TEDDY CAMEL WAS TWELVE hours overdue on his income tax, he'd also be late for meeting Eddie, Mary, and Annie at The Ground Floor.

Concerned about what Elizabeth Rockwell had said indicating Growler might've already visited the other people who testified against him, Camel was knocking on the front door of a brown-shingled bungalow owned by Judith and Lawrence Rainey who didn't answer Camel's knock. The Raineys were an older couple, maybe they didn't hear him, maybe they were around back.

Camel walked along the side of the house, checking in windows as he went but seeing no sign of anyone home. He entered the backyard, no one here either but he noticed a cigar on the ground and wondered who had dropped it. Climbing the steps and knocking on the back door, Camel ran through possibilities as he waited . . . what led to the murder of that seventeen-year-old girl, was she in on the theft of that solid-gold elephant or was she trying to blackmail someone with those secret sex pictures? When Camel asked Parker Gray about an elephant, Gray didn't tip to it, he was worried about photographs. Did McCleany and Gray run a bogus investigation seven years ago to protect the real killer . . . one of Hope's lovers, someone she caught with that hidden camera rig, someone rich enough to buy off McCleany and Gray, with enough political power to move Parker Gray up the ranks to associate superintendent?

No one showed at the back door, Camel starting around for the front again when he looked down a flight of concrete steps to a basement door. He went down there and saw that the door had been jimmied. Pushing it open he caught a funny smell. Sincerely wishing he had Eddie's .45 with him, Camel entered the basement and saw what looked to be red paint on the floor. He knelt. It was dried blood leading to a washing machine and dryer which also had blood on their lids.

Careful not to leave tracks or fingerprints, Camel walked over there and used a handkerchief to lift those lids . . . Mr. and Mrs. Rainey.

33

FASCINATED BY GROWLER'S PREDICAMENT, BY THIS TERRIBLE THING SHE'D somehow managed to accomplish, Annie hadn't yet grabbed her blouse or run from the room . . . as if hypnotized she continued watching even as Growler reached down inside of himself where seven years of revenge burned, finding there the energy and madness he needed to grab his ankle and pull, Growler screaming mouth open and teeth bared as the head of that spike nail ripped flesh all the way through his foot and out the bottom.

Annie fascinated by this too . . . stunned and fascinated and *still there in the room* even as a voice from some logic compartment in her brain urged her to leave, run, go, *now.*

Growler was looking at his bleeding foot, then turned a red-wrath face toward Annie and promised her, "I'm going to cripple you."

She believed him, Annie believed this promise more sincerely than she believed any promise a man had ever made to her.

He kept both arms out for balance, putting weight on his right foot, allowing only the heel of that mangled left foot to touch the floor . . . leaving bloodprints across the floor.

Annie finally did what she should've done those critical few seconds ago, running from the room . . . no time to grab her blouse now, Annie running onto the balcony around the atrium, running for the stairway.

Growler followed . . . limping, dragging his foot, screaming further terrible promises to her.

She made it down the stairway without tripping, to the front doors which were locked. Must be a way to open them from the inside but in her panic and with Growler bellowing his way down the steps Annie couldn't figure it out . . . rushing back through the corridors the way she came, to that storage room, out the window, feeling no self-consciousness about being naked to the waist, too scared for modesty, running around to the side of Cul-De-Sac, to the truck, getting seated behind the wheel . . . and only then remembering she'd tried to open that chest with the truck key and then left it on the floor upstairs.

Annie looked at Cul-De-Sac, no sign of Growler yet. Paul used to keep a spare key in a magnetic holder stuck under a fender . . . was it the left front fender? She got out and searched, kept glancing at the building . . . which way would he be coming from, the front, the back, out the side door? Where is it, where is that little key box, under the other fender? No, *here*. She slid back the top, dropped the key, picked it up just in time to see Growler opening a door to the side of Cul-De-Sac no more than twenty feet from where she stood.

Annie got into the truck, fumbled getting the key into the ignition, told herself not to flood the engine, thank God it started on the first crank . . . one more quick glance at the hobbling Growler, he was almost to the truck as Annie dropped the transmission into gear and hit the gas, popped the clutch, throwing gravel as she swung around and headed out the lane.

When she checked her side mirror she didn't see Growler back by the side of the building, where'd he go? She looked into the rearview mirror and got her answer: the naked son-of-a-bitch was there on the bumper trying to get his wounded left foot up over the tailgate.

Annie jammed the accelerator hard to the floor but it was too late, Growler already aboard.

34

CAMEL DROVE TO A PAY PHONE AND CALLED IN AN ANONYMOUS TIP TO the Arlington police, telling the dispatcher what could be found in the washer and dryer in the Raineys' basement and also in the closet upstairs. At another pay phone he called the Nefferings but got the answering machine . . . Mary and Eddie must've already left to take Annie to The Ground Floor for lunch.

Camel got back into the Fairlane and checked Kenneth Norton's address, he could swing by on the way back to The Ground Floor. Except maybe that wasn't smart. The safe thing to do would be go have lunch with Eddie, Mary, and Annie. Camel started the engine and listened to the sound of the exhaust, underwater rumbling. He pulled away from the curb wondering if he'd ever learn to do the smart, safe thing.

Camel was getting accustomed to the heavy old Ford with its oversized steering wheel, and although he liked the car's afterburner acceleration he drove carefully in deference to how much the Fairlane meant to Eddie.

Knowing the general area around Norton's address, Camel still couldn't find Lee Street so he stopped at a convenience store where the long-haired pimply young clerk offered a heavy-lidded bored look over the top of an illustrated swimsuit catalog . . . until Camel asked, "Isn't Lee Street around here?"

The clerk put the catalog down and stood up behind the counter like a soldier coming to attention. "One block up, take a left, Lee Street's two blocks over."

Camel told him thanks and the clerk responded with a crisp, "You're welcome sir."

He drove to the apartment complex, found the building, went up to Norton's apartment, and knocked on the door. Camel waited, didn't get an answer. The smart thing, just leave. He shouldn't be getting involved in any of this, not when he's out on bail for a manslaughter charge . . . but ever since Annie showed up, since he started working on this case, Camel felt more alive, more juiced, hungrier and hornier than he had in years. He wasn't going to leave until he had a look in Norton's apartment.

Camel went downstairs to see the building manager, a man in his late sixties, dressed in a blue shirt and tan slacks, smelling of cologne, obviously proud of his long white hair which he had combed with a sort of double wave all along one side. Camel flashed his license but put it away before the guy had time to memorize his name.

"I wondered if someone would be by to check on Mr. Norton," the manager said after he stepped back into his apartment to get a set of keys, the masters.

"Why's that?"

"I had two noise complaints filed against Mr. Norton."

"When?"

"When was the noise or when were the complaints filed?"

"The noise."

"Last night around eight. Mr. Norton is normally such a good tenant, never a complaint against him since he moved in. That's why I was wondering if there had been . . . foul play." Using the term embarrassed him.

At the door to Norton's apartment the manager knocked and called Norton's name. "We never go into a tenant's residence unless we have a compelling reason."

"This is compelling believe me."

The manager unlocked the door and opened it a crack. "Mr. Norton! Oh Mr. Norton!"

Camel pushed the door the rest of the way open . . . first thing he and the manager saw were red stains streaked in a path across the white carpet.

"Oh my . . . Mr. Norton had this carpet installed at his own expense, I can't imagine—"

Camel interrupted him with an arm across the manager's chest, easing him back out into the hallway as Camel went into the apartment. A naked man presumably Norton was tied to a chair in the kitchen, his back to Camel. From the dining alcove it looked as if Norton's head must've been hanging forward, that's why Camel couldn't see it. Then he stepped into the kitchen and saw Norton looking up at him from the floor.

Camel went through the apartment before returning to the hallway.

"Everything okay?" the manager asked hopefully.

Camel told him everything wasn't okay, the apartment needed to be locked up again and the police needed to be called.

"Is Mr. Norton in there?"

Yeah in two pieces. "Call nine-one-one and report a homicide."

"Oh my."

"Don't let anyone in this apartment until the police arrive."

"No I won't. Where are you going . . . I mean in case the other officers ask."

"I'm officially out of my jurisdiction here, I need authorization before I can start processing the crime scene."

The manager nodded his head so vigorously at this gibberish that the waves in his white hair shook . . . but did not dislodge. "What's your name again, I didn't quite catch it on your badge."

"Parker Gray . . . state police."

"Oh yeah I remember now."

35

HALFWAY OUT THE LANE ANNIE JAMMED BOTH FEET ON THE BRAKE PEDAL slamming the truck into a gravelly skid that succeeded only in throwing Growler farther into the truck bed . . . and there he held on one-handed to a side rail, crouching like an evil troll naked and wild-eyed and bloody-footed.

When he started crabbing forward, Annie locked her door and hit the accelerator again, knocking Growler off his good foot and onto his bare ass. She weaved violently side to side, rolling him around back there, smearing blood, the determined bastard managing to get up and crawl forward until he was at the cab's back window, pounding on it with the butt of his palm.

Annie sped out of the lane hitting one of the brick pillars a glancing blow as she made a screeching right turn that again rolled Growler but failed to eject him from the truck.

She was on a county road, no traffic, when she checked the rearview mirror again and didn't see him . . . then, *Christ,* there he was right at the driver's window, standing one-footed on the running board, holding one-handed to the side mirror, demented face pressing against the glass, black hair blowing in the airstream. Annie had neglected to lock the triangular vent window, Growler pushed it open and reached in with his left arm.

He was trying to grab her, she screamed and slapped at his hand, he went for the steering wheel . . . and that's when Annie once again used both feet to lock the brakes.

Growler flew forward, his arm catching in the vent window. Annie heard the bone break like cracking a green stick wrapped in a blanket and she saw the unnatural way that arm bent when it was pulled from the vent window by Growler's forward momentum . . . as if the arm had two elbows, one bending toward his body, one bending away.

He lay on the road, he could've been dead was how quietly he lay on the road. Annie drove away checking repeatedly to make sure that Growler was still back there in the road, then she picked up speed and headed for civilization. She was shaking from adrenaline and relief and the cold, Annie's hand so trembly she could barely work the truck's heater controls . . . the day that had once been filled with so much sun and sky was cloudy now and cold.

When she began encountering traffic Annie didn't know exactly what to do, should she just stop and flag someone down or wait until she sees a police car? In a crazy way she almost wished Growler was still back there in the truck bed because then she wouldn't have to explain why she didn't have a blouse on, what she was running from . . . Growler would be all the explanation she needed, no one would doubt he'd been trying to kill her. But now, without Growler, she'd have to tell the whole complicated story.

Because the truck's cab rode high, people in cars couldn't see the extent of Annie's predicament, but when two young men in another pickup started to pass, the passenger did a double take and their truck slowed to keep pace with hers.

Annie rolled down her window, the passenger in the other truck did the same. He was grinning, twenty years old . . . blond hair and a sunburnt face.

"I need help!" Annie shouted. "I need to get to the police!"

"Nice tits!" he shouted back.

Furious, Annie accelerated and lost the other truck in traffic. She kept searching for a patrol car, didn't know where the nearest police station was, didn't want to get out of the truck to make a phone call. She considered alternatives, a church, a fire station, a hospital, but didn't see any of those and continued driving aimlessly, numbed by what she'd been through, until she began recognizing certain landmarks and realized she was only a few miles from the shopping center where Teddy had his office . . . that's where she'd go. Teddy might still be in jail but Eddie Neffering would be at his bar, The Ground Floor . . . Eddie would help her.

Annie turned into the shopping center's vast parking lot, while she was looking up trying to remember which high-rise was Teddy's her pickup broadsided a late model Lincoln.

She hadn't been traveling more than five or six miles an hour but the collision threw her forward, bumping her head on the windshield which didn't break. She sat there trembling.

The driver of the Lincoln emerged, reached back into the car to help his wife out, then slammed the door with both hands. The couple were in their late fifties, well-to-do.

He came over to Annie's truck, the man holding his peace only to make sure she wasn't injured then he intended to release a tirade, irresponsibility would be its theme . . . but when he saw she was naked from the waist up he forgot everything he was going to say.

Annie leaned back in the seat and touched her forehead. Her fingers came away sooty but no blood on them. She looked curiously at the man's very white face.

His wife came hurrying up to the truck just as the man was opening Annie's door. "Good God," the woman said. "What's going on here!"

The husband stammered as if he and Annie had been caught in a compromising position.

"I've been . . ." Annie started to say. But she decided not to launch any explanations, she simply told the astonished couple, "I need help, get the police."

They continued standing at the open door, other drivers were getting out of their cars and coming over for a look.

Aware of an audience the woman suddenly demanded of Annie, "What are you, some kind of . . . *freak?*"

This moved her husband toward sympathy. "Are you hurt?" he asked, reaching out to Annie.

"Phillip!"

He withdrew his hand.

The growing crowd pushed in closer as word spread about a topless woman in a pickup truck, the front ranks exchanging angry looks with those who were pressing them from the back, those who hadn't had a peek yet.

Annie felt powerless to do anything except sit with her hands over her breasts and wait for deliverance . . . when it finally came in form of a large black man wearing the uniform of a private security firm she could've wept with relief.

He had no trouble pushing his way through the crowd and when he saw Annie he asked an old question, "What's going on here?"

First to speak were the Republicans from the Lincoln, they'd held tenaciously to their front-rank positions repeatedly telling others in the crowd, "It was *our* car she hit."

Which is exactly what they told the shopping mall's security guard.

"She was driving around *topless,*" the wife said, then added extravagantly, "Look at her filthy face, I think she's on drugs."

The guard stood in the truck's open doorway, his bulk effectively blocking the view, sorely disappointing those in the crowd who had just worked their way to the front and now felt cheated out of seeing a *topless* woman.

"Ma'am, are you hurt?"

Annie searched his broad round face for sympathy. "I was attacked by a man, I just got away from him."

"Near here?" The guard looked around as if the assailant might still be in the crowd.

"No, I drove here because I didn't know where else to go, I

couldn't find a police car, a friend of mine works in one of these office buildings."

The guard removed a radio from his belt. "We'll get you fixed up in just a minute."

"Thank you."

Not until the arrival of four more security guards were the gawkers dispersed. The big black man had returned to his car for a jacket, which he put around Annie's shoulders. Closing the large jacket over her bare breasts, she looked at the ID plate on his shirt and said, "Thank you Mr. Kempis."

"Not a problem ma'am. What's your name?"

"Annie Milton."

"And who were you coming here to see?"

"Teddy Camel. Actually his friend Eddie Neffering who owns a bar in one of these office buildings." When she saw Kempis's troubled expression Annie asked, "Do you know them?"

"I don't . . . hold on a minute, will you?" He stepped away from the truck and was on his radio a long time, coming back to Annie and telling her, "Maybe you should come wait in my car."

She followed him to the private patrol car and asked if she should get in the backseat or front. He said it was up to her and Annie got in front.

Kempis drove to a far corner of the lot where no other cars were parked, Annie becoming suspicious and then telling herself don't be silly. "Will the ambulance be able to find us over here?"

"How bad are you hurt?"

"I guess I don't need to go to the hospital, mainly I want a long hot shower, get some clothes on, find out if Growler is—"

"Who?"

"The man who attacked me. I injured his foot, I think I broke his arm too."

"Sounds like he got the worst of it, tangling with you."

"I would've killed him if I could."

"And who is this guy Growler?"

Annie didn't know where to begin that long story, she was huddling in Kempis's big blue jacket, shivering as if the cold originated from inside her. "Do you think we could have some heat."

"Sure." He started the car, turned on the heater. "What's he look like, this Growler?"

"He didn't have any clothes on, his right foot is bleeding, his left arm is broken, he's got a tattoo of the devil on his belly and down to his groin."

Kempis laughed a little, said something about how the man shouldn't be hard to find. "And what's Teddy Camel got to do with all this?"

"You *do* know him?"

Kempis looked embarrassed. "Teddy's been getting a lot of attention lately . . . there was a man killed in his office yesterday."

Annie's turn to be embarrassed. She decided not to mention that the man who shot himself in Teddy's office was her husband.

Kempis fielded a few radio calls but other than that they sat there in silence. Annie looked at her dirty palms, the first two fingers and thumb of her left hand were red and swollen from where she'd hit them with the hammer while punching out those rivets. In her mind Annie replayed what she'd done to Growler, it seemed impossible now that she'd driven a nail through his foot but she did . . . and was proud of it too. She turned to Kempis. "Are we waiting for an ambulance or what?"

He replied without looking at her. "I thought the state police should be involved, I called them."

"I wish you'd told me that, I could've given them directions to where I left Growler. I don't even know if he's still alive, he's the one who needs an ambulance, Jesus I should've . . . can you send someone out there now, I don't want to be responsible for that man dying."

"I thought you said you would've killed him if—"

"Yes . . . but the idea that he's lying on the road—"

"The state police will handle it."

"Yes but—"

"Here he is now."

Annie looked up to see an unmarked patrol car pulling in next to where they were parked. The man who got out was wearing a suit, not a uniform.

"That's Parker Gray," Kempis said. "He's associate superintendent—"

"I know who he is."

36

WHEN CAMEL REACHED THE SHOPPING MALL HE HAD TO SLOW DOWN AND weave traffic, there'd been a fender-bender in the parking lot. He could see one of the damaged vehicles, an old pickup, but didn't connect it to Annie who, Camel assumed, was with the Nefferings. He drove on, worried about putting a scratch on this Fairlane, Eddie would never forgive him . . . Camel maneuvering more carefully than ever into the parking garage, on up to level 4. He walked the ramp down. Cautious about the weenie wagger, women in groups of three and four gave Camel the eye. He recognized them from the building but didn't know any of the women to speak to, to reassure them he wasn't the pervert. Hell of a place to call home he thought as he entered The Ground Floor. He wished he didn't live in an office building, he wished he owned a house. If wishes were dishes . . . Camel walking to the bar and asking for Eddie.

"He's still gone," the young bartender told him . . . the kid had blond hair over a sweetly vacuous face, he looked almost exactly like Troy Donahue but wouldn't have a clue who that was.

Camel asked for the phone, called the Nefferings' number, got the answering machine again. "Eddie leave a message for me?"

The bartender said no. "He got a call from Mary this morning, went home, haven't heard from him since."

"How'd he get home, I got his car."

"Don't know . . . a cab?"

Camel thought Eddie can't be happy about paying for a cab that far. He told the kid he was going to drive out to Eddie's house. "If we miss each other and he shows up here you explain that's where I've gone."

The bartender promised he would.

Camel decided he'd go up to his office suite first, shower and change clothes . . . see how the state police detectives left the place. Riding the elevator thirteen floors to 14 he was reminded once again—he thought about this nearly every trip he made—how the modern world can still find room for superstition. He walked to his office door, unlocked and opened it, turned on the lights . . . the place had been tossed. What the hell were the detectives looking for: furniture upside down, cabinets emptied of their drawers, files scattered out on the floor . . . Camel couldn't figure what this kind of all-out search had to do with the charges against him.

He opened the adjoining door to his living quarters, that room had been tossed too. When he stepped through the doorway two things happened . . . Camel smelled cigar smoke and he got hit hard enough in the stomach that he dropped to both knees and one hand, the other hand holding where he'd been hit as his lungs worked on getting in some air.

His position on the floor allowed Camel to see from the knees down the guy who'd just hit him: lime green slacks and white shoes. When one of those white shoes came up and kicked Camel's shoulder he obligingly rolled over onto his side and kept balled up as protection against being kicked again.

The guy who leaned down to search him clearly knew what he was doing . . . Camel figured a cop.

"Houdini," Camel said.

"What?"

He managed to come over into a sitting position but still had a tough time breathing. "That's what killed Houdini."

"The sam hill you talking about?"

"Getting hit in the stomach when he wasn't ready for it."

"Oh yeah I heard that, some bar wasn't it?" The guy took the cigar from his mouth and tossed it over into the sink.

Camel waited for his breathing to regulate before continuing. "Houdini had such control over his muscles he'd let guys take a free shot hitting him in the stomach—"

"Except this one guy hit him before Houdini had a chance to tighten up and it busted his guts, killed him . . . that the story you mean?"

Camel said yeah that was the story.

The guy was about sixty, wearing a pink short-sleeved shirt and a white golfer's cap, his face was wide and flat and florid, he had little blue eyes and a big potato nose . . . Annie had said a guy like this, a golfer, was snooping around the office.

"I hit pretty good for a man of my age don't I?"

Camel agreed he did.

"You know, I'm sort of like that guy who did Houdini, I can kill someone with one punch too."

Camel wondered if he should get to his feet or stay down here on the floor.

"You got 'em?" the guy asked.

Here's the tricky part, Camel thought . . . if I say I don't have a clue what you're talking about then he's going to start kicking me but if I pretend to know what the deal is and we skip the third degree to go right into negotiations, then how long will it be before he catches on I'm clueless?

"If they're in either of these two rooms I sure as hell can't find them," he said before kicking Camel in the side.

Damn that one hurt too . . . then it came to Camel. "Gerald Mc-Cleany."

"Too clever for your own good that's what you are."

"Yeah well . . ."

"Everything coming together in a neat little package except for you snooping around, what's your angle anyway?"

"How about if I stand up?"

From a pocket McCleany drew his stainless steel, snubnose .38, then said, "Okay by me."

Camel stood but not straight.

"I guess Milton didn't like what he saw when he caught you here with his wife," McCleany said.

"You responsible for setting that up?"

The golfer grinned.

Camel asked him, "How did Paul Milton get involved in all of this?"

"You're the detective."

"That's the part I haven't figured out," Camel admitted.

"Milton belonged to a religious group, worked getting guys paroled from prison, helping rehabilitate them."

"I guess it didn't take in Growler's case."

McCleany laughed then wiped at his face. "You indicated to Parker Gray you had certain knowledge about certain photographs so I got two questions for you, where's the little lady and where's the dirty pictures?"

"Why are you and Gray so interested in those pictures, who you trying to protect?"

McCleany laughed again. "Jesus you want me to write out a confession or what?"

"You could just tell me, you don't have to actually write it out."

"I'm going to shoot you is what I'm going to do, then cut your head off so it looks like Growler did it . . . or as an alternative to that you can tell me where the pictures are, assuming you have them or know where they are—do you?"

"If I tell you you'll shoot me and cut my head off anyway, what's the percentage in that?"

"Maybe I won't. Figure it this way, you're a smart guy. If I got the pictures then why would I have to kill you, it's just your word against mine I was ever even here . . . and you're about to become a felon for shooting Milton in the mouth, me I'm a respected retired law enforcement officer, who do you think's going to be believed?"

"So I give you the pictures and you drop out of my life, don't bother Annie again, that the deal?"

"Sure."

Lying. Of course he was lying. "I don't know where the photographs are."

McCleany's shoulders sagged to show how disappointed he was in Camel. "Stand up there against the wall."

Camel wasn't sure if he should . . . until McCleany pointed the snubnose at his face. As Camel put his back against the wall he said, "I got something else I can deal you for."

"Just stand there and shut up." McCleany walked backward to Camel's overturned bed, grabbed a golf club he'd left on the floor, produced a rubber tee and golf ball, teed the ball, addressed it, gauged Camel's position and distance, put the .38 revolver back in his pocket . . . and hit that ball so hard it went right through the drywall just a few feet to the right of Camel's head.

"Jesus."

McCleany got another ball from his pocket, teed it up. "You seen them yourself, the pictures?"

"No—"

He addressed the ball, getting ready to swing.

"Are you trying to hit me," Camel asked, "or you just aiming close enough to scare me?"

McCleany chuckled like he thought that was a pretty funny question . . . and this time when he hit the ball it smacked Camel on the right bicep, stung like a turbo-powered bumblebee.

"I guess I'm aiming to hit you," McCleany said proudly, producing another ball and teeing it.

"One of those hits me in the head, it could kill me."

"Yeah, kind of a dumb way to die too." He looked up from the ball and eyed Camel. "You thinking about rushing me, seeing if you can get here before I can draw the thirty-eight and shoot you?"

"I was considering it."

McCleany nodded as if this was a reasonable option for Camel to be considering. "It'd be close."

"What exactly is the point you're trying to make?" Camel asked.

He stepped back from the ball. "You know, I heard about you when you worked homicide, heard you were a real firestorm . . . I guess the fire went out huh?"

Camel didn't say anything.

"Used to be called the Human Lie Detector isn't that right?"

Camel didn't confirm or deny it.

"Well look me in the eye and see if I'm telling the truth . . . I will kill you to get those pictures."

He wasn't lying.

McCleany went back to addressing the ball.

Camel said, "You don't know about the elephant do you?"

Another shoulder sag. "The what?"

"The whole reason Growler came back to Cul-De-Sac, so he could get a solid-gold elephant he hid before his cousin was killed, before he went to prison."

"What is this bullshit—"

"You investigated Hope Penner's murder, you never saw her uncle's collection of chess sets?"

"Yeah, J.L. had a fortune in . . ." McCleany clicked. "Yeah I remember him talking about a chess piece, an elephant, he said it was worth more than anything else he owned." And that idiot Paul Milton had babbled something about an elephant too. While McCleany was recalling this, Camel reached next to the door frame and pulled down on the fire alarm, setting off a loud clanging out in the hallway.

McCleany wearily put the club head on the floor, spread his feet and rested both hands on the butt of the grip like he was posing as a dandy, like he should be wearing a top hat. "Well that was a Mickey Mouse thing to do."

"I can't hear you," Camel said. "The alarm's ringing."

McCleany came Camel's way, holding the club in his left hand, with his right he was bringing out the stainless steel revolver.

"Security will be here in less than two minutes," Camel said, checking his watch. "Elevators are turned off automatically, you'll run into security on your way down the steps. Even if they don't stop you they'll have your description . . . which might come in handy when the investigation starts, who shot me."

McCleany stopped. "Got it all figured out."

"Wasn't that tough."

McCleany was shaking his head to indicate his continued disappointment in Camel. "You know that *really* was a chickenshit thing to do," he said. "I mean, it's the kind of stunt a high school sissy pulls when the bullies are roughing him up in the hallway, he goes for the fire alarm."

"Yeah well . . ."

The golfer came within a club's length of Camel who pointedly checked his watch again.

"I ain't done with you or your girlfriend," McCleany promised, holding the club head right in Camel's face.

Since Camel had moved slowly and painfully ever since being punched in the stomach McCleany was caught off guard when Camel's hand snaked out so quickly, grabbing the club, yanking it away, turning it around to hold the club as you would a baseball bat, swinging for the golfer's head.

McCleany ducked. "Grip's all wrong," he told Camel as he raised the revolver . . . Camel swinging a second time, striking a forearm and knocking the .38 loose.

"Never took a lesson in my life," Camel said quietly. McCleany started to say something smart too but decided to leave without further comment when Camel picked up the .38.

Camel didn't follow. The security guards would be here soon, maybe not within two minutes, a time Camel had picked out of the air, but soon enough, and he didn't want to be caught holding a revolver . . . he had enough to explain setting off a fire alarm in the office where a man had killed himself just last night.

Something else he had to deal with too, the three bodies he found today and whatever loose ends went with them . . . a neighbor might've spotted him at the Raineys' house, the manager of Norton's apartment building can describe him, and Camel is going to look suspiciously like an accessory unless he can explain what he was doing at the crime scenes, tell someone in authority how he came to find those bodies. He knew a judge he could trust and decided that would be his next order of business . . . calling the judge.

When Camel heard security coming he stashed the .38 and went out into the hall to meet them . . . three guys running, Jake Kempis in the lead.

37

"YOU LIED TO ME," SHE TOLD JAKE KEMPIS.

"Mrs. Milton the state police have jurisdiction—"

"No, I thought you were a nice man," Annie said, starting to remove Kempis's jacket, "but you're not . . . you lied to me."

He said for Annie to go ahead and keep the jacket and she did but only because she had no alternative. Annie didn't thank him.

Parker Gray looked shattered when he opened the door to Kempis's car. "Mrs. Milton I wonder if you could come with me please."

He'd been horrible to her during the questioning about Paul's death and Annie didn't want to go anywhere with him. "I was attacked," she said without looking at Parker's face.

"Yes I know." He extended a hand but Annie stepped from the car without his help. Gray leaned down and said, "Thanks Jake."

Annie leaned down too. "Yeah, thanks Jake."

"I'm sorry ma'am."

Parker Gray took her to his car. When she was seated in the front passenger side she asked if all this was still connected to Paul's death.

"All of what?"

"Am I under arrest?"

"No, nothing like that." He rubbed his face with both hands. "I got a little of the story from Kempis, I need to hear it from you huh?"

"I want to be taken to the Nefferings' house, that's where I was staying."

"You give me directions, I'll drive you there." But he made no move to start the car.

"Let's go then."

"Were you raped?"

"No but—"

"I could still take you to the hospital if you want."

"I've told you what I want, I want to go to the Nefferings' house, I want a hot shower . . . is Teddy still in jail?"

Gray started the engine and turned on the headlights but didn't move the car. During the interrogation following Paul's suicide, Gray offered lurid theories about Annie and Teddy, making Annie feel guiltier than she already did. He speculated that Teddy killed Paul, that Annie engineered the whole scenario to get rid of a husband and regain an old lover . . . Annie had been physically afraid of him as if any moment he might start slapping her around.

But now he spoke to her in a soft voice. "What happened to you this afternoon Mrs. Milton?"

Annie told him about going to Cul-De-Sac, finding the chest, finding papers about the organization Paul belonged to, Our Brothers' Keepers, the group that apparently helped get Growler out of prison, finding pornographic photographs in the chest—

Gray swung around so quickly that she flinched back against the door. "Where are those photographs right now?" he demanded.

"Still in Paul's workshop as far as I know." She told Gray about Growler threatening her, his horrible tattoo, how she nailed his foot to the floor and even then barely escaped when he jumped into the back of her truck. "I don't know if he's dead or what, when I left he was lying in the road. Have you sent someone out to check on him?"

Gray replied with a question of his own. "You've told me everything huh?"

"Yes." Everything except finding the elephant, which Annie

wanted for herself because Paul had died to get it for her and in her mind that elephant had become Paul's memorial . . . and also because it was worth three million dollars.

Gray asked her again to tell him everything that had happened between her and Growler, what she found in that chest, everything . . . and Annie did, everything except the elephant. Gray listened without comment, seemingly distracted and saddened by something other than what Annie was saying. His dark suit was rumpled, a red tie loose at the neck, he needed a shave and a shower and sleep . . . he looked haggard in a soul-troubled way that reminded Annie of her mother in those days following the funeral of Annie's father.

Gray moved the shift lever to Drive but held his foot on the brake, reluctant to leave. "You sure you don't want to be seen by a doctor huh?" he said after a long wait.

"Except for this bump on my forehead I'm fine."

Another pause before he spoke. "I'll drive you wherever you want to go."

Annie thanked him.

Gray took his foot off the brake pedal allowing the car to ease forward. Out on the road he continued at such a slow pace that drivers who managed to pass him did so with glares on their faces while the ones forced to pile up behind used their horns, their brights. Gray didn't notice, his mind elsewhere . . . it was like he'd forgotten Annie was in the car.

When he finally spoke he acted as if someone was forcing him to ask the question. "Those photographs, that young woman having sex with different men you said . . . you recognize any of the men?"

"No."

"That was a quick answer."

"Well I didn't—"

"You take a good long look at each picture huh?"

"Not really."

He pulled off to the side of the road without using a turn signal, a maneuver that earned him a horn and a finger from the driver behind. Leaving the car running and in gear, he turned to Annie. "How many pictures did you find?" Still trying to be careful with her, Gray held his face in what passed for a kindly expression . . . but Annie could tell it was becoming increasingly difficult for him to stay calm.

"I told you, there were eleven snapshots."

"Eleven different men with Hope."

"Hope? She was the girl who was killed—"

"And you looked at each of those eleven different men, could you see their faces really well?"

"To tell you the truth I was mainly trying to determine if Paul was—"

"What the fuck your husband got to do with this huh?"

"I don't know, I don't know why he had those pictures—"

"Was Growler in any of the photographs?"

"I don't think so."

"You don't *think* so?"

"I was looking to see if Paul—"

"You didn't recognize anyone huh?"

"Why do you keep asking me that, I told you—"

"Don't bullshit me on this."

"I thought one of the men was vaguely familiar but I couldn't place him."

Gray grabbed the steering wheel and hit the accelerator, pulling a U-turn and traveling now above the speed limit back in the opposite direction.

She asked where they were going.

He didn't answer.

She told him she changed her mind, she wanted to see a doctor after all.

No reaction from Gray.

"You offered to take me to a hospital, that's where I want to go."

Nothing.

"Please, you said you'd take me to a hospital or wherever I wanted to go . . . take me to the Nefferings' house."

Gray didn't answer, he was concentrating on driving and on

something else, whatever was troubling him, whatever decision he was trying to make.

After a few more miles Annie recognized the route they were taking. "No, I don't want to go there."

"I'll just pick up those pictures, then take you—"

"No, this isn't right! That man, Growler—"

"He won't hurt you."

"Don't take me back there, *please.*"

But Gray obviously wasn't going to change his mind and Annie had to settle for curling up in the seat, feeling small and vulnerable in Kempis's oversized jacket.

■　　■　　■

SHE MADE GRAY stop the car before turning into Cul-De-Sac's lane, Annie wanted to show him the exact spot where Growler had been thrown from the truck. He wasn't there . . . no body, no blood.

"I bet he walked back to Cul-De-Sac," Annie said, her voice rising. "He was naked, he was hurt bad . . . he *had* to go back to Cul-De-Sac, he's there right now, he's—"

"He won't hurt you as long as I'm around."

"You don't understand, I don't even want to *see* him."

"Mrs. Milton, those photographs are critical to an investigation—"

"*What* investigation, you won't tell me anything! Is Teddy still in jail? Why did Paul have those photographs?"

"The charges against Camel are being dropped."

"Why did you keep insisting he killed Paul?"

"I was obligated to explore that possibility."

"Obligated to charge him with murder?"

"It wasn't a homicide charge and I told you huh . . . all charges are being dropped. The photographs are important for another reason, unrelated case."

"Unrelated case? Then what in hell am I doing here?"

He told her to get back in the car. Gray drove to the side of Cul-De-Sac where he stopped and killed the engine, turned off the headlights. "Get out."

Annie told him she intended to file a complaint. "You're putting me in danger bringing me here, this isn't right."

"Do you know what vehicle Growler is driving?"

She didn't answer.

He reached over and grabbed her by the hair. "What's he driving huh?"

Annie was almost as frightened of Gray as she had been of Growler . . . why was this happening to her?

"Mrs. Milton." He shook her by the hair. "His car huh?"

"I didn't see what he was driving."

"How's he get around, there's no vehicle here now."

"I don't know."

Gray released her. "I thought you said he was crippled, how'd he make it back here from the county road?"

"I don't know." Annie was confused and weary . . . she just wanted this all to be over with.

"Get out of the car."

"Please don't make me go back in that building."

"You're safer in there with me than out here by yourself."

He was right. They left the car and walked to the side door Growler had left open, Gray went in first . . . he'd taken out a semi-automatic pistol. Annie held onto the back of his suit jacket and stayed close, that's how they walked through Cul-De-Sac, up the stairway, to the workshop on the second floor.

The nail Annie had hammered through Growler's foot still stuck up from the floor, the chest was still there, papers and spike nails still scattered around it, and when Gray wasn't looking Annie glanced at the shelf and saw that the elephant was still where Growler had placed it, between a circular saw and an electric sander . . . but the photographs were gone.

"Goddamn you lady, you have no idea—"

"Growler must've taken them."

After putting the pistol away, Gray grabbed Annie and shook her hard.

"Please . . . why are you doing this?" Why was everyone doing horrible things to her?

Gray let go. "You're telling the truth about what you did to his foot?"

"There's the nail, it's still in the floor!"

"And breaking his arm?"

"Yes it was definitely broken."

"So maybe he crippled his way back here from the county road but then couldn't get any farther, he's holed up somewhere in the building."

"Yes!" It seemed to be what Gray wanted to hear.

"That little bastard knew a million places to hide in this building."

"Yes he's hiding here, you should call in your troopers to search the place, every inch of it."

He looked at her and finally made up his mind about whatever had been troubling him. "Yeah, right . . . we'll go on that assumption huh . . . Growler hiding somewhere in Cul-De-Sac, got the pictures with him."

She agreed again, anything to get out of here.

"Tell you what, I'm going to lock you in this room—"

She couldn't believe it, Annie thought she must've misunderstood what he just said.

But Gray repeated that he intended to lock her in the room. "For your own safety, so Growler can't get to you . . . I'll take a look around—"

"No! You call for reinforcements or do whatever you have to do but I want to be taken away from here before—"

Gray was already moving toward the door, Annie tried to beat him out of the room but he grabbed the back of the jacket. "I'm sorry," he said, pushing her away and then slamming the door with Annie inside. She heard the padlock close.

Using both hands Annie beat on the inside of the door and kicked it, threatening Gray and then begging him not to leave her here.

"I'm sorry huh?" he said through the door.

She cursed him.

"You'll be safe in there." Leaving the key in the lock, Gray walked away.

Annie kept hollering for him, refusing to believe he'd really left her here. She turned around, the windowless room putting her at a loss what to do. Turning to the door and pounding on it again she called for Gray and waited and called for him again . . . nothing. Annie went to the shelf and held the elephant in her hands for a few seconds before hiding it behind the circular saw, probably a futile gesture because what good would a gold-and-jeweled elephant do her if Growler got back in this room . . . after what she'd done to him he'd kill her for sure. Annie remembered his voice when he promised to cripple her. *What if he's here in this room . . . hiding?*

She looked around, really only one place to hide . . . a big walk-in closet to the right of the fireplace. Annie went over there and gingerly opened the door, the closet full of old furniture and moldy bedding . . . unlikely anyone could hide in there but just to be sure she clicked the lock and shut the closet's door.

She still didn't feel safe, nothing and no one in the world not even Teddy Camel could make her feel safe here in Cul-De-Sac.

38

JAKE KEMPIS TURNED OFF THE FIRE ALARM AND SENT THE OTHER TWO SE-
curity guards away before asking Camel what'd happened.

"I came in and the guy who tossed the office was still here. I
pulled the alarm to get rid of him."

"Who was it, what was he looking for?"

Camel didn't reply. His stomach was tender from being
punched by McCleany, whenever he moved his right arm the
bicep hurt from where the golf ball had struck him, he was tired,
he wanted to see Annie . . . Camel didn't think he owed Kempis an
explanation. "Listen Jake if you got to write a report or whatever
about the alarm, go ahead and do it but I have to meet some people so I'm leaving."

"You're not going to brush me off like that. Sit down, I have to
make a call."

"Yeah you make your call, meanwhile I'm—"

Kempis took out a canister of pepper spray. "Sit down Teddy,
I'm calling the state police, where's your phone?"

"What is this shit?" Camel asked coldly.

"Come on, you should've known better than to come here after
escaping jail, now where's the—"

"Escaping? Jake, use your head . . . I'm out on bail."

"No, Parker Gray said—"

"You know anyone else at the state police beside Gray?"

"Yeah, couple guys I been working with on that appointment."

"Gray's not going to get you any appointments, he's going to get your ass in trouble is what he's going to get you. Give those other guys you know a call, ask 'em to check if I'm not out on bail."

Kempis wasn't sure about it but followed Camel into the other office, to where the phone had been knocked on the floor. "Go on," Camel told him, "do yourself a favor, make the call."

Kempis did, was put on hold, got through, talked to someone for less than a minute . . . then told Camel, "Gray's been suspended."

"Bingo."

"Okay I'll ask you straight out, what's this all about?"

"I still don't know all the details except I know Parker Gray and his former partner Gerald McCleany screwed up a homicide investigation seven years ago."

"Screwed up as in . . . ?"

"As in framing a man for the murder, protecting the real killer, I don't know . . . but it's all coming down on their heads now and they're both scrambling to keep out from under it."

"I don't understand—"

"Jake I don't either, I'm still trying to put the pieces together. Gray lied to you about me escaping, his partner McCleany is the one who tossed this place . . . you don't want to be involved with them believe me."

Kempis put the pepper spray back on his utility belt.

"You want to hear how you can get that appointment to the academy all on your own?" Camel asked.

"I'm listening."

"Three bodies have been found today, murder victims, decapitations—"

"Who? Where?"

"You said you were listening."

Kempis nodded.

"I'm going to tell you who killed those people. You take this information to the jurisdictions handling the investigations, be a hero."

"And your angle?"

"I want you to give me a couple hours, an hour . . . I have to get to a judge and explain how I happened to find the bodies. I already got that manslaughter charge against me and I can't afford—"

"That charge has been dropped."

Camel was surprised to hear it.

"The guy I just talked to, who told me Gray was suspended? When I asked if you were really out on bail he said you didn't need bail 'cause the charges against you were dropped."

"Okay, good, now let me tell you what I know about these killings—"

"Oh shit."

He waited to hear whatever bad news Kempis had just remembered.

"Friend of yours, Annie Milton?"

Camel went cold in the belly.

"She was assaulted this afternoon and came here trying to—"

He pointed a finger at Kempis's face so he would concentrate on the two questions Camel wanted answered before anything else was said, "Where is she now, what's her condition?"

"She's okay, I turned her over to Parker Gray." Kempis watched Camel's face for a reaction.

"Come on, talk to me Jake."

"Parker and McCleany came to see me, said they could grease me an appointment to the academy if I did a little work for them . . . keep an eye on you, report whatever happens around here involving you, so when Mrs. Milton got in that wreck I called Gray and he came and got her."

"Where'd he take her, he wouldn't use a state police facility if he's been suspended."

"Teddy I didn't know he'd been—"

Camel had already turned away from Kempis to search through the debris around his desk until he found the sheet of paper on which Annie had written the phone number at Cul-De-Sac, directions how to get there . . . these were for Camel when he was still planning to go get Annie's husband and bring him back here to thrash out the truth.

Kempis came over. "I assumed Gray was taking her to a substation for—"

"No he took her back to Cul-De-Sac, some property Annie owns."

"How do you know?"

"I know." Camel grabbed the phone and punched in the number . . . busy. He tried it again, still busy, then got an operator and told her it was a police emergency she'd have to break in on the call. The operator referred the request to a supervisor who told Camel there was no call to break in on, the busy signal was a result of a malfunction on the line.

Phone ripped out. Camel went to where he'd stashed Mc-Cleany's .38, Kempis trailing him and saying, "I'm coming with you Teddy."

"Jake this isn't your—"

"I gave them the key to your office."

Camel looked at him. "That's how McCleany got in to toss the place . . . McCleany also gave a copy of the key to Annie's husband."

"I fucked up."

"Yeah you did."

"So give me a chance to square it."

"All right," Camel said, moving to the door.

"You want to hear what Mrs. Milton told me about who assaulted her?"

Camel was already in the hallway. "Tell me walking."

■   ■   ■

ON THE WAY to Cul-De-Sac, following Annie's directions which Jake Kempis read for him, Camel drove the '65 Fairlane faster than he should have . . . thunder road. They got lost, had to retrace the route, it was dead dark before they found the turnoff to

Cul-De-Sac's lane marked as Annie had indicated with two brick pillars, one of them looked like it'd been sideswiped. The graveled lane ran straight for half a mile into a little bowl of a valley, no other houses in sight. From over the treed hills walling this valley shined a dull glow of commerce that reflected onto the underside of the night sky, ruining all hope of ever seeing Orion.

Although once centerpiece of a 220-acre estate Cul-De-Sac now sat on only an acre's land to call its own, the surrounding valley and hillsides remained unbuilt-upon because they were deeded to people rich enough to employ land as a buffer, keeping shopping centers and suburban sprawls (all that light from over the hills) away from their horse farms and fox hunts.

Camel doused his headlights and drove around to the side of the building, parking behind a car with its trunk open.

"That's Gray's," Kempis said. "The one he took Mrs. Milton off in."

Camel walked over and looked in the truck which was empty but smelled heavily of gasoline.

Kempis smelled it too. "He got a leak in his tank?"

Pointing to two round indentions in the trunk's mat, Camel said, "Hauling cans of gas."

"What're we going to do, call the sheriff's department?"

"I don't know who else is in on this with Gray and McCleany, first thing we're going to do is find Annie . . . then we'll worry about who to notify."

Camel and Kempis went to the side of Cul-De-Sac and tried two doors, both locked.

"What do you think?" Kempis asked.

"Find a way in."

"I wish I had more than a can of pepper spray."

"Listen Jake you walk around the building that way, don't use a flashlight, check for any door that might be unlocked but don't open it, don't go in. We'll meet around back. You okay?"

Kempis said he was.

"All right, see you around back."

Camel pulled McCleany's little stainless steel revolver from his pocket, he had already familiarized himself with it . . . a Smith & Wesson Model 640, .38 Special, loaded with five hollow points. Walking around the back of the building, stopping frequently to listen, looking for signs of occupation, Camel spotted a window that was open.

Not waiting for Kempis he climbed in and threaded his way carefully through a storage room full of boxes and filing cabinets and broken chairs, Camel finally stepping out into a hallway lit by bulbs burning dimly like they weren't getting enough juice, the smell of gasoline a lot stronger here in the corridor where a man with his back to Camel was holding a five-gallon container, pouring gas out on the floor.

"Parker," Camel said quietly.

He stopped pouring and straightened up, the gas container still in his hand.

"Put the can down, turn around, keep your hands where I can see them . . . you know the drill."

Gray did as he was told except on one crucial point . . . after placing the gas can on the floor he managed to sneak a hand inside his suit coat and, when he turned to face Camel, Gray was holding a 9mm semiautomatic.

39

"MURRAY DEAR WHAT *ARE* YOU DOING?"

Elizabeth Rockwell was just coming out of the bathroom when she heard a booming floor-thump in the back bedroom . . . she'd warned Murray repeatedly about his weights, they belonged in the garage not the house.

"Murray?"

The door to the bedroom was closed, Murray wasn't answering her . . . until he made a strange sound, like a pig grunting. That was a new one even for Murray.

Walking toward the bedroom Elizabeth wasn't pleased to hear another crashing thump, another pig grunt. "Murray darling Mommy's had a bad day, she has a splitting headache and isn't in the mood for silly buggers."

Just then the bedroom door opened, presenting Elizabeth with the second most extraordinary sight she'd ever seen in her life . . . the most extraordinary being when she walked into Donald Growler's room seven years ago and found Hope's head on a shelf.

He stood there half naked, wearing black trousers but no shirt and no shoes. Strips of white cloth torn perhaps from a sheet and soaked through with blood wrapped Growler's left foot. He held his left arm crooked and close to his body like a broken wing that was swollen in one specific spot as if the forearm were a snake that had swallowed a softball . . . the swollen area horribly discolored. Growler's hair was wild, in his right hand he held a machete that Elizabeth recognized . . . Murray had seen it in a catalog and pestered her until she bought it for him, he said he could use it to "clear brush," though of course there was no brush around Elizabeth's house and Murray ended up keeping the machete in the garage where he would occasionally play with it, maybe pretending he was leading a safari and fighting off natives, you never knew what films played in Murray's mind. Blood was everywhere on Growler, it specked and splattered his torso . . . and that normally handsome face looked like half the sufferings of hell, his expression mixing pain and anger and betrayal with a kind of wild demonic joy.

The black trousers were loose and rode low on his hips and Elizabeth could see, just above the waistband, tattooed blue on Growler's lower belly, the eyes and horns of Satan . . . as if Satan were peeking out from Growler's pants, maybe to guide him what should be done next.

Her pistol was back in the kitchen drawer.

"Where's Murray?" she asked.

"I know who killed Hope," Growler said.

"Where's Murray?"

"You're going to make a phone call, arrange a meeting at Cul-De-Sac." Considering Growler's ruined condition he spoke with amazing clarity and calm . . . having within the last hour used his entire stash of cocaine, some externally on his spiked foot, the rest internally up his nostrils, an amount of powder that should've wired him like Broadway but in fact simply managed to counterbalance what he would have otherwise been suffering.

"Please tell me you haven't hurt Murray, he's just a boy."

"Murray's in on the bed," Growler said reassuringly. "Now let's make that call. Then we'll go to Cul-De-Sac and—"

"I want to talk to Murray."

"Need you to drive because the last cabbie I had really freaked out—"

"I want to talk to Murray first."

"Jesus." Growler turned to speak into the bedroom. "Murray, say something to Mommy."

40

IT WAS A VARIATION ON THE CLASSIC MEXICAN STANDOFF . . . CAMEL AND Gray each holding a side arm but neither man pointing his weapon at the other, their respective handguns kept down at their sides ready to be brought up and fired if it came to that.

"What're you doing here huh?" Gray asked with a sour expression, as if Camel owed him a lot of money from a long time ago.

"Where's Annie?"

"She's safe."

"Safe where?"

Parker Gray shook his head and worked his mouth like he was biting the insides of his cheek . . . Camel had seen men looking and acting the way Gray was now, men who were suspects in a felony crime and obviously worried about being charged but you could see their minds were still scrambling, they were still thinking I can beat this.

"Destroying evidence?" Camel asked, indicating the gas can at Parker's feet . . . another can, presumably full, at the end of the corridor.

"Doing what I should've done a long time ago . . . this place has been the ruin of me."

Camel remembered the phrase from an old song. " 'The House of the Rising Sun.' "

"What?"

"It's been the ruin of many a poor boy."

"What're you talking about huh?"

"Before your time I guess . . . where's Annie?"

"I told you she's safe."

"You stashed her someplace, then came here to burn down this building?"

Gray didn't answer.

"Hoping those pictures get destroyed in the process."

"All the trouble I got, you Sherlocking my ass on top of it. Why don't you just leave huh?"

"Tell me where Annie is and I will."

"I could arrest you right now for violating bail."

"Charges against me have been dropped, you're on suspension . . . your whole world caving in because of those photographs."

"Jesus you're asking for it," Gray warned, his right arm tensing as he weighed the chances of raising that 9mm and shooting Camel before Camel shot him.

"Seven years ago you were screwing that girl, Hope Penner, and you got caught on film, got blackmailed into covering up for whoever really killed her . . . or was it you Gray? Killed that little girl and then butchered her to make it look like Growler—"

"I didn't kill her!" Gray's arm tensed again then relaxed, he wasn't going to shoot Camel . . . or burn Cul-De-Sac either. His mind had stopped scrambling for a way out of this, there was no way out except dead. "She wasn't a little girl."

"Seventeen—"

"Seventeen going on forty."

Camel said nothing.

"I know what that sounds like, some asshole on a statutory. But the truth is I was twenty-nine years old and Hope was seventeen but she was twice my age in maturity. You want to hear how pathetic I was with that girl?"

"I want to know where Annie is, is what I want to know."

"Hope was beautiful . . . and smart and talented. She spoke three or four languages, a master at chess, played the piano, when she wanted to she could make you feel like you were the only man left alive on earth, like everything you said was wisdom and . . ." Gray's memories flew around in that dreamland for a few moments before falling onto a hard reality. "Of course I didn't know she was fucking everybody else along with me, didn't know she was taking pictures of it, didn't know that whole side of her. I'd seen Hope a little drunk on champagne and I thought that was the extent of her wildness, getting tipsy on champagne, I didn't know she was into blow, God knows what else. So here's how pathetic I was with her, Camel . . . I asked Hope to marry me. Said I'd divorce my wife, wait until custody arrangements were made with our kids, wait until Hope turned eighteen, then Hope and I could get married. You know what she says to me huh? She holds my head on her chest and says, 'You're so sweet.' There I was, been a trooper for almost six years, just made detective, married nine years, three children . . . and this seventeen-year-old *girl* was comforting me like I was the lovesick kid and she was the older woman. An older woman who . . . I don't know, who was charmed and a little amused that this puppy was proposing marriage to her."

"So she turned you down and you killed her."

"No . . . asshole. I loved her, I would've never—"

"Her uncle killed her and blackmailed you into—"

"You're not all that good as a detective are you huh?"

"McCleany."

"How many guesses you get?"

"You covered for your partner."

His shoulders slumped. "Biggest mistake of my life. Among the other ten million things I didn't know about Hope, she was fucking that fat slob McCleany too. *How could she?*" Gray's eyes were wet. "J. L. Penner hired us, McCleany and me, to do security work for him, not strictly kosher but Penner paid well, liked having cops around, on his payroll, that's how McCleany and I got to know Hope. We were here at Cul-De-Sac for something, turned into an all-night party, I got drunk and passed out, McCleany got drunker but didn't pass out, instead he shows up in Hope's room and figures he's going to knock off a piece . . . Jesus."

"Hey Parker why don't we—"

He held up his left hand, the one not holding the pistol. "Except this particular morning Hope wasn't in the mood to get pawed over by that drunken slob. As charming as Hope could be, she could be ten times as mean if you pissed her off. She said some things that put McCleany over the edge, plus he was drunk enough . . . he said he hit her just once but that it killed her."

"Houdini."

"Huh?"

"Nothing."

"Truth be told I don't think McCleany 'accidentally' killed her with one punch, I think he was in a rage and beat her head against the floor . . . but however it happened he killed her, comes to me and says we're going to pin it on the weird nephew, Donald Growler. I said bullshit . . . I never liked McCleany to start with, I could've killed him myself for what he did to Hope, but he'd already been in conference with J.L. who knew about the secret camera rig. I guess J.L. and Hope used to look at the pictures for yuks . . . and when McCleany started showing me the photographs, all those men Hope was fucking, the things she was doing with all those men, things she'd done with me . . . I went a little crazy."

"Felt she'd betrayed you."

"Played me for a fool. And I'd asked her to marry me? I kept thinking how she and her uncle must've got a *big* laugh out of that one."

"So you and McCleany framed Growler for the killing."

"McCleany wanted to do it for obvious reasons, so he wouldn't get charged with Hope's murder, and J.L. wanted to do it so he'd inherit Hope's share of Cul-De-Sac . . . and I went along with them because they said they had all kinds of pictures of me and Hope."

"They *said?*"

Gray nodded. "At first it seemed easy, Growler this weird twenty-six-year-old who was still a kid the way he acted, who kept a collection of animal heads in his room, had a lot of strange friends, he was either queer or bisexual. The frame seemed a natural. Mc-Cleany did the actual . . ."

"Cut off her head."

Gray wasn't able to answer aloud, had to nod.

"McCleany put her head in Growler's room."

Another nod, then Gray found his voice again. "J.L. promised he would destroy all incriminating photographs but obviously that was a lie. We made so many mistakes . . . found out *after* the evidence was planted that Donald wasn't even at Cul-De-Sac, he spent the night with a friend of his."

"Kenneth Norton."

"Yeah. So we were forced to come down on Kenny's nervous ass, he had a boyfriend at the time, an underage kid, and we threaten to arrange hard time for Norton unless he withdraws as Growler's alibi . . . we told Norton a bunch of mumbo jumbo, I don't know if he believed it or not, he was mainly just scared of us . . . we told him Growler had really killed Hope but the time of death had been screwed up by the medical examiner and Growler was going to get off on a technicality unless Norton cooperated."

"Perjure himself."

"We ran the same line by the Raineys, a couple who worked for J.L., got them to establish that Donald went into Hope's room around the time of the murder. I never thought it would fly. Really. I was convinced the whole frame would just collapse, I was planning to kill myself. But fuck me if it didn't hold together."

"Until now."

"Until everybody and their frigging brother comes crawling out of the woodwork . . . Growler, the Milton couple, you."

"Where's Annie?"

"She's locked upstairs, a room on the second floor."

Camel hadn't tipped to it, that Annie was here. When Gray said he'd put her somewhere safe Camel assumed that was somewhere *else*. "You son-of-a-bitch you were going to burn this building with Annie in it?"

Gray looked a little surprised too as if just then owning up to himself the consequences of what he'd intended to do.

Camel told him to drop the goddamn automatic.

Gray stared eye-to-eye for an uncomfortably long time, more than six seconds, Camel sensing a decision being made . . . something serious coming his way. "Don't—"

But Gray already was . . . bringing up the 9mm, forcing Camel to do the same with that shiny .38 in *his* hand: cowboys.

41

SHE HAD BROKEN THE HABIT THREE YEARS AGO WHEN SHE MARRIED PAUL
but now as she scouted the room for a place to pee Annie was once
again biting her nails. She opened the door to that walk-in closet
full of old furniture and stood in front of a full-length mirror,
cracked on the diagonal and leaning against the closet wall. Annie
opened the big blue jacket she was wearing.

Looking at her reflection she made no vain wishes for an inch
or two correction here and there, what bothered her was she
didn't recognize those hollowed eyes looking out from a soot-
blackened face, the ratty hair and blotchy skin, knot-nippled
breasts sagging as if drained dry. Annie wondered if she washed
her face and stood up straight and sucked in her tummy and
smiled a thousand watts . . . would it look like me again?

She'd been waiting for Parker Gray to return and let her out,
she was wishing Teddy Camel would come rescue her . . . it seemed
she was always waiting, wishing for a man.

Back when they spent that summer together Teddy told Annie
to get a career because a good career would never disappoint her
while a man usually would. (Actually he said *always* would but she
remembered it as usually.) Annie had always worked hard, holding
down an office job during the day and raking in big tips as a cock-

tail waitress at night. She took classes at a college where she met Paul and she banked most of her money hoping that one day she'd have enough to travel the world. That had always been her dream, to travel.

Then she married Paul and used all she'd accumulated to finance his renovations business, losing everything including her credit rating. Now her husband was dead and Annie had all those debts to pay because her name was on every loan paper and Paul didn't carry insurance. Annie wanted the elephant. Wrong or not, she intended to have it . . . that was one decision she'd made while locked in this room. Whatever money the elephant would bring, Annie would consider it compensation for what she'd been through . . . compensation for what Growler did to her.

She thought of him limping his way back to this room, he would do more than rape her, he would fulfill his promise to cripple her. Annie realized she was waiting for that to happen too, always waiting for men.

She used to think their predictability made them easy to manipulate . . . all men the same in that each thought he was special . . . hey, baby, I march to the beat of a different drummer . . . yeah you and the rest of the army. Golf pros and corporate executives, pretty boys and tough cops, judges and stepfathers . . . Annie could make them blush and stammer, break into nervous sweats and flare nostrils like stallions with their brains addled by the smell of estrus.

She thought of the girl in those photographs, looking over the shoulders of men and mugging for the camera . . . did she think men were easy too?

But if they're so easy why do they keep winning? One of those men killed that girl. And in a lifetime of dealing with men Annie never remembered coming out ahead either. It was as if she'd been playing poker with men, thinking she was taking every hand, but now at age thirty-five she looks down and sees no chips in front of her.

Definitely had to pee. She went further into the closet, between an old chest and a wooden chair with its seat rotted out. Annie pulled up the jacket, dropped her jeans, and squatted . . . keeping the closet door ajar because she wanted to watch the door to the room, hoping it wouldn't open to reveal Donald Growler standing there or hoping it *would* open for Teddy Camel or Parker Gray to come in and tell her you're safe now.

On camping trips Annie had peed squatting like this but she had never peed on a floor and discovered it required serious concentration . . . her urine stream starting and stopping and then just when it got going steadily she heard two shots, boom-boom, that shut off the flow like closing a tap.

She stood and felt wet on her thighs as she pulled up the jeans then ran across the room and put an ear to the door, hearing nothing more. The sound of the shots had been muffled but Annie knew it was gunfire coming from somewhere in the building. Parker Gray shooting Growler? Or the other way around? Whoever was the survivor would be coming to this room . . . Gray because he knew Annie was here and Growler to reclaim the elephant. She stepped back from the door wondering which man it would be this time.

Annie returned to the closet forgetting about where she'd peed and stepping in it, biting her nails again as she looked for a hiding spot somewhere in that jumble of old furniture. Against the back wall was a tall pile of old blankets blue with mold, Annie made her way there and pulled at the top blankets, filling the air with the smell of mold and revealing an upright piano. She could crouch next to it and cover herself, maybe someone glancing in the closet wouldn't bother coming back here to check what was under those blankets.

Annie closed the closet door and opened her eyes very wide, surprised by the darkness, how very complete it was. Feeling her way among pieces of furniture she bumped so hard against the piano that a few loose hammers struck their strings creating dampered notes . . . and when those false notes faded was when Annie heard the piano buzzing.

42

IN THE IMMEDIATE AFTERMATH OF THE SHOOTING CAMEL CREDITED being alive to the simplicity of a design patented in 1835 by Mr. Colt because even if Parker Gray's semiautomatic was cocked and locked, which Camel assumed it was, Gray still had to thumb-off a safety while Camel armed with a revolver could simply point and pull. It was the ever-readiness of Mr. Colt's design, Camel figured, that gave him the edge over Gray and made Camel the cowboy left standing. But he was wrong.

Just as he'd been taught to do Camel had fired at the center of his target, Gray getting two rounds in the gut, quickly covering his stomach with a forearm, looking down at the sudden blood then up at Camel with questioning eyes.

By the time Camel reached him Gray was slowly folding onto his right side like something made of snow melting. He tried to break the fall but ended up dropping knee-hard in the gas-splashed corridor.

Camel bent down and moved Gray's arm to see that one round had hit his western-style belt buckle, holing the buckle and entering flesh but only superficially while the second round went on in unimpeded making a neat entry wound just to the left of Gray's navel. The kind of wide-mouthed hollow points with which Mc-

Cleany's .38 revolver had been loaded are designed to spread on contact for two advantages . . . one, they won't penetrate most walls so you don't end up shooting someone in the next room when you didn't even know the guy was there and, two, after a hollow point enters flesh through a small hole it spreads open its mouth and starts chewing up tissue like a Mixmaster set on purée . . . except Parker Gray in his current condition wouldn't of course list this second point as an advantage.

Camel was on his knees next to Gray who said, "Oh Christ call an ambulance huh?"

Camel placed Gray's forearm back over the wound and debated telling him the truth: too late for ambulances, you got maybe a couple of minutes before you bleed to death or die of shock.

"Jesus." He groaned and said Jesus again. "I thought you didn't feel the pain until later, isn't that what everybody says huh?"

Camel took the pistol from Gray's hand. The thumb safety was on as Camel had thought but the 9mm was not cocked and locked, no round in the chamber, the hammer still seated. Gray must've known the pistol was not ready to fire, which meant, regardless of the efficiency of Mr. Colt's patented revolver, Camel had not out-cowboyed anyone . . . Gray had used him to commit suicide.

There on the floor on his side he began contracting slow-motion into the fetal position like something wet drying up. "Jesus . . . you think it's going to get worse than this huh?" He meant the pain.

"You're not going to make it Parker."

"Don't say that," Gray pleaded, his voice whispering out from somewhere within that fetal curl, commenting again how much it hurt. "Call an ambulance huh, there's still a chance . . ."

"No there's not."

"Hardhearted bastard."

"You're dying, what can I say?"

"You fucked me up good."

Camel thought, you fucked yourself.

Gray's blood mixed with gasoline on the floor making a

petroleum-protein pool spreading out to confirm Camel's prognosis . . . you can't leak that much blood and live.

"Teddy."

Hearing his name in a voice so softly pathetic made Camel's face twinge like Steve McQueen's when he played a bad character regretting he was about to do something good. "Parker, you Catholic?"

Gray nodded.

"Want to confess?"

"I already told you everything—"

"I'm not talking about who killed that girl, I mean—"

"My soul?"

"Last rites. You don't necessarily need a priest, any Catholic can perform them in a pinch."

"In a pinch huh," Gray said like it was a joke except of course neither man laughed. He paused to consider then agreed, "Okay."

Camel and Gray stumbled through what they remembered of confession and final rites. Afterward Gray held tightly to Camel's hand and said, "She's upstairs in a corner room on the second floor, I left the key in the padlock . . . I'm sorry."

"You were going to burn her alive."

"I'm sorry."

Camel didn't say anything, didn't let him off the hook.

"Hey Teddy you're seriously fucked too . . . shooting me like this."

Gray was right. The manslaughter charge relating to Paul Milton's death might have been dropped but now Camel had fatally shot a state police associate superintendent, the man who pushed for Camel's arrest, and it's going to look like Camel did it for revenge, going to be hell's own time proving justifiable self-defense, proving that Gray had used Camel to commit suicide.

"Give me something to write on," Gray said.

Camel dug out a notepad and pen.

"Oh Christ . . . Teddy . . . going into . . . is this it huh . . . really dying?"

Camel didn't answer except to cradle Gray's head.

"You got it, something to write with?"

He held pen and pad ready.

Gray blinked a couple of times like he was thinking things through. "I'm going to write, 'Teddy Camel shot me in self-defense.' I'll write it was justifiable . . . no crime committed. Help me huh, I'm doing this to save your ass."

Camel had to bend Gray's fingers around the pen, then steady the notepad on the floor as Gray forced himself to write . . . interrupted by a spasm that quickly drew him back into that fetal curl. "Dying," he said with a sense of astonishment.

"Yeah," Camel confirmed, wondering too late if simply on principle he should've called an ambulance . . . then he remembered the phone here at Cul-De-Sac was disabled.

Gray had collapsed onto the notepad. When he was still, was dead, Camel dug it out. Gray had scrawled his signature followed by this: *Teddy Camel shot me in—*" But that's as far as he made it. Didn't get to "self-defense," much less "justifiable" or "no crime was committed." Show this to a prosecutor and she could argue Gray intended to finish his dying statement any number of ways: *Teddy Camel shot me in . . .* cold blood.

Camel tore off the page anyway, put it in a pocket and checked his watch, ten P.M. on the nose. As he was standing he heard a noise behind him, Camel wheeling to see Jake Kempis there in the corridor.

"Jesus Teddy what've you done?"

Killed a man, Camel thought, the full awareness of it sinking in, soaking right through to his core . . . I have just now killed a man.

43

AT 9:20 P.M. THEY WERE ALL THREE IN ELIZABETH'S CHINA BLUE CADIL-
lac, Murray on the front seat with his head on Elizabeth's lap as
she drove, Donald Growler sprawled in the back holding his left
arm on a diagonal pressing close across stomach and chest, that
softball hematoma indicating where the bone had broken, halfway
between wrist and elbow, his left foot offering up another source
of pain along with enough blood to make the bandaging squishy.

Still he wasn't hurting now as bad as he did after being thrown
from Annie's truck and then limping naked and winged back to
Cul-De-Sac. Upon getting there he went immediately to the cellar
for his stash of drugs and alcohol, dusting the foot wound top and
bottom with almost a gram of cocaine which not only stemmed the
pain but also slowed the bleeding, though Growler now wished he
still had that gram of magic to put up his nose because the pain
from his various wounds, psychological and physical, were all returning with a vengeance.

Just hold on until it's done he told himself as he leaned forward
to make sure Elizabeth was still driving toward Cul-De-Sac and not
taking a detour to a police station. Back at her house, when he
forced her to make that telephone call, she had performed flawlessly.

.   .   .

"THIS IS ELIZABETH Rockwell," she announced in that tight-jawed patrician manner of hers. "Do you remember me?"

"Of course I remember you Elizabeth."

"I have some photographs I think you should see."

No comment.

"You're in these photographs . . . with Hope."

Still no comment.

"You do remember the photographs?"

"Who else has seen them?"

"I don't think you want this discussed on the phone do you? I'll be at Cul-De-Sac within the hour, meet me there and come alone."

.   .   .

ARRIVING AT CUL-DE-SAC, Growler instructed Elizabeth to stop in front of the building, he wanted her Cadillac prominently displayed . . . neither he nor Elizabeth saw the two cars parked around at the side.

When Growler leaned forward from the backseat he regretted most painfully that all his medicines had worn so thin.

Elizabeth sat behind the wheel stroking Murray's silky ponytail.

"You going to wake up the big guy or not?" Growler asked.

She turned and gave him the strangest look before announcing in a curiously distracted and formal voice, "I've never known anyone as aggrieved as you Donald."

He brought his good right arm around to smack her in the face. "Aggrieved . . . *aggrieved?*" He didn't know where to start. "You bet your ass I'm aggrieved . . . aggrieved all the way from these goddamn Frankenstein teeth I had put in my mouth . . . all the way down to that spike-nail hole in my foot is how bad I'm aggrieved . . . seven years pulling a train for a crime I didn't commit is how I'm aggrieved . . . backstabbed by my best friend, betrayed by my partner St. Paul, everyone lying to me and about me . . . aggrieved, *aggrieved,* I'll show you aggrieved, now get out of the fucking car." As an afterthought he hit her in the face again.

When Growler stepped from the car door he inadvertently put weight on his left foot which sent back enough pain voltage that he collapsed onto his right knee and dropped the machete . . . was it the paranoia again or did he really hear Elizabeth laughing at him from the front seat, that bitch is asking for it.

"Get out of the car!"

As she did, Murray's head rolled off her lap and onto the cold April ground with a solid thump, no bounce.

Growler's turn to laugh. "Pick it up."

"Donald . . ."

He alternated words with open-handed smacks to the back of her head: "Pick . . . it . . . up . . . you . . . rotten . . . cunt."

She required a moment to regain her bearings then said, "I've never been called that in my life."

When Growler retrieved the machete and put it to her face Elizabeth lifted Murray's head by the ponytail.

Growler laughed again. "Come on."

She carried the head away from her body though Elizabeth's skirt and blouse were already elaborately stained, Murray having leaked enough blood to fill several fat children.

"What're you going to do to me?" she asked once they were inside.

"Anticipation sharpens pain, you sure you want to know?"

He was right, she didn't want to know.

Growler told her anyway. "I'm going to take you around back to the storage room . . . remember the storage room where I grabbed your tit, remember testifying about it at the trial, making me out as a some kind of sex—"

"I told the truth at your trial."

"You want the truth Mommy . . . I'm going to cut off your head."

She didn't doubt it.

Walking the overheated and cluttered hallways of Cul-De-Sac, Growler limping and pushing Elizabeth on ahead of him, they made their way around to the rear of the building where they turned a corner and nearly tripped on a five-gallon can of gas . . . down the corridor two men stood talking over the body of a third.

Growler couldn't tell who was on the floor and didn't know either of the other two men but he wasn't all that surprised to see them here . . . the conspiracy against him must include a huge cast, maybe every single person in the world.

He picked up the gas can one-handed and with considerable effort managed to begin soaking Elizabeth.

44

BEES, SHE THOUGHT. THE PIANO'S BUZZING HAD BEGUN SOFTLY LIKE A fluorescent hum but as Annie stumbled backward to get away, knocking over a bookshelf that fell against the piano, the buzzing grew louder and more urgent, angrier. She desperately wanted out of the closet, out of the dark, away from bees.

As a child, attending a Girl Scout Jamboree, Annie had been playing on old wooden steps when her foot went through a rotten board and onto a hornets' nest in the ground beneath the steps. She was instantly swarmed, stung a dozen times, very nearly going into shock as she was rushed to a hospital. What she remembered most about the incident was not the pain of the stings but the panic of having those hornets all over her, in her hair, not being able to escape them no matter how she flailed her arms and ran and screamed. She'd been stung a few times in her life since then without suffering any allergic reactions but Annie was left with a deep-seated dread of bees.

Which was why she lurched so wildly for the closet door, knocking over more furniture, barking her shins but not caring, desperate to get out of there, turning the handle but unable to get the door open . . . had it locked upon closing or was someone in Paul's workshop, someone who had locked her in?

As the buzzing-whine grew louder behind her she kept rattling the handle, throwing her shoulder against the door, shouting to be let out. And when the first one landed on her face Annie very nearly went mad with panic.

■   ■   ■

JAKE KEMPIS HAD walked all the way around Cul-De-Sac, stopping near the open window at the back of the building, where he waited as Camel had told him to. But when he heard gunshots Kempis went in through that window . . . and now he was looking at Camel holding a revolver and standing over Parker Gray's body. "Jesus Teddy what've you done?"

Camel's face held a stricken expression for just a moment, then he seemed to recover, walking over to Kempis and cooly handing him a small sheet of paper.

Half-convinced Camel intended to kill him too, Kempis didn't even glance at the paper until Camel insisted, "Go ahead and read it."

Kempis finally did: Gray's signature over an incomplete statement: *Teddy Camel shot me in—*

"He didn't get a chance to finish," Camel was saying. "If he'd lived long enough he was going to say it wasn't my fault. Read it again, tell me how you think he meant to complete it."

Kempis looked at Gray's body, all that blood over the front of his shirt, then back at the note which he read softly aloud, "*Teddy Camel shot me in* . . . the stomach?"

Camel was disappointed but not surprised. "In *self-defense,* that's what he was going to write."

Although deeply unconvinced Kempis nodded. "I understand now." Returning the note he said, "I guess we'd better call someone . . . you want to hand me that revolver?"

"Jake, it *was* self-defense."

"Okay except I'd still feel better if you gave me that revolver."

Camel handed it over grips-first but immediately picked up Gray's semiautomatic. "We'll go get Annie, she's locked in a room upstairs, then—"

He was interrupted by the sound of a woman loudly gasping, Camel and Kempis both turning to see Elizabeth Rockwell down there at the end of the corridor, a man standing behind her soaking Elizabeth with gasoline. It was the shock of that cold liquid on her shoulders and back that had made her gasp.

And it was the shock of seeing what she held in her right hand that made Jake Kempis say Sweet Jesus.

45

ON HER ASHEN FACE WAS AN EXPRESSION OF PROFOUND BEWILDERMENT, both eyes blackened, her blouse bloodstained like a map of Minnesota's lakes, shoulders hunched and shivering from the gasoline, Elizabeth Rockwell still holding Murray's head.

"Step in that doorway," Camel told Jake Kempis. "Get ready to open fire."

"On who?" Kempis didn't know any of these players, didn't know who the enemy was . . . the woman with the head, the man with the gas, both of them?

"Just don't hit the woman," Camel said, racking the slide on Gray's 9mm, thumbing off the safety, pointing the muzzle toward Growler, and telling Kempis again, "Don't fire until you get a clean shot at the man behind her."

When Growler resumed pouring gasoline on Elizabeth she reacted this time by dropping Murray's head and starting to run toward Camel . . . but Growler grabbed her.

"Hey Donald I know you didn't kill your cousin!" Camel called from the other end of the hallway.

What did it matter now, Growler wondered . . . because although he finally knew the answers to the questions that'd been eating at his brain for seven years, *knowing* had brought him no peace. He took out a silver lighter and rolled the wheel against the flint, sparking a flame.

"Don't do it!" Camel told him.

"Have to," he muttered . . . have to kill Elizabeth, kill Hope's murderer, kill St. Paul's wife . . . then maybe that hungry little beetle would crawl back out of his ear and maybe then he could sleep. Sleep would be good. To his ravaged mind the prospect of sleep was like the promise of heaven.

"If you hurt her, Jake and I'll both open fire. But that doesn't have to happen, just put the lighter away and—"

"And what . . . you got nothing to offer me!"

"I'll help you nail who framed you, here's one of them on the floor . . . Parker Gray."

"He's not who I want."

"We'll get the other one too."

"Then what!" Growler shouted.

"Make sure he pays for what he did to you."

"You mean like this?" Growler said, tossing the lighter onto Elizabeth's skirt.

46

THEY WERE ALL AROUND HER FACE AND IN HER HAIR AND AT HER EARS too, though oddly they hadn't started stinging yet . . . little solace to Annie because the horror of it was having them *on her,* especially being trapped in the dark like this, their insistent buzzing seeming to drive through her ears and right into her brain as she sunk to the floor and lifted Kempis's big jacket over her head like a protective dome, Annie brushing wildly at the ones there under the jacket with her as she screamed for help or just screamed because what else could she do but scream.

47

ELIZABETH ROCKWELL SCREAMING WHEN SHE CAUGHT ON FIRE, THE lighter having ignited her before bouncing to the floor still holding on to its flame as it landed next to Growler's right pants' cuff which he had inadvertently splashed with gasoline, Growler now on fire too but not like Elizabeth Rockwell who had become a living pyre.

When Growler stepped away from Elizabeth to beat at his pants' leg, Camel and Kempis both opened fire . . . both hitting their target which then hit the floor howling.

Elizabeth still screaming lifted her arms out from her sides in a terror-and-panic pose reminiscent of that famous photograph of the Vietnamese girl who'd been burned with napalm, Elizabeth rushing toward Camel like one of hell's angels straight from home and still fiery.

He realized of course she was coming to him for salvation but he also realized that if she reached him, here in this section of corridor which Parker Gray had soaked with gasoline, the entire corridor would go up in flame.

Quickly dropping the pistol he turned to a pile of white canvas tarps, grabbed one, and ran to meet Elizabeth, her heat even from ten feet away enough to warm his face and dry moisture from his eyes.

Most of her clothing had already burned off, she was naked in front and all the more blindingly on fire as her movement fed oxygen to the flames making them intensely blue.

In nearly thirty years as a cop Camel had handled drunks and psychos but never had he been charged by anything quite as terrifying as that burning woman with fiery arms reaching his way.

He lifted the canvas tarp between them like a protective curtain and neatly snared the still-screaming Elizabeth, embracing her, bringing the tarp around in the back and then using his weight to collapse her, getting Elizabeth on the floor and furiously tucking in the tarp to deny fire its breath.

Flames kept leaping out from the edges of the canvas, burning a hole in Camel's shirt high on his chest, the skin there turning immediately red, hurting . . . and before completing the grisly task of extinguishing Elizabeth he also got scorched just above the beltline.

Camel stood to check his clothes for fire then glanced at Growler down the corridor on his back. "Go see if the poor bastard's dead," Camel told Kempis who was just now coming out from the protection of that doorway. "If he's alive cuff him to a radiator . . . you got cuffs?"

Kempis said he did then stayed standing there staring wildly at Camel.

"Jake, go on!"

Holding his breath Camel lifted the tarp to see what was left recognizable as Elizabeth Rockwell . . . her face had been scorched, skin blackened, lips burned away so that teeth showed, most of her nose gone too, leaving gaping nostril holes.

Let her be dead, he prayed . . . but Elizabeth opened her lids to look at him with hazel eyes that appeared impossibly wet and alive in contrast to the black-burnt flesh of her face.

"Hold on," he told those eyes. "I'm going to get you to the hospital."

Kempis returned and asked how she was, though he wouldn't

look over Camel's shoulders to see for himself. "I think we both hit him in the legs," Kempis said excitedly, "but with all the other wounds it's hard to tell, like he's been through a meat grinder, his pants were still on fire, I had to put it out—"

"Jake is he dead?"

"Yeah I think so, or just about."

Camel fought to hold his temper. "Go back and cuff him anyway." He tucked the tarp more tightly around Elizabeth and when Kempis returned, Camel told him, "We got two things to do, get this woman to the hospital and get Annie out of this building. You know the nearest hospital?"

Jake ventured a look at Elizabeth's face and spoke quickly, "I'll get Annie, where is she?"

No time to argue the point. "Okay listen to me," Camel said as he prepared to lift Elizabeth. "Gray said Annie's in a corner room on the second floor, you find her then use Gray's car to drive Annie to The Ground Floor."

"Where's his keys?"

"I don't know Jake, probably in his pocket, *find them.*" Camel was taking Elizabeth in his arms, Kempis looking away. "Just make sure you get Annie to The Ground Floor."

"What about the guy we shot, I mean I fired because you told me to, I don't even know who he is, what he's done—"

"Go upstairs and get Annie," Camel said as he carried Elizabeth down the hallway.

Kempis followed. "Teddy—"

"Jake, he's the one who killed all those people I told you about, the decapitations . . . just leave him there, all you have to worry about is getting Annie out of here and taking her to Eddie's place. I'll meet you and we'll call this in from there."

"All right."

When Elizabeth began slipping, Camel boosted her higher in his arms, his fingers slipping off the tarp to scrape loose a chunk of crisped flesh that felt like soft warm pork barbecue. He had to will himself not to drop her in disgust.

He carried Elizabeth outside and then around to Eddie's Fair-

lane placing her as carefully as he could into the backseat, keeping the tarp around her, Camel thinking the interior is going to be
ruined now, Eddie will never get this smell out. He looked down
at hazel eyes watching him from somewhere far away.

Camel got in the driver's side and slid behind the wheel, started
the engine, snapped the lap belt closed, looked back at what had
once been Elizabeth Rockwell, then took off.

He was going too fast when he got to the two-lane county highway, braking hard and making a sliding right turn that nearly
clipped one of the brick pillars. The hospital waited another fifteen, twenty miles away, Camel almost sure she would die of shock
before he got her there but he also felt obligated to try . . . Parker
Gray had died while Camel, in typical cold logic, knelt beside him
waiting for the inevitable, this time he was going to race the inevitable to a hospital.

The highway wound through a forest, Camel driving as fast as he
could and still stay on the road, glancing in the rearview mirror
and Jesus Christ there she was, RIGHT THERE . . . Elizabeth's face
leaning over the seat back right there at Camel's shoulder, he wondered how in God's name did she find the strength to sit up . . .
the fire had transformed that face into a horror mask, blackened
with little left of her lips or nose, most of that gray blond hair
burned off, ears only remnant folds of charred flesh, her teeth
grinning white. Camel might've survived the shock of having that
fright-face suddenly at his shoulder but when he saw her eyes he
jerked away from Elizabeth and lost control of the car . . . because
while her head was held rigidly forward, as if she was leaning to see
out the windshield, her eyes were straining to the left, bulging
from the sockets to find him, to plead with him, as if those un-
damaged eyes desperately wanted Camel's help getting out of that
ruined face.

The Fairlane was fishtailing while Camel worked the brakes to
slow down without going into a completely uncontrolled skid.
These maneuvers were only partly successful because while he did
manage to get almost stopped, at the last moment the car veered
off and hit a tree dead center . . . with sufficient impact to rocket

Elizabeth over the front seat and into the windshield, which instantly spider-webbed into a thousand cracks but did not break out . . . Camel's lap belt limiting him to hitting his face against the steering wheel.

Pinpoints of light exploded in front of his eyes and he kept saying, "Jesus." Not taking the name in vain but saying, "Jesus, Jesus" as a prayer, the most earnest he'd ever prayed . . . and continued praying as he got out of the car, went around to the passenger side, propped Elizabeth in the front seat, and retrieved the canvas tarp to put over her.

She had remained dead silent until now when she said, "Oh." Camel thought he should offer a reassuring word, none came to mind.

Elizabeth held a hand toward him, he didn't know what she wanted, wasn't sure she knew either. He tried to push her hand back so he could close the door but she kept reaching for him, finally he grabbed her wrist and forced it inside . . . his palm coming away wet with serum.

Wiping that hand on his pants Camel walked to the front of the car, bumper bent in a wide-mouth U around the tree. Steaming green antifreeze bleeding onto the ground told Camel the radiator had taken a crippling hit but, amazingly, the car started. He reversed onto the road and took off again.

A mile later the temperature gauge had pegged itself way over past H, these small-block V-8s notorious for running hot even with a good radiator, engine's heat coming through the fire wall to roast his legs, Camel wondering how it must have felt on hers.

No choice but to throttle on full bore waiting any moment now for the engine to seize but the old Ford motored its heart out delivering Camel and his damaged cargo right to the hospital's emergency room entrance.

He looked at Elizabeth and again wanted to say something but she was beyond words.

Running to the hospital's double glass doors, he encountered two orderlies just exiting.

"What happened to you?" one of them asked with a casualness

that Camel found maddening. "Somebody Joe Louis your ass, didn't they?"

He had no idea what the orderly meant, Camel hadn't yet felt pain from his nose, broken on the steering wheel in the crash, and was unaware of blood creeking down his face.

The orderlies each took an arm.

He pried their hands off.

"You on something buddy?" one of them asked. "What've you been taking?"

He looked at their faces, they appeared to be concerned for him but wary too, expecting Camel to turn violent at any moment. He knew what he had to say . . . there's a severely burned woman out in the car.

When they tried again to get Camel inside he settled for raising his right arm and pointing at the car.

They saw the busted windshield on the passenger side.

"Someone in there?" one of them asked.

He nodded.

"Worse shape than you?"

Camel nodded again, closing his eyes with the relief of finally being understood.

They grabbed a gurney and ran to the car, Camel following. When the first orderly opened the door Elizabeth started to fall out and the second orderly had to reach down and grab her. When he saw what he had in his hands, he said, "Jesus."

Camel thought yeah I know that prayer.

They got Elizabeth on the gurney and rushed her inside, Camel arriving at the treatment room just behind a doctor, young guy with orange-red hair that stuck high all over his head like a comic wig, who lifted the tarp and mumbled, "Jesus."

Everybody praying tonight.

Quickly recovering his composure the doctor began giving orders to the nurses, yelling for the orderlies to put through for a helicopter because the best he could do was stabilize the patient for a flight to the nearest burn center.

As the nurses assembled equipment Elizabeth turned her head

and found Camel. She unbent one burned arm and reached for him as she'd done after the crash. The doctor turned and looked at Camel. Nurses staring too. Everyone still for a moment as if frozen in a living tableau . . . then just as abruptly all their animation returned, the emergency room once again filled with clatter and activity as the nurses brought in IV drips and hypos, sponges and sterile wraps, the doctor nudging Camel aside and telling him, "Go across the hall to the other treatment room, I'll get someone to take a look at you as soon as we can."

"I'm fine," Camel said just before doing a most astonishing thing, the first time he'd ever done it in a long life full of all possible opportunities and provocations: he fainted.

48

WHEN THE ELECTRICITY IN CUL-DE-SAC WENT OUT JAKE KEMPIS PULLED A
flashlight from his utility belt and it worked just fine . . . but he
wished he had an even bigger one, an even brighter one.

The man he and Camel had shot was not dead, Growler had regained consciousness to scream at Kempis who went over and
tried to figure out if he should do something for the guy, take him
to a hospital or at least try to stop the bleeding from the bullet
wounds or what.

"Hey look at this," Growler said indicating the front of his
trousers. He wasn't wearing a shirt and Kempis could see enough
of the tattoo to know what was being depicted. "Better let me loose
or the ol' debil get you nigger."

Jeez, Kempis thought, right away with the *nigger* . . . assholes like
this were so goddamn predictable. Kempis turned and walked
down the corridor, no longer feeling guilty about leaving the bastard cuffed to a radiator . . . while Growler called after him, "Ol'
debil live in dese walls, you listen, you hear him scratching to get
out."

It was while Jake was searching for a stairway that the electricity went out and he started second-guessing himself about how
he placed the cuffs on Growler . . . maybe he didn't tighten them

sufficiently, maybe the bastard got loose and turned off the electricity.

Coming around to the front of the building Kempis saw the double doors to the outside and thought about leaving . . . but he'd promised Camel he'd find Annie and Kempis intended to keep that promise.

What's to worry about anyway, he had the flashlight in his left hand and he was well armed, the .38 revolver he'd used to shoot Growler was in Kempis's right hand and the 9mm Camel had dropped to the floor was tucked in Kempis's belt . . . but he wished for even more guns, even bigger ones.

Jake turned toward the stairway.

Mrs. Milton was supposed to be in a corner room on the second level, Kempis almost to the first step when he heard a noise behind him, like something hard tapping along on the wood floors, almost as if an animal was following him, its nails clicking on the floor . . . it could've been hooves but most likely it was Kempis's imagination. He turned, shined his light, saw nothing, and headed once more for the stairs . . . there it was again.

"Mrs. Milton?"

No answer.

He wanted to be a state trooper, all his life Jake Kempis had been a ballsy guy, very little frightened him . . . but now he wished for even more courage, even bigger balls.

49

CAMEL AWOKE WITH A START, A MUSCLE TWITCH LIKE WHEN YOU'RE COM-
ing out of a dream about stepping off a cliff. He was in a hospital
room, lying on a bed but atop the covers and dressed except for
his shoes which had been removed and his sports coat which was
on a nearby chair. Camel's first thought was of Annie . . . she's
okay, Kempis has already taken her to The Ground Floor. Then he
thought of Elizabeth Rockwell and wondered if she'd made it.

The only injury to himself that he was aware of initially was the
one to his pride, the embarrassment of having fainted, but when
Camel sat up he got reminded of everything else that hurt . . .
burns high on his chest and above the belt-line, his stomach still
sore from where he'd been sucker-punched by McCleany, his right
bicep aching where the golf ball had hit, and most especially his
nose, swollen and bandaged as if doctors had grafted an eggplant
onto his face.

Adrenaline and a focused concentration had masked these various injuries while Camel dealt with everything that happened at
Cul-De-Sac, with getting Elizabeth to the hospital, but now as he
swung around to sit on the edge of the bed he felt each individual
source of pain.

His shoes were there on the floor, Camel slipping off the bed and sitting in the chair to put them on. How long had he been out, were Kempis and Annie waiting for him at The Ground Floor . . . had Kempis already notified the state police about Parker Gray's death?

I'm going to get nailed for that, Camel thought. Even if it eventually comes out that Gray helped frame Growler for the murder seven years ago, that's not going to let me off the hook for killing Gray. It'll look like I did it because he pushed to have me arrested for shooting Paul Milton, like I did it for revenge.

Camel closed his eyes and put his head back to think. Gray was the first man he'd killed without wanting to, the first man he'd killed who didn't need killing . . . and Camel felt sick to his soul. But he didn't intend to go to prison over it, Camel would repent on his own schedule.

When a young nurse walked by the room's open doorway and saw Camel sitting in the chair, she backed up, looked again, and came into the room flashing a big white smile, "How you feeling?"

He opened his eyes and said he felt fine.

She kept smiling, nice teeth like Annie's.

"How long have I been out?"

She checked her watch and shrugged. "Ten minutes?"

She had to be kidding. Camel said, "You got to be kidding."

She shook her pretty head and hit that toothy smile again . . . Camel liked looking at her.

"Always darkest before the dawn," she said, apropos of what, he wasn't sure. She felt his pulse, placed a cool hand on his fevered brow, Camel understanding then why rich old men bequeath everything to their nurses. This one's name tag said she was Crystal Packard, Camel figured her at barely twenty.

"We di'n't even take off your clothes," she informed him. "Just your shoes so they wouldn' dirty up the bed. But we di'n't put you in a hospital gown and all . . . doctor said you'd be coming around in a few minutes. He was right, huh? He fixed your nose. I di'n't hear if it was broken or not but you'll have two black eyes I'm sure."

Camel asked about Elizabeth Rockwell.

"You'll have to talk with doctor." Like many in the health profession Crystal consistently dropped articles when referring to doctors . . . the way other people drop articles when referring to God.

"Are you saying you don't know whether she made it or not . . . or you don't want to tell me?"

"Was she your wife?"

"*Was?* She's dead?"

Crystal had a little bobbed nose and small brown eyes, over-dyed blond hair arranged in a short, perky style . . . when she tried to force this button-cute face into a somber expression the result came across as an exaggerated pout. "I could get you some counseling."

"What?"

"Counseling. You want some?" she asked, as if offering ice water.

"No." Camel stood and put on his sports coat.

She told him he couldn't leave just yet.

"Why not?"

"Doctor has to say it's okay."

"I haven't been admitted, I don't have to be discharged."

"I think you better wait right here," she insisted, turning on low nonmarking heels and walking out of the room, Camel watching her go. The word "pneumatic" came to mind.

And then right behind pneumatic . . . Elizabeth Rockwell came to mind. He had always harbored a private dread of being burned and seeing it happen to Elizabeth was like experiencing a childhood nightmare, unable to wake up and make it stop. Checking the scorches on his chest and above his belt-line he saw they were no worse than bad sunburns, then he touched his face again, the bandaged nose felt both numb *and* painful if that was possible. He had an axe-in-the-skull headache . . . and knowledge of more to come.

Camel stopped at the doorway to the room and looked down a corridor to see Nurse Packard talking with a state trooper in full uniform, an impossibly young man whose face was bland and gentle, eyes brown and bovine, hair dark and thinning . . . he'd be bald before he was forty. Seeing them standing together like that Camel thought the trooper and the nurse made a breeding-program-compatible couple except the trooper's nose was even smaller than Crystal's and you had to wonder if their babies would have any noses at all.

She pointed back toward Camel's room.

He didn't want to start answering questions yet, Camel still didn't know what to say about Parker Gray and he still wanted to make sure Annie was okay.

He hurried to the bathroom, flipped on the light, opened a tap, then stepped out and closed the door, returning quickly to hide behind the door to the room just as the trooper walked in.

With Camel close enough to touch him the trooper stood there looking at the room's three empty beds, then at the closed door to the bathroom. A light was shining under that door and you could clearly hear water running. When the trooper headed for the bathroom Camel slipped out.

Luckily Crystal wasn't at the nurses' station when he walked by, Camel taking the steps down because he didn't want to chance waiting for an elevator.

Evading that trooper was probably stupid he thought as he left the hospital . . . but he was working on a plan how he might avoid being charged in Parker Gray's death and to make it fly he needed to have a very serious talk with Jake Kempis.

Camel was heading for the street, looking for a cab, when from behind him someone called his name.

50

"MRS. MILTON?"

Hearing her name being called from the other side of the closet door Annie screamed to be let out . . . she didn't care who was there, which man it was this time, she wanted *out*.

When the door opened Annie came rushing into the room but still kept the jacket protectively over her head. "Bees!" she shouted. *"Bees!"* Then she was embraced by whoever had opened the door and he laughed and told her, "No, honey, they're just flies."

Cluster flies, the kind that swarm livestock in the summer, that will cover a horse's face by the hundreds . . . big fat flies that cluster in hibernation-like swarms inside the walls of buildings and if these clusters are disturbed the flies will buzz loudly like bees and try to reform their clusters. In the closet they swarmed Annie's face not to attack her but in an effort to find each other and reassemble.

She finally pulled the jacket down from her head and saw that dozens of the flies were still buzzing around her, flies just like those that were behind that rotting window shade she pulled down, that settled on Paul and got caught in his hair. Not swattable little domestic houseflies, these were heavy and loud and if you squashed one of them there'd be a mess to clean up, they were that big.

In Annie's hair now, she brushed at them wildly and said, "No! No!" Not bees, thank God they weren't bees, but she still didn't want them on her, she was still repulsed whenever one landed in her ear or on her lip.

As Annie continued flailing at the flies, ducking her head to escape them, the man who'd let her out of the closet laughed again and grabbed Annie's wrists. "Honey they're just flies."

She looked up at him.

"Just big ol' fat flies," he said, brushing at her hair with one hand as he held her right wrist with his other hand. "You remember me?"

Annie did, of course she did.

51

WHEN CAMEL TURNED AROUND THE FIRST THING NEFFERING SAID WAS, "What happened to your nose?"

"Broke it in a car wreck."

"Yeah the reason I'm here, got a call about my car being in an accident . . . how bad?"

"Bad."

"Totaled?"

"I don't know, probably." He handed over the keys which Eddie accepted like the personal effects of a recently departed loved one.

"You come from home or The Ground Floor?" Camel asked.

Eddie kept looking down at the keys.

Thinking of the trooper who was searching for him right at this moment, Camel said, "We got to get out of here." He started walking, Eddie following slowly. "Come on we got to go *now*."

When Eddie caught up he said, "I don't know where Annie is."

"It's okay, she was out at Cul-De-Sac but Jake Kempis took her to your place."

"She's been missing since morning, I've spent most of the day looking for her . . . Jake took her to my house?"

"No, The Ground Floor."

"Teddy I just came from there."

Camel stopped, checked his watch.

Neffering asked him what's going on.

"They've had plenty of time to get to The Ground Floor . . . you driving Mary's Mustang? Where's it parked?"

"You wrecked the Fairlane." Neffering saying this to make sure he had it straight, to confirm it was really true.

"Eddie let's get to Mary's car, I'll tell you on the way."

"Can I see the Fairlane first, where is it?"

"No time."

"You said Annie's okay?"

"I thought so but she and Jake should've been at your place by now."

"We got time to take a quick look at the Fairlane?"

"No."

"Why?"

"Because I just gave a state trooper the slip there in the hospital and any second now he's going to be coming out here to grab my sorry ass."

Eddie nodded. "Car's over there."

In Eddie's wife's new red Mustang, on the way to The Ground Floor, Camel explained some of what had happened . . . but not everything because he didn't want to make Eddie vulnerable to an accessory charge.

When they got to the shopping mall's parking garage Camel thought about showing Eddie the sheet of paper from the notepad, ask him to read it and give an opinion on how he thought Gray intended to finish the statement.

"How much trouble you in?" Eddie asked.

"Lots." Camel decided he couldn't let any of that trouble wash over on Eddie . . . couldn't tell him about killing Gray. "Let's go see if they showed up yet."

Camel and Neffering went into The Ground Floor but Annie and Jake weren't there, no one had heard from them.

"Something must've gone wrong after I left," Camel told Eddie. "I need that forty-five . . . and the keys to Mary's Mustang."

Neffering looked away, his big brushy mustache drooping.

"I know, Eddie, *I know*. You went my bail, I wrecked your Fairlane, now I want your other car and your forty-five . . . I know I'm being a pain in the ass but this is important, I have to get back out to Cul-De-Sac."

"I'll come with."

"Not possible. Now gimme the car keys or I'll take a fucking cab."

"Teddy you can't make demands like that, not to the only friend you got in the world."

"Then who can I make them to?"

Eddie shook his head. "I brought the forty-five from home, I'll get it then I'll walk out to the car with you." He waited for a thank-you.

"Come on Eddie I'm in a hurry."

■   ■   ■

CAMEL HAD THE forty-five in one pocket, the keys to the Mustang in another . . . he and Eddie were just coming off the elevator when they both saw a little guy heading their way. He was five and a half feet tall, wearing a London Fog raincoat, had thinning dark hair, face like a well-groomed weasel.

"Weenie wagger," Eddie said almost in passing because, with everything else that was happening, catching weenie waggers had fallen low on the priority list.

But Camel reacted differently, seeing the pervert galvanized him into action . . . running toward the guy, Eddie hurrying to keep up.

At first the weenie wagger looked scared then he realized these were the same two lugs around whom he had run circles last time they met up . . . the pervert smiling as he skipped backward and sang out, "If it ain't Slow and Slower . . . see ya boys!" To mock Camel he shaped his thumb and forefinger into a pistol and pretended to shoot.

Camel raised the .45 and shot for real, two quick rounds into the concrete at the weenie wagger's feet . . . made a hell of a noise there in that low-roofed garage, the pervert lucky the bullets didn't ricochet up into his legs. In fact when chips of concrete peppered him the little guy thought he *was* shot, yelping and tripping backward to fall on his skinny ass.

Neffering said, "Jesus Teddy."

Camel walked to the pervert. "You work around here don't you?"

He didn't answer, too busy checking his legs for blood, for bullet wounds.

"Better find another job," Camel told him. "I don't want to see you again, never again, because if I ever see you again . . ." Something in Camel snapped loose, he kicked the guy knocking him flat on his back. "I'll fucking castrate you." As if to perform that very operation with gunfire he shot repeatedly into the concrete between the pervert's legs, chips and chunks flying everywhere, the sound deafening. In the echoing aftermath of all that gunfire Camel said, "Never again." Voice of God, Old Testament.

Eddie grabbed Camel's gun hand and raised it to point up at the ceiling before telling the pervert, "Better get out of here."

He didn't have to be told a second time, the little guy quickly on his feet, running without looking back.

"Like the bad old days," Eddie said, releasing Teddy's hand once the pervert was out of sight. "Camel's back."

He popped the clip and asked Eddie, "You got more ammo?"

52

MIDNIGHT, BOTTOM OF THE BAG, CAMEL DRIVING UP CUL-DE-SAC'S LANE,
dousing the Mustang's headlights, worried about Annie and won-
dering about Jake, how deeply he was in on this with Parker Gray.
Jake was the one snooping around for information right after
Camel started making calls about that old homicide at Cul-
De-Sac, Jake used his position as a security guard to get keys to
Camel's office, Jake was the one who turned Annie over to Parker
Gray, and Jake wouldn't take Elizabeth to the hospital, he insisted
on staying at Cul-De-Sac to get Annie. As Camel slowly drove up
the lane he tried figure it out . . . Jake did all of this to get an ap-
pointment to the academy? Was he in on the conspiracy? Or was
Growler still alive, maybe Jake didn't cuff him after all and
Growler somehow . . .

Camel felt a burning pain in the middle of his chest, like his
heart was on fire . . . the only thing he cared about in this whole
mess was Annie's safety, what did it matter to him that Growler had
been framed, that Parker Gray had been living a lie for seven years
. . . people are framing each other and lying and conspiring all the
time, fuck 'em, he cared only about Annie, he should've seen to
her first, made sure she was okay *then* worry about Elizabeth, *then*
worry about getting off the hook for having shot Gray.

A film of sweat covered his face. *Take care of your own first . . . when did I forget that fucking lesson?*

Stopping the Mustang a hundred yards from Cul-De-Sac, Camel killed the engine and sat there wishing for a cigarette. After checking the .45 for maybe the sixth time he got out of Mary's Mustang and walked the rest of the way. A late-model Cadillac and a beat-up Chevy Nova were parked in front of the building, Camel didn't remember seeing them before but of course he'd left in a hurry, Elizabeth Rockwell smoking in the backseat.

Gray's car was still parked to the side, its trunk still open. Camel entered the building through that window in the back, keeping the .45 cocked and locked in his right hand as he opened the storage room door with his left. The corridor still smelled of gas, Parker Gray's body was still there on the floor, so was Murray's head . . . but Donald Growler was gone.

The possibilities made Camel feel hollowed out inside as he hurried around through mazelike corridors, turning on lights as he went, reaching the huge atrium at the center of Cul-De-Sac. One of the five-gallon cans of gasoline had been carried from the back corridor and placed here at the bottom of the stairway. And next to that can of gas was Jake Kempis, his throat gashed. "Jake," Camel said softly. But he didn't have time for regrets or sympathy, Camel was ruthlessly focused now . . . one thing and one thing only, Annie. Starting up those steps, he shouted her name.

■   ■   ■

WHEN HE REACHED the second floor he stopped. Heard something, a door being opened and closed. He waited. *There,* Camel immediately crouching and pointing Eddie's .45.

"Whoa hoss," the man said, holding both arms out to his sides. "I ain't armed." Still wearing his stupid golfing clothes, pink shirt and green slacks, tonight McCleany even had on a pair of cleated golfing shoes.

"What're you doing here?" Camel demanded. "Where's Annie?"

"I got called here by Elizabeth Rockwell . . . I arrive but Elizabeth's not around, instead I find my old partner shot dead in the gut, some guy's head on the floor I don't even know who he is."

"Murray."

"Who?"

"Where's Annie?"

"And a spade at the bottom of the steps, throat cut, I don't know who he is either."

"Goddamn it McCleany, where's Annie?"

When McCleany started to lift a cigar to his mouth, Camel warned him, "Keep your hands out to the sides."

"I told you I wasn't armed. What happened to your nose?"

"Where is she?"

McCleany went ahead and put the cigar between his teeth, grinning.

"You think I won't shoot you?" Camel asked.

"Yeah yeah, you'll shoot me, you'll kill me, you'll rip my head off and shit down my throat, you'll make me wish I was never born, you'll, you'll . . . everybody so goddamn tough these days, wouldn't make a pimple on the ass of the guys I used to know." He lit the cigar. "You know I ain't armed 'cause you're the one took that little thirty-eight away from me, damn near broke my arm doing it . . . and second thing is, mad as you might be at me for punching you in the stomach and whatever else you think I've done, what you got against me ain't nothing compared to what you got against Donny Growler."

Camel waited to hear it.

"That ain't my gun, what'd you do with that little revolver you took off me?"

"Jake had it."

"Who?"

"The guy at the bottom of the steps, come on McCleany you're lying to me."

"Am I? Growler is up here in a room with your lady friend, am I lying about that pal?"

He wasn't. "But Growler was half dead, no way he could've overpowered Jake and crawled—"

"Never want to underestimate your basic psychopath."

For one of the few times in his life Camel wasn't sure if he was being lied to . . . too much riding on it.

"When you go in that room you'll see for yourself."

"What room, where?"

McCleany drew heavily on the cigar, talking while exhaling blue smoke. "Donny Boy never liked firearms, I'm wondering if it wasn't *you* who shot Parker." McCleany smiled, took another drag. " 'Course you could always blame it on Growler anyway, poor boy comes in handy for blaming things on."

Camel thumbed off the safety.

"Easy there cowboy."

And aimed at McCleany's head.

"You pointing that big forty-five at my brainpan don't change what Growler did to your lady friend."

"Where is she?" Give him another five seconds to tell me, Camel decided, then I'll shoot him and go look for Annie myself.

Sensing that a potentially fatal decision had been reached, McCleany took the cigar from his mouth and spoke seriously. "I was trying to prepare you for what you're going to find. Donald Growler's been a bad boy since he got out of prison, decapitated an old married couple, also his former best friend—"

"I know all that."

"But what you don't know Teddy, what I'm trying to ease in and tell you . . . he also killed your Annie."

"No."

"I'm afraid so, I tried—"

"Where . . . not another word, just tell me where."

"Down there, corner room."

"Let's go."

McCleany led the way, keeping his hands out to his sides, the cigar clenched between his teeth. "You're not going to want to see this, Growler cut her head off."

Camel didn't believe him, *refused* to believe him.

They got to the door and McCleany turned. "You okay son?"

"Open it." The door had been fitted with a heavy hasp and pad-lock but the padlock was left open.

"I messed Growler up real bad for you," McCleany said. "At least you'll have the satisfaction of—"

Camel motioned with the .45.

"Hoss I really don't think you need to see what's in that room, you want my opinion."

An unnatural thirst came over Camel, he felt like he didn't have spit enough to swallow, his throat closing up on him, unable to tell McCleany again to open the door.

"He used a homemade garrote to cut her head off," McCleany said flatly. "If I'd been just five or ten minutes earlier . . ."

Camel shoved him aside and pushed open the door, stepped into the room.

On a big black couch sat Donald Growler. Camel assumed it was Growler: left foot bandaged, swollen left arm, gunshot wounds, pants' leg burned off . . . you couldn't tell by the face it was Growler because that face had been beaten featureless. Annie was there too, her head on Growler's lap.

53

IT WAS MCCLEANY WHO HAD LET ANNIE OUT OF THE CLOSET AND PUT HIS arms around her when she was becoming hysterical about the flies . . . then asked her if she remembered him.

Of course she did, the golfer who'd been snooping around Teddy's office. He was still wearing golfing attire tonight, including cleated shoes.

He took Annie to the couch and sat next to her as she kept digging at her ear and wiping her mouth, convinced she was still covered with flies.

Under the pretense of helping her brush them off, McCleany pawed Annie's breasts and ran blunt fingers up her legs . . . laughing when she slapped at his hands and told him to leave her alone.

"We met in Camel's office."

"I remember you." She also remembered him from the photographs . . . McCleany was one of the men in those snapshots with that teenage girl, his was the face she recognized but couldn't place until now. He was seven years younger in that photograph but Annie had no trouble identifying him.

McCleany hustled his balls. "Too bad time's so short, I'd fuck you."

Life had become such an obscenity for her, she covered her face with both hands.

"I see you bite your nails, disgusting habit . . . now where are the fucking pictures?"

Everyone wanting those photographs, they were the reason Parker Gray brought her back here . . . Annie didn't know where they were, Growler must've taken them.

McCleany moved close to her. "How come you're wearing this big blue jacket?" He groped under it. "No bra huh, let me see." He wasn't smoking but smelled heavily of cigars, Annie figured it must've been his cigar in the fireplace. "Come on, red, just a quick peek."

"Leave me alone, please leave me alone."

"Take off that jacket and your jeans, we'll start some serious negotiations."

She looked him right in the eye. "You pig."

McCleany's face clouded briefly before breaking out in a large leering smile. "Give me the pictures baby and I'll let you walk out of here, otherwise—"

"I don't know where they are," she said, pushing away his hands and trying to stand.

He pulled her back down.

"The pictures were here in this room earlier . . ." Her voice broke, Annie forcing herself to continue. "When Parker Gray brought me back . . . the pictures were gone . . . Growler must have them . . . I don't know . . . *I don't know.*"

"My old partner Gray is dead downstairs, somebody's head is there in the hallway and I don't even know who it is, what the hell went on here tonight?"

"I don't know, I've been locked in this room."

"Five minutes after I get here I catch a nigger snooping around with *my thirty-eight* in his hand, so you know what I did, I pulled a fuse and came up on him in the dark where you think the nigger would have the advantage—"

"I don't know what you're talking about."

"Slitting a nigger's throat."

She closed her eyes.

"You said you found the pictures here in this room?"

"Yes," Annie replied without opening her eyes.

"Maybe they're still here but I'm tired of looking for them. Tell you what sweetheart, I'm going to bring Donny in, see if he can contribute to the conversation." McCleany hauled himself off the couch and looked around the workshop until he found a roll of duct tape that he used to wrap Annie's ankles and wrists. "I'll be right back, red." When he walked out of the room his cleats clicked on the floor like an animal's toenails.

Annie sat there too mentally wrecked to plot even an improbable escape, all she could do is wonder where Teddy was.

"Had to haul the poor bastard all the way up here on my back because he's in no shape to walk," McCleany announced as he came back into the room with Growler over his shoulder. "Shot twice, leg burned, one foot bandaged, broken arm . . . who you figure did all that to him?"

I did part of it, she thought . . . broke his arm and stabbed his foot, though she didn't tell this to McCleany.

He dropped Growler on the couch next to her. Annie had expected to be terrified upon seeing him again but how can you fear someone who's been battered the way Growler had, beaten very nearly senseless.

"Found him cuffed to a radiator downstairs, the keys in the nigger's pocket," McCleany said, breathing hard. "Thought I'd have a heart attack carrying ol' Donny boy up here."

"Is he dead?" Annie asked.

"Let's see." McCleany used the cleated golf shoes to stomp repeatedly on Growler's bandaged left foot, the one Annie had pierced . . . Growler moaning as he tried pathetically to lift that foot out of harm's way.

"Still alive," McCleany said jauntily.

"What'd you do to him?"

" 'Bout what I'm going to do to you . . . except I got a few special things in mind for your sweet little red-haired ass." McCleany pulled out an eighteen-inch length of electrical cable roughly the diameter of a fat hot dog. "Found this downstairs, used it to put the nigger to sleep before I slit his throat . . . *then* I used it on our friend Donny but give the devil his due he didn't lie to me, didn't claim not to know where the pictures were, he just wouldn't tell me. Can't seem to change the bastard's mind." Without ceremony, making no threats and asking no questions, McCleany struck Growler across the face.

"Please don't," Annie begged.

"You fucking him?"

She glared at McCleany.

"All he's got to do is tell me where the pictures are. Hey Donny, they still somewhere here in this room?"

Growler's glazed eyes managed to focus partially, he was conscious enough to mutter an obscenity.

McCleany once again stomped those cleats hard onto Growler's injured foot, then swung that makeshift sap back and forth across his face, McCleany seemingly willing if not able (chest pains made him grimace as he worked the sap) to continue until Growler had no face left at all.

Although Annie's wrists and ankles were bound she kept trying to get up, get away, McCleany pushing her back down, Annie sprayed and speckled with Growler's blood as she jammed a nail-gnawed thumb over each ear in vain attempt to keep out the *thwap-thwap* of that cable hitting blood-wet flesh . . . the sound worse even than the incessant buzzing of those fat black cluster flies, she really was convinced she'd lose her mind before the night was out.

For McCleany, beating Growler was no longer a way to find those pictures, it had become an end in itself, beating him and beating him until Growler became transcendent . . . injured and in pain even before being carried into this room he existed now in another circle entirely beyond injuries and pain, beyond imagination, his brain unable to measure the exact dimensions of the information sent its way by snapped bones and pierced flesh, gunshot wounds and third-degree burns and this constant slap of a copper cable across the face . . . Growler's brain having given up trying to compute pain except to conclude we've reached the bottom of the bag, we live now in a world of hurt.

He wanted to die. His mind didn't argue the point, okay let's die. But life clung perversely to him.

McCleany finally had to stop, purple-faced as he stumbled back from the couch. Annie took down her hands. Growler was no longer recognizable, his right eye had been dislodged from its socket and that once fine straight nose had been smashed into a flap of bloody torn skin hanging in the middle of his face.

McCleany was astonished with unaccustomed exertion and Annie wondered what the tortured must think when seeing the torturer exhausted.

"He's not going to tell you anything," she said to McCleany.

"I already figured that part out."

"Just let him . . ." What, she wondered . . . let him alone, let him die?

"Oh I could've done a lot more damage if I wasn't using my left hand, your old boyfriend nearly broke my right arm."

"Teddy? Where is he, what've you done to him?"

"If I were you little sister I'd be worried about my own sweet ass 'cause you're next."

The ancient radiators in this room generated overly abundant heat but Annie shivered as if that big leather couch was solid ice.

Moving backward McCleany staggered again and put a hand out to catch himself, he really was shattered. After checking his wristwatch he cursed then brought out from his back pocket a length of guitar string fastened on both ends with wooden handles.

"Our hero here," McCleany told Annie, "used this to decapitate his old friend Kenny, at least that's what Donny Boy said when I took it out of his pocket downstairs. Had the balls to tell me he was planning to use it on my neck too, ain't that right sport?"

The only sound from Growler was a pained mewling.

Before she realized what he intended to do, McCleany went around to the back of the couch and slipped the wire over Annie's head.

"You got about thirty seconds to tell me where those pictures are, then I'm going to squeeze off your head and leave you here as another one of Donny boy's victims."

Why didn't anyone believe her? "I don't know where they are, I swear to—" "God" got choked off, Annie trying to dig her fingertips between the wire and her neck.

McCleany braced himself for a good grip on the garrote's handles. "Adios, red."

54

SEEING HER THERE ON THE COUCH VERY NEARLY BROUGHT CAMEL TO
tears. "Annie," he said. *"Annie."*

Having lingered behind, McCleany now quickly pulled the .38
revolver, which he'd had with him all along, and used it to disarm
Camel, telling him, "Sucker," before pushing him into the room,
closing the door, snapping the padlock into place.

Camel remained focused on Annie as he hurried to the couch
and took her head in his hands. Speaking her name over and over
he carefully removed the duct tape from her mouth.

"Thank God," she said. "Thank God you're here."

He helped her sit up, Annie's dark red hair matted with even
darker red blood that had pooled in Growler's lap. Camel unwrapped the tape from her hands and ankles, examining Annie
for wounds, finding none . . . all the blood must be Growler's,
Camel wondering if he was dead.

He asked her what'd happened and in a gush of words she told
him about hiding in the closet, knocking into the piano and dis-
turbing all those fat flies . . . that man, the golfer she'd seen in
Teddy's office, he was one of the men in those photographs. "You
don't have any idea what I'm talking about do you?"

He assured her he did so Annie continued, explaining how the golfer taped her wrists and ankles before leaving to carry Growler up here, beating him with a cable, demanding to know where the photographs were. "He put that wire around my neck and was going to kill me but then we heard you holler my name."

When I was coming up the steps, Camel remembered.

"God it was the sweetest thing I've ever heard in my life Teddy, you calling my name. He took the wire off my neck, taped my mouth and left the room . . . who *is* he?"

"Gerald McCleany, Parker Gray's ex-partner . . . McCleany's the one who killed that girl here seven years ago and he wants those pictures because they're proof—"

Growler muttered something.

"Still alive," Camel said with a sense of wonder.

Annie put her arms around Camel. "That man, McCleany, he beat him so bad."

"McCleany didn't do all the damage, I shot Growler and so did Jake Kempis."

"And I drove a nail through his foot, broke his arm . . ."

Growler managed a strangled laugh.

Camel stood. "Is that Jake Kempis's?"

"Yes." Annie ran a hand along the jacket's sleeve. "McCleany said he killed a black man . . ."

"It was Jake, he's downstairs. Annie, was Parker Gray in any of those pictures?"

"Not that I remember."

"Gray told me he was in love with her, I bet she never took any photographs of him . . . the poor bastard was blackmailed into helping McCleany for no good reason." Camel grasped Annie gently by the shoulders. "Do you know where the pictures are?"

She looked at him with wild eyes. "Teddy not you too, if I knew—"

"Okay, all right . . . I had to ask because we could've used them to trade with McCleany, he's going to burn this place to the ground, finish what Parker Gray intended to do and we need—"

Growler grunted, managed to raise a hand and motion for Camel. Growler's right eye was out of its socket, unseeing, but his left eye fixed on Camel who bent close and listened, couldn't understand him at first, listened again, then a third time, finally got it.

Annie asked, "What's he saying?"

"Where the photographs are."

"Where?"

Camel moved Growler aside and lifted one of the couch's big leather cushions . . . revealing the eleven snapshots.

"They were there all the time," she said in amazement. "Why didn't he just say so?"

"Growler, where's the elephant?"

He shook his head.

"If we had the elephant *and* the pictures," Camel said, "we might be able to bargain our way out of here."

After a moment's hesitation Annie hurried to the tool shelves, moved the circular saw, brought the elephant to Teddy. "This is why Paul killed himself."

It was bigger than Camel had imagined.

She asked him, "Can you make it work, McCleany gets the elephant and pictures, he lets us walk out of here?"

"If he's greedy enough he might go for the bait."

"Bait?" Annie asked.

"Yeah I got an idea." Camel went to the shelves and grabbed two extension cords while Annie hesitantly approached the couch, leaning down cautiously to ask Growler, "Why didn't you just tell him where the pictures were, he would've stopped hitting you." Growler didn't answer. Flies had found his face and although Annie waved them away they were eager to return, Growler somehow managing to look pleased with himself . . . Lord of the Flies.

Camel was over at the big brick chimney, moving the fire screen which was in three sections and could be laid flat, when Annie asked him what he was doing.

"McCleany went to get the gasoline, he's going to be pouring five gallons of gas under that door there and then setting us all on fire . . . I saw a woman get burned to death tonight, believe me you don't want to die like that."

"How can I help?"

"Run these cords along the wall then take the fire screen over to the door." Camel made Growler sit up. "Listen to me." Growler's good left eye had closed. Camel didn't dare shake him, he was too fragile. "Donald, can you hear me?" The left eye came open, his head tilted forward.

Camel noticed the huge blue tattoo on his lower belly but couldn't make out what that tattoo was supposed to be, too much blood.

"Donald . . . I know why you ended up like this, people lied about you, lied about what you did to your cousin, lied about where you were that day, lied all through your trial."

He was nodding as Camel spoke, thank God someone finally believes me.

"Nobody hates a lie worse than I do, but even I can't imagine how you must've felt, a whole big goddamn world of lies and you were forced to carry it seven bad years."

For Growler hearing this was like receiving grace, he kept leaning forward until his bloody face pressed Camel's shoulder.

"Most of the people who lied about you were forced or tricked into it by McCleany, he's the one who killed Hope."

Growler nodded.

"And now he's going to get away with it, you killed all the wrong people and McCleany's home free."

Growler brought his head away from Camel. "No."

"Unless you help me."

"Pictures . . ."

"Yeah the pictures will link McCleany to the victim but those pictures are about to get burned up along with everything else in this room including us. I might be able to bargain with him, but he's going to want me and Annie where he can keep an eye on us . . . that leaves you to do it."

Growler fell back on the couch.

"Come on, sit up, I need you over there by that wall." Waiting for Growler to respond, Camel watched Annie position the fire screen on the floor near the door to the hallway. "Put the elephant and pictures on it," he told her before turning back to Growler. "God-damn it sit up."

He tried but couldn't.

"Help him," Annie said.

"He's got to do it on his own." But Growler couldn't move. Camel came close, talking right into his grotesque face. "You son-of-a-bitch, strong enough to kill old people, angry enough to kill your best friend and set a woman on fire . . . but you're not strong enough or angry enough to nail the man who's responsible for everything that's happened to you, you're going to let him get off scot-free because you can't even sit up you candyass—"

"Teddy—"

"Shut up Annie." He turned back to Growler. "She doesn't un-derstand about lies, not the way you and I do, now sit up and get mad all over again you fucking pansy."

Growler began making low sounds deep in his chest, animal sounds, warning growls, the rumbling of anger and determination like a weight lifter talking himself into lifting more than he ever has in his life . . . Growler coming off the couch, stumbling but staying upright, a clumsy Frankenstein raging at the world for hav-ing created him, mad all over again just like Camel said.

Camel led him to the far wall, sitting him there, explaining twice what had to be done. "It's simple enough but you have to do it at exactly the right time so don't fucking fade on me."

He indicated he wouldn't.

Camel took out his pocketknife and began stripping insulation from an extension cord, telling Annie how everything was going to work . . . if it worked.

She heard something out in the hallway. *"He's coming."*

Camel kept cutting. "Go over there to the door and tell him you found the elephant, Growler you stay there on the floor and act like you're dead." Growler managed another strangled laugh and Camel squinted a smile too . . . yeah, he thought, won't be much of an acting job. But if Growler couldn't stay alive for another few minutes then they were all dead.

55

BY THE TIME MCCLEANY HAULED THAT FIVE-GALLON CAN OF GAS UP THE stairs and to the door he was heaving for breath . . . goddamn, he thought, wouldn't it be a pisser if after all this I keeled over from a heart attack right now. But then as he gave the prospect some serious consideration he felt a tug of conscience because if he really was about to die from a coronary, maybe he shouldn't kill those people in this room after all. McCleany stood there with a queer expression on his face wondering where this sudden fucking wave of humanity came from.

When he got his breath back he felt better, more like his old self as he began pouring gasoline under the door and into the room.

"Can you hear me?" Annie shouted from inside.

"Yeah I hear you, red." McCleany kept pouring.

"I found the elephant! It's here in the room."

He put the gas can on the floor.

"It's worth three million dollars," she continued. "Solid gold with diamonds and rubies and . . . it's beautiful, you can have it if you let us go."

McCleany remembered Camel and Paul Milton both having made references to an elephant. He hefted the gas can and began pouring again . . . it's the chess piece J. L. Penner owned, the one

J.L. had said was worth more than everything else in his collection put together. Did they really have it there in the room with them?

Camel was at the door now, telling McCleany, "Growler gave me the photographs before he died. I'll turn them over to you, those pictures are the only hard evidence against you, everything else you can deny, your word against ours. When we were in my office that's the deal you wanted, you get the pictures and leave us alone. You can have this elephant too, just let us walk out of here."

McCleany finished emptying the can without answering. Stepping well away from the gasoline he thumbnailed a kitchen match to relight his cigar. "Camel you must take me for a complete idiot."

"You're an idiot if you leave this elephant to burn in the fire, yeah. Everything's right here on the floor in front of the door, just open up and—"

"You got another side arm on you . . . I know you're up to something."

"I'm up to saving my ass is what I'm up to McCleany. I don't have a weapon. Open the door and take a look, see if I'm not playing this straight with you." He continued talking, urging McCleany to be reasonable . . . Camel was good at this, nudging people toward the reasonable, and McCleany listened carefully while puffing on the cigar.

"If you know my reputation," Camel told him, "you know I don't lie . . . I'm playing this straight with you."

He removed the cigar from his mouth. "If I open this door I want to see all three of you standing in the middle of the room with your hands on top of your heads, if I don't, if those pictures and that elephant aren't all right there on the floor I swear to God I'll start shooting and then torch you all to hell."

"Annie and I are in the middle of the room right now! Can you hear me?"

"Where's Growler?"

"I told you he's dead, laying over there against the wall. Everything's just the way you want it Gerald, we got a deal?"

McCleany unlocked the padlock, lifted it out, doing all this with his left hand, the .38 in his right, using it to push open the door while he kept himself to the side in case Camel did have another weapon.

With the door open McCleany knelt down and quickly peeked around the jamb ready to shoot . . . but Camel and Annie were out in the middle of the room as promised, hands on their heads, Growler lying over against a wall.

On the floor right there by the doorway where it got soaked with gasoline was a fire screen and on it were eleven snapshots and an elephant eight inches long and about the same height, solid gold, foot and trunk raised in triumph, studded with jewels. "I'll be damned," McCleany muttered.

"You take the elephant," Camel was telling him, "and you take the pictures, then let us go . . . after that I don't care if you burn this place, fly to South America or what. We have a deal?"

"Yeah sure," McCleany said as he stepped onto the fire screen, keeping the revolver pointed at Annie and Camel, kneeling down to look at one of the photographs. "She was a sweet piece of ass."

"That elephant's the real McCoy," Camel said. "Gold."

McCleany stuffed the photographs in a pocket.

"Solid gold," Camel said.

When McCleany put his hand on the elephant to lift it, Camel shouted, *"Liar!"* . . . and McCleany died instantly.

56

LIGHTNING WAS THE REASON CAMEL'S FATHER GAVE FOR NEVER PURSUING the game of golf. He'd been at the 1975 Western Open in Chicago when Lee Trevino and Jerry Heard were struck by lightning. "Cleats," Camel's father would always say whenever he told the story. "Lightning hits anywhere nearby and your goddamn cleats ground you."

■ ■ ■

EXCEPT FOR ONE disastrous consequence Camel had not foreseen, the gig came off pretty much as he had planned it.

Getting McCleany to open the door was the toughest part, he could've torched the room and destroyed the photographs without ever putting himself at risk but Camel counted on the elephant being an irresistible incentive. Who could be presented with a chunk of gold like that and not want to touch it?

■ ■ ■

CAMEL HAD CUT off the receptacle end of an extension cord and had split the black hot wire from the white neutral wire, wrapping bare copper from the hot wire around one back leg of the ele-

phant. The fireplace screen had been laid flat on the floor and
Camel attached the extension cord's neutral wire to it. After that
was done, hot wire connected to the elephant and neutral wire to
the screen, the other end of the cord was plugged into a second
extension cord that was hidden along the wall and run around to
an electrical outlet where Growler was sprawled feigning death. At
the agreed upon signal, Camel shouting *liar,* Growler plugged in
the extension cord, elcctricity then seeking to complete its circuit
from hot to neutral, from the copper wire through an even better
conductor of electricity: the gold elephant. McCleany, standing on
the fire screen in his golf cleats and holding the elephant in his
greed-wet hand made the connection . . . and got zapped by 20
amps flowing at 120 volts. The shock might only have disabled a
healthy man . . . it was McCleany's heart giving out that killed him.

Lying on the floor next to the receptacle Growler had willed
himself to stay alive. Hearing the signal from Camel and finding
the strength to push that plug into the receptacle, knowing it was
going to zap McCleany, that's when Growler even with all his
wounds, the insupportable pain, realizing his own death was minutes away . . . it was at that moment Growler's seven-year burden
lifted and he felt blessedly free.

The disastrous consequence Camel had failed to foresee in de-
vising and executing this booby trap was McCleany's cigar. When
he got juiced, leaping up still holding the elephant, McCleany had
that cigar firmly clenched between his teeth . . . and when he fell
flat and hard on his broad red face, the cigar splintered into a
shower of glowing coals that ignited the gasoline.

■   ■   ■

WITH ALL THAT gas burning right there in the doorway, illuminating the room, in less than a minute the fire would be too high, too
hot for anyone to escape . . . Camel working quickly, first telling
Annie to get the hell out of there and then gathering the photographs from McCleany's pocket and checking his pulse . . . dead.
He searched him for weapons, finding all three: McCleany's own

.38, Gray's 9mm, and Eddie's .45. Camel went to Growler and pulled out the plug before checking *his* pulse . . . bastard still alive, unfuckingbelieveable. He debated leaving him there to burn but then hefted Growler onto his shoulder . . . when Camel turned around and saw Annie still in the room he shouted at her, "Get the hell out of here!"

She was kneeling at the elephant. "Is it safe to touch it?"

"We don't have time—"

"Is it safe!"

"Yes."

She unwound the wire from the elephant's back leg and wrestled it from McCleany's dead grasp.

"Annie, throw the cushions from the couch in the doorway, we'll use them to step through the fire."

She did that, then tucked the sculpture close to her body like a fullback with a football . . . using her other hand to hold the jacket closed, Annie running nimbly from one cushion to the next, escaping injury completely.

Camel didn't fare as well. Carrying Growler made him clumsy, he slipped off one cushion and tripped, the fire scorching his clothes. But he quickly righted himself and hauled Growler down the hallway-balcony to where Annie waited. They looked back at the doorway, the fire having become so intense that no one could've made it through there now.

On their way out of Cul-De-Sac, Camel was forced repeatedly to stop and rest. Annie asked him if he wanted to put Growler down, he said if he did that he'd never get him back up again.

"What'd you do to your nose?"

"I'll tell you all about it outside, come on I can make it the rest of the way now."

Camel carrying Growler, Annie leading, they went through the big double doors at the front of Cul-De-Sac, across the wide porch, down the steps, and were well away from the building before Camel lowered Growler to the ground.

"What're we going to do?" Annie asked.

"Sit right here on the grass and watch the goddamn place burn to the ground I hope."

She looked back at Cul-De-Sac, no outward sign of the fire yet but the way it had been burning, with that big atrium functioning as a chimney to draw the fire upward, flames would be showing out the roof within minutes.

Camel checked Growler's pulse again, thready but still ticking. "I can't believe it," he said. "I couldn't save Elizabeth Rockwell—or Jake Kempis or Parker Gray for that matter—but this bastard I manage to bring out alive."

"I almost feel sorry for him," Annie said.

"I don't."

"No you wouldn't."

Growler coughed and beckoned Camel close. "McCleany?"

"Dead as dead."

"Innocent," Growler whispered, referring to himself.

"You *were* innocent, now you're on your way to hell."

"Teddy!" Annie said, shocked by the harshness of telling that to a dying man.

But Growler indicated his own agreement with Camel . . . and then died without comment, ceremony, or grace.

"Is he gone?" Annie asked.

"Yeah."

Sitting on the grass next to Camel, watching for signs of Cul-De-Sac's destruction, Annie cradled the gold elephant in her lap as if it were a child she had saved from that burning building.

Camel meanwhile was plotting, running the possibilities, totaling body counts . . . ten dead. Growler had killed five: the Raineys, Kenny Norton, Elizabeth Rockwell, and Murray. There would be little doubt about those homicides. Paul Milton's death would be ruled a suicide. Whoever was ultimately responsible for Growler's death, no one would much care . . . he'd be labeled a mad-dog killer and good riddance. McCleany killed Jake Kempis, probably with a knife that would be found on whatever was left of McCleany's body. Which left two final victims, McCleany himself and Parker Gray, both of whom Camel had killed. McCleany would be easy enough, Camel was forced to electrocute him in self-defense and Annie could testify to what had happened up in that room . . . she could tell the truth. Parker Gray was another matter entirely.

"I intend to keep this elephant," she said.

Camel didn't comment.

"Growler claimed it was worth three million dollars."

"Yeah, that's what Elizabeth Rockwell said too."

"It's mine now."

"Actually it's not."

She knew it was futile to argue a point of ethics with him but Annie stubbornly said, "I'm keeping it just the same."

Camel was back to thinking about Parker Gray, whom he'd shot with McCleany's .38 . . .

I'll say McCleany did it. I'll say the reason I slipped away from that trooper at the hospital is because I didn't trust anyone with the state police, not after I discovered Parker Gray and Gerald Mc-Cleany had framed Growler for a murder that McCleany committed. The former partners must've had a falling out because McCleany killed Gray, that's what I'll say. If necessary I might even claim I saw him do it. I'll say that after murdering Gray, McCleany used his own .38 and Gray's 9mm to put two rounds in Growler. Jake Kempis isn't around to contradict me, I'll lie my way out of this.

Camel hadn't looked at the eleven snapshots in his pocket yet but from what Elizabeth Rockwell indicated they probably included some prominent men who seven years ago were screwing a seventeen-year-old girl who then became a murder victim . . . this whole affair will be like something the cat coughed onto the carpet in polite company, everyone's going to want it cleaned up and cleared away with a minimum of comment.

All I have to do is tell the lies people want to hear.

When Annie leaned against him he put an arm around her shoulder.

"I feel so guilty that Paul got himself involved in this for me," she said. "I don't understand why, I never nagged him about money, I always tried . . ." She wept.

"Don't put yourself on the line for any of this," Camel told her. "Paul did what he did, he's responsible."

She wiped at her eyes. "I wish I could be so sure of everything the way you are."

He didn't feel sure of anything.

"Always so hard," Annie continued. "Telling that dying man he was going to hell . . . that was a hard thing to say."

But Camel didn't feel hard, he felt soft and weak. "What do you think you'll do now?" he asked.

She said she didn't know. "I've always wanted to travel."

"Travel's good."

They watched as flames showed themselves in a whole bank of Cul-De-Sac's windows.

Annie asked him what he intended to tell the police when they got here.

Lies, he thought, lots of them.

"Teddy?"

"Yeah?"

"I mean about this elephant. I know better than to ask you to lie for me."

Go ahead, he thought . . . I will. Ask me to travel around the world with you, I'll do that too.

"But I *am* asking you not to mention it one way or the other, give me a shot at keeping this elephant for myself . . . or do you consider that the same as lying?"

He thought it probably *was* the same as lying but he didn't tell that to Annie.

She rested her head on his chest. They were both watching when the building's windows shattered from the intense heat sending glass like hard sharp tears down the front of Cul-De-Sac, freeing smoky yellow flames to leap from those windows as if they'd been dying for air.

She asked him if he would ever lie about *anything*.

He said he never would.

"Then tell me this, do you love me?"

Before answering, he gently turned her head so she could see his face.

ABOUT THE AUTHOR

DAVID MARTIN is the author of *The Crying Heart Tattoo, Final Harbor, Tethered, The Beginning of Sorrows,* and three international bestsellers: *Lie to Me, Bring Me Children,* and *Tap, Tap.* He and his wife, Arabel, operate a working farm in West Virginia.